1 Adolphus

Adolphus
by
Lionel Ross

ISBN: 978-0-9574346-7-7

Adolphus
by
Lionel Ross

ISBN: 978-0-9574346-7-7

Published by

i2i Publishing. Manchester.
www.i2ipublishing.co.uk

Glossary of German Military Terms:

Die Fliegertruppen des Deutschen Kaiserreiches (German Air Force) in World War 1.

Militärgerichtsbarkeit (Military Court)

Ranks in the Imperial German Army 1914-18

Gefreiter - *Lance-Corporal*
Feldwebel – *Sergeant*
Oberleutnant – *First Lieutenant*
Hauptmann – *Captain*
Major – *Major (pronounce Mayor)*
Oberst-Leutnant – *Lieutenant Colonel*
Oberst - *Colonel*

AUTHORS NOTE:

There must be some terrible weakness in the nature of man that makes him capable of killing and maiming his fellow in the name of patriotism or religion. The war of 1914-1918 was described at its conclusion as *'the war to end all wars.'* How hollow that sentence reads in the light of subsequent history. The Great War planted the seeds of an even greater conflict with even greater inhumanity, to follow just twenty years later. Now, a hundred years on, human beings are still imbued with the desire to murder those whose culture, nationality, faith, image and background varies, even slightly from their own.

Will we never learn???

Dedication:

This story is for Luise, my constant inspiration.

Chapter One

Manchester July 1912

An Unexpected Guest

It had been a hard week for Jacob, peddling his jewellery around the Lancashire mining and textile mill towns. Not that every week wasn't hard. The goods he offered were a luxury for people, who hardly had two halfpennies to rub together, but they still wanted to buy Jacob's silver wedding rings, engagement rings, bracelets and necklaces for their girl friends, fiancées and spouses; at least most of them did; that is providing they could pay weekly! Credit was an essential part of his business and Jacob counted most of his customers as friends. They rarely let him down.

The others, the ones who went straight to the pub with their earnings, as soon as they came out of the mines and mills, were never his customers.

How could a man do that to his wife and hungry family? Jacob often thought.

It was Thursday July 25th 1912 and he had gone directly from Exchange Station to catch the late evening prayers service at the Synagogue. This only took twenty minutes and helped to relax him from the pressures of the day.

By nine thirty he was home and being greeted by Leah, his wife of twenty five years. As usual, a hot meal awaited him and with the two youngest of their four children fed, the couple ate together and enjoyed the exchange of information about their respective days.

Just after ten o'clock there was a knock at the front door.

"Probably some poor soul looking for help," Jacob sighed pulling, himself somewhat wearily out of the dining chair.

This was nothing unusual and there were many desperately poor people in the area that had arrived over the last few years. Most were completely destitute, after fleeing persecution in Eastern Europe.

Jacob opened the front door to see before him a young man dressed in the height of fashion. His whole appearance exuded wealth and privilege.

"Guten Abend," he said in a heavy German accent. "You are Herr Jacob Bergman?"

"Yes, indeed," Jacob replied completely mystified as to whom this young man might be. Arrivals at his door starving and in rags were nothing unusual but this man hardly looked as if he sought charity.

The young man stepped forward and to Jacob's astonishment flung his arms around him and planted a big wet kiss on each of Jacob's cheeks. Then taking Jacob's two hands in his he leaned back and announced,

"I am Adolphus Bergmann, your nephew from Berlin."

Jacob was rarely lost for words and for a few moments he gazed at the new arrival as if unable to assimilate the information that this young man had just supplied. Suddenly, he remembered his manners.

"My dear boy," he began, "Come inside! What are you doing here in Manchester?"

Adolphus smiled and bowed as he followed the older man into the house.

"Do you speak Yiddish?" Jacob enquired as soon as Adolphus was comfortably seated.

"Nein!" his nephew replied in heavily accented English. "I speak German and some English but my parents never spoke to me in Yiddish. I know they spoke it when they took us to visit my grandparents in Lithuania and of course it was originally a German dialect; but Nein! My language is German."

"Anyway," Jacob replied, "How about a cup of tea and something to eat? We are strictly kosher as I am sure you are."

Adolphus looked slightly uncomfortable as he answered with a watery smile that he would very much appreciate a cup of coffee and maybe a little cake.

At this stage Jacob suddenly remembered that he had not introduced the visitor to his wife, Leah.

"Excuse me for a minute," he told his nephew.

He returned to the kitchen where Leah was still tidying away the dinner pots.

"We have a visitor," he announced to Leah. "It's my nephew Adolphus Bergmann, Kalman's son, from Berlin. A fine young man! You should see how he is dressed; in the height of fashion. My brother Kalman must have done well in Germany. We must be the poor members of the family. Come in, come in and meet him," he said as he ushered Leah into the front parlour.

Leah quickly removed her apron and patted her hair as she followed her husband into the main entertaining room of the house.

Adolphus arose from the armchair with alacrity, clicked his heels, bowed and said,

"Delighted to meet you, Tante."

Well his manners are impeccable, Leah decided. *And what a good looking young man he is. I wonder if he is already married as he would make a lovely husband for our Rachel.*

"Please sit down," she told him smiling. "We're delighted to meet you."

Adolphus gave another of his little bows and settled back into the large armchair.

"Leah," Jacob suggested, "if you go and make a nice cup of tea for our guest and some of that delicious cake that you baked yesterday, I will ask about our German relatives."

Adolphus then proceeded to tell his uncle about his family in Berlin. Jacob had learned that his older brother was doing well in the German capital from their occasional exchange of letters but Kalman was a poor correspondent and apart from news of births, weddings, sickness and death he supplied little personal information.

"My father is in the shoe business," Adolphus explained. "We have two factories and fifty three shops in the main cities of Germany. We have recently expanded into France and Austria. I am here to investigate the possibilities for our shoes in England."

"I am also a reserve officer in the army of his Imperial Majesty the Kaiser," he continued proudly.

By this time Leah had returned and deposited the small tray replete with tea pot and cake on a small table alongside their guest.

"Danke Schon!" the young German said. "I am sorry but I don't drink tea. Is it possible to have a cup of good German coffee?"

"Certainly," Leah replied, thinking to herself that their nephew may have some good manners but had little difficulty in setting them aside and embarrassing his hosts.

"Have you booked a hotel?" Jacob enquired. "If you had written to tell us of your visit you could have stayed here."

"Ja! Tonight I stay at the Midland. They say it is very good," he explained.

"However," he continued, "tomorrow I can move here to be with my dear family."

"Good," Jacob replied, "So that is settled. We will expect you with your luggage at about five o'clock. Tomorrow night is Shabbos (the Sabbath) and we dine after Shul at eight o'clock. Once you have unpacked you can accompany me to Shul with your cousins."

Once again Adolphus looked a little uncomfortable and then bethought himself to enquire,

"Ach! My cousins! Of course I have cousins. Please tell me about your children."

Leah and Jacob Bergman had been blessed with a fairly average size family, as families went in the early twentieth century. Leah had given birth to six children but, as was tragically common in those days, only four had survived early childhood. The oldest was Abraham who preferred to be known as Alfred. He was twenty three and recently married to Anne (nee Cohen). The next in line was Rachel. She was twenty two and unmarried. This was a great disappointment to her parents who had assumed that a girl with her good looks would have been snapped up by the age of eighteen or nineteen, at the latest. Rachel however, had other ideas and the procession of possible suitors introduced by her parents was rejected outright.

Rachel had a totally different agenda. She had started attending meetings of the WSPU to campaign for votes for women and was deeply influenced by Christabel and Emmeline Pankhurst in their campaigns for women's rights. Jacob and Leah were by no means typical early twentieth century parents and they turned a blind eye to their daughter's political activities. That was until the week before Adolphus arrived, when on Thursday 18th July 1912 all the news had been about one Mary Leigh, a WSPU member who had thrown a hatchet at the Prime Minister, Herbert Henry Asquith.

Jacob was furious. This was an unusual event and Leah could count on the fingers of one hand the number of previous occasions when her husband had lost his temper. He was a gentle man who believed in persuasion rather than anger when he felt his children needed correction, and on the whole, this approach worked well in his family.

Rachel worked in a drapery store in the centre of the city and arrived home that evening to be greeted by her quiet reasonable father suddenly transformed into a seething mass of indignation.

She walked through the door to find him pacing up and down the hall.

"Young lady, I want to talk to you," he bellowed and he almost dragged her into the front parlour.

A shocked Rachel was unaware of the news, not having been able to purchase a Manchester Evening News before boarding a bus for home. Jacob, of course, had the paper and thrust it into his daughter's hands.

"Look at this. You are consorting with murderers and anarchists. This Votes for Women nonsense has got to stop. I'm not going to sit back and watch you finish up in prison. I want you to promise me here and now that you will have nothing more to do with these Meshuganers."

Rachel was deeply shocked both by the news and the effect that it had had on her father. She stood in the parlour, reading the front page of the newspaper over and over again.

Eventually she looked up into her father's face and replied,

"Please do not think that all suffragettes are like this crazy woman. I attend meetings and I listen to the Pankhurst sisters and their colleagues. I am also quite capable of addressing small meetings myself but I would never, never ever, resort to violence."

Jacob was beginning to calm down but he was completely determined that Rachel must sever all connections with WSPU. As he recovered his usual equanimity he told his daughter to take off her coat and sit down so that they could discuss the whole affair.

Jacob was very persuasive; after all, he was a salesman, albeit of jewellery, and after an hour-long discussion Rachel promised to resign from the WSPU and find other more peaceful ways of promoting the cause.

At this point Leah entered the parlour and joined in the discussion.

"You know what you need, don't you?" she told her daughter.

"What Mum?" Rachel enquired, knowing exactly what her mother would reply.

"A nice Yiddisher husband," Leah promptly answered, grinning broadly.

"Well find me one," Rachel replied, smiling with relief that the confrontation with her father was over.

"I wish I could," Leah replied, grinning. "Maybe you are just a little too fussy. You have met some lovely young men but by you, there is always something wrong with them. Some are too tall; some are too small, too dark, too fair, too clever, and not clever enough! Or you don't like their mothers or fathers. Maybe they are too poor or even too rich; it is always the same. I wonder if the man who is right for you has been born."

And that is where the two matters lay when cousin Adolphus arrived, just one week later.

Chapter Two

Manchester July 1912

An Empty Chair

Jacob was pacing up and down the hall wondering what had become of his newly arrived nephew. He had sent his sons on ahead of him so that he could personally escort Adolphus to Synagogue for the Friday evening service that was always the highlight of Jacob's week. He had been looking forward to introducing his nephew to his friends. They would be most impressed by this smart and obviously wealthy member of the Bergman family from far-away Berlin. But where was he? He pondered.

I will give him another five minutes, he decided, *and then I must leave.*

Suddenly there was a loud knock on the front door and Jacob ran to open it exclaiming,

"So there you are. I was getting......"

And then he saw it was not his nephew but a telegraph-boy, who quickly handed him an envelope explaining,

"Telegram for Mr Bergman!"

Jacob was not a frequent recipient of telegrams and when those rare communications did arrive they usually heralded bad news concerning the death of some long-parted and now departed relative. He feverishly tore open the envelope, removed the contents to read:

```
Dear Uncle - stop - Cannot now come this
evening but will arrive at 10 o'clock on
Sunday morning - stop - Best wishes - stop -
Adolphus
```

Jacob ran into the kitchen to tell Leah that their relative would not be joining them for the Sabbath and dashed off to Synagogue, a deeply disappointed man.

Over dinner later that night the family discussed the situation. Alfred and Anne, and indeed Rachel had all been intrigued to learn of their glamorous cousin. The two younger sons, Joe who was sixteen and Ike who had celebrated his Barmitzvah that year, had been very excited to hear of the new arrival.

"It's very strange," Jacob commented, as he sipped his chicken soup, "How is he going to make Shabbos in the Midland Hotel? And what will he do for food? There's no kosher food there."

Leah, who had an instinct in such matters suggested,

"Maybe he is one of those Reform Jews. There are a quite a few of them here in Manchester; you know their Synagogue is just off Cheetham Hill Road. Mrs Goldbloom told me that there are many more of them in Germany. She says they don't keep Kosher and they hardly ever go to Shul."

"Well, it is all very strange," Jacob replied. "First he turns up without warning, hints he would like to stay with us and then prefers to spend the Sabbath among strangers; all very strange!" He repeated.

The Germans, whether Jews or gentiles, seem to have an almost fanatical approach to punctuality and true to this tradition Adolphus arrived on the stroke of ten o'clock on Sunday morning. He bounded up the steps followed by the cab driver struggling with the young German's luggage. He gave a resounding rat-a-tat-tat on the door knocker and greeted Uncle Jacob with a short bow and kisses on both cheeks.

"Uncle," he began, "I am so sorry about Friday but I had an important meeting to attend with a colleague from Frankfurt."

Jacob was shocked. He lived in a community of religious Jews, all of whom had arrived some twenty to thirty years earlier from Eastern Europe. The idea of attending business meetings on the Sabbath and staying in a hotel without kosher food was anathema to him.

"Couldn't your meeting have waited until today or tomorrow?" he enquired, "searching his nephew's face for some sign of guilt or discomfort.

"Nein! Unmöglich!" Adolphus answered. "It was a very important meeting."

Jacob sighed and thought about his brother in far-off Berlin and the way he had brought up his son.

"Anyway, come in and I will show you to your room."

Then Adolphus remembered the poor cab-driver standing on the top step with his luggage.

"How much do I owe you?" he asked.

He pulled out a bulging wallet and gave the man a most generous tip.

"Do me a favour," he said. "Put my bags in the hall near the stairs."

The cabby nodded and obediently followed the instruction.

"Well," Jacob commented resignedly, "you are here now so I will show you to your room and then you can meet the rest of the family."

Half an hour later, Adolphus came down stairs after meticulously hanging his collection of suits, shirts and ties in an empty wardrobe. The room allocated to him had been that of Jacob's oldest and newly married son Alfred, and was certainly comfortable and well-appointed according to the standards of the day and location.

"I hope you'll be comfortable," his host announced.

"Oh! Ja! It may not be the Midland Hotel but it will do me fine," Adolphus replied.

"Now, how about a cup of coffee?" Jacob enquired remembering that Adolphus did not drink tea.

"Ja! That would be good," he replied and settled himself into Jacob's usual easy-chair.

"You had better meet your cousins now," Jacob suggested and left the room to tell Rachel and the two young boys to come into the sitting-room to be introduced.

The boys arrived first and formally shook hands with their cousin. A minute later Rachel entered.

"And who is this young lady?" Adolphus enquired, rising with some rapidity to greet his pretty cousin.

"This is our daughter Rachel," Leah replied as she entered the room behind her daughter.

"Ach! I did not know I had such a beautiful cousin," Adolphus said, bowing courteously.

Rachel blushed and replied primly that she was pleased to meet him.

"Please sit down," he said, pointing to the chair nearest to where he had been seated.

He then proceeded to ignore his Uncle and Aunt and the two boys and gave all his attention to Rachel.

She was naturally very flattered by this attention and could not help but to be impressed by her worldly German cousin with his smart fashionable clothes, so different from the other young men she met.

"Ach, so!" Adolphus began. "So you are the beautiful Rachel, the cousin I knew nothing of. I gather you are not married so what do you do to fill your time?"

Rachel blushed. "I work in a drapery store in town," she explained.

"And what do you do in your spare time?" her cousin enquired.

"I have been quite involved in the Votes for Women movement," she told him.

"You mean you are one of those, what do you call them? Ach, yes, suffragettes," he replied with a somewhat shocked and disapproving expression.

This was the opportunity for Jacob to enter the conversation.

"I am not very happy about this activity of Rachel," he pronounced. "These women mean well, but they are becoming more and more aggressive and I have asked Rachel to be very careful about whom she associates with."

Rachel looked at her father very unhappily while Jacob decided that his German nephew was not all bad after all.

Adolphus turned to address his uncle.

"It seems to me that Rachel should be more involved in the usual activities of young ladies. Maybe I could take her to the films; I noticed that the new French film Richard III with James Keane is on here." Jacob nodded and Adolphus turned to Rachel, smiling.

"Would you like that? We could go tomorrow evening."

Rachel felt somewhat uncomfortable. Her father much preferred to leave her in the company of a man they hardly knew, even though he was apparently a relative, than have her involved in serious work to improve the social and political fabric of British women. However, she quickly decided, this Adolphus was certainly good-looking and charming and her friends would think her quite odd to turn down such an invitation.

"Yes," Rachel replied, "that would be lovely. I like Shakespeare and I studied Richard III at school."

"Gut! " Adolphus replied smiling broadly. This charming young English cousin was an unexpected bonus.

"Gut!" Adolphus repeated. "I saw the picture-house on Saturday night and outside it said there is, what they call 'First House,' at six o'clock."

Rachel wondered why they could not go to the second house but felt it would be discourteous to question the arrangements.

So, at a quarter past five, after an early dinner, the pair set out for the Scala Picture House in Withington.

Rachel had changed from her severe black skirt and crisp cotton blouse and had donned her new frock, originally intended to be retained to be worn for Synagogue at New Year. It was, she felt, particularly elegant in pale blue with navy stripes on the bodice. Adolphus too, had changed into a tweed suit that made him look far more English than the formal German clothes he usually wore.

Rachel imagined they would take a tram to the centre of the city and another out to south Manchester and was amazed to find that as soon as they arrived on Cheetham Hill Road, Adolphus hailed a cab. This seemed like unheard of extravagance to Rachel, but as a well-mannered young lady, she accepted the method of transport without comment.

The film was, of course silent, but with the combination of prompt cards, superb acting and mood music, the cousins left the cinema having thoroughly enjoyed the experience.

Once again Adolphus hailed a cab and within half an hour they were back home in the Bergman's front room.

Adolphus had been the perfect attentive escort throughout the evening and Rachel was a little surprised that he quickly excused himself from her presence. She could clearly hear his footsteps on the stairs as he repaired to his bedroom. However, both of Rachel's parents and her older brother wanted to hear all about the evening and the film and it was well after nine when Adolphus again opened the sitting room door to announce that he had to go out and not to wait up for him.

Jacob looked surprised and went to fetch a latch-key for their guest.

"Where on earth do you have to go at this time of night?" he enquired.

"I have to meet a business colleague," his nephew explained, pocketed the key and quickly left the house.

Joe was the only one who heard their guest return at almost two o'clock in the morning. Joe was a great reader and devoured every book that came his way. As a result, when he should have been fast-asleep in bed, he was pouring over Oliver Twist by Charles Dickens. He heard the front door creak as Adolphus opened it and he jumped out of bed to watch his cousin through a crack in the barely open door as he crept by on the landing. Joe could see that their guest was carrying a black box and a file of papers. The young man was desperately curious to discover what these items might be and decided to try to ascertain the reason why Adolphus behaved in such a mysterious manner. However, for the rest of that week the strange guest hardly left the house. He spent hours telling members of the family about his parents and siblings in Berlin. Otherwise he seemed to be involved in writing long reports which the family assumed were about his business. These were, of course, written in German with its special Fraktur script and as such completely unintelligible to most English speaking people. Both Jacob and Leah also spoke Yiddish which was largely based on the German language but that was always written in Hebrew characters. In any case, unlike their middle son Joe, they would never have dreamed of spying on their visitor. If Adolphus did not wish to explain what he was doing and why he was there, that was his prerogative.

Eventually Joe managed to slip into the bedroom of his cousin while the latter was out at one of his daytime meetings. However, there was no sign of the black box or the documents.

In the meantime over the ensuing weeks a certain developing closeness was discernible between Rachel and her German cousin. They both seemed to be particularly happy with each other's company.

When the Sabbath came round again the nephew accompanied his Uncle Jacob and cousins to the Synagogue which pleased Jacob, although he was somewhat shocked to discover that Adolphus had no idea how to pray in Hebrew. *My brother has been too busy making money to give his son a proper Jewish education,* he decided.

Within a month Adolphus had settled into being a member of the family in more than name. His manners were a trifle odd for English taste but a bond was growing with all the English Bergmans and especially with Rachel.

Rather than displease his host he had started to attend Synagogue with him and secretly began to enjoy the experience. If he was going to accept his Uncle's hospitality for a few months he needed to do everything possible to keep Uncle Jacob sweet. Apart from his main reason for his visit to Manchester, a well-guarded secret from his English relatives, he had fallen head-over-heels in love with his cousin Rachel.

Chapter Three

Manchester November 1912

Taken into Custody

Adolphus settled into a routine. By day he would take a cab to meetings which he told the family were about expanding their chain of shoe shops into England. In the evening he would take his cousin Rachel to the cinema or theatre and sometimes they would dine out, although Rachel's insistence on eating only kosher food made this activity very restricting.

After two or three months his demeanour had softened and he now appeared much less Germanic. In short, he became a more than acceptable member of the family and was treated with friendship and affection.

There was only one matter that was still causing concern and that was his twice weekly nocturnal activity. Just like on their first evening out together, he would bring Rachel home early and then slip quietly out of the house from which he would be absent for three or four hours.

"I have to meet my new English store managers," he explained. "They are working elsewhere until our first stores open, so I have to meet up with them late, after we have all dined."

Jacob, Leah and Rachel had little difficulty in accepting this explanation or at least in convincing themselves that this was the truth. However, Joe was highly suspicious of the whole matter and resolved to investigate further as soon as the opportunity arose.

Joe had his opportunity a week later. It was a Tuesday evening and the young man pleaded fatigue and told his parents that he would have an early night. This was a great surprise to Jacob and Leah, as the boy was always full of energy and normally had to be nagged to go to bed so that he would be fit for school the following morning.

Once in his room Joe selected a warm jacket and gym pumps and lay on his bed waiting.

At quarter past nine he heard Adolphus return from the theatre with Rachel and then just five minutes later he heard Adolphus on the landing and entering his bedroom. Joe knew his cousin's nocturnal routine by then, so he slipped on a jacket and running shoes and crept out of the house. After just ten minutes his quarry also left the family home. He walked briskly to the main road and waited on the corner. After a further five minutes Joe heard the sound of one of those new horseless carriage cabs approaching. It stopped on the corner and Adolphus climbed in. The cab then set off in the direction of the city, only a mile away and with its speed strictly regulated, the athletic Joe had no problem in trotting a little way behind.

Much to Joe's surprise the motor chugged along Market Street and through Piccadilly showing no intention of stopping within the city centre. The cab eventually stopped at its destination, a mile or so out of town in an area known as Ardwick Green. This area contained two theatres, but it was a complete mystery to Joe why his cousin should wish to visit another theatre, when he had only returned from an outing to a similar place with his sister Rachel, just an hour or so earlier.

The cab was now outside the Hippodrome and Joe watched as Adolphus disembarked. He paid the driver who then set-off back in the direction of town. Adolphus, however, made no attempt to enter the theatre and took up a position outside the establishment after glancing at his watch.

Joe stood patiently, peeping around the corner, thoroughly intrigued until, after a wait of some ten minutes a tall man came striding along the pavement to join Adolphus. Then to Joe's surprise they walked away from the theatre and entered the small park that gave its name to Ardwick Green. Joe, keeping a safe distance, followed them until they stopped near the park entrance at the far side. They were now opposite a large building that looked for all the world like a castle. Joe had approached as near as he dared to the two men and watched in amazement, from behind a large tree trunk, as Adolphus handed the black box he had been carrying to his companion. Then Joe realised what the black box was – a camera; a Kodak Brownie box camera.

Joe's astonishment only increased as Adolphus' companion walked towards the castle-like building and started taking photographs of the exterior. Adolphus had seated himself on a park bench and waited for his friend to return. In the meantime the man was now out of sight having walked round to the rear of the large building.

It was getting colder in the night air, when after a good forty-five minutes the photographer returned. He handed the camera back to Adolphus as the pair retraced their steps to a cab-rank at the side of the Hippodrome. To do this they walked almost within touching distance of Joe's tree. The young man kept as still and quiet as he could but could clearly hear the pair speaking, in what Joe suspected to be German, as they passed within his ear-shot.

Five minutes later the two men sped off, back towards town in a horse-drawn cab.

What was so interesting about the building that they had photographed? Joe pondered and resolved to take a closer look, before setting off back through the city to his home.

As soon as Joe left the park he could see the identity of the building. It was an army base, in fact the headquarters of the 8th Ardwick Battalion of the Manchester Regiment. He still wondered why it should have been of such interest to cousin Adolphus and his friend. Maybe they were studying architecture and Joe knew from school that Manchester had many wonderful buildings?

Anyway, he was cold and decided to start a brisk walk towards home, some two miles away. As he fastened his top button he was startled by a deep voice immediately behind him.

"And what are you doing here, sonny Jim," the voice enquired.

Joe looked round to see a large middle-aged policeman complete with helmet and cloak.

"I was just out for a walk in the park," Joe quickly explained.

"Well then, why the sudden interest in Ardwick barracks?" the Bobby demanded.

"I thought it was a nice building," Joe replied lamely beginning to realise that he may be in trouble.

"Well my lad," the policeman said. "I think you had better come with me to the station. I think you were up to no good; that's what I think. Are you going to come quietly or shall I arrest you?"

"I'll come quietly," Joe stammered and the pair set off for a short walk to the police station.

Inside they were greeted by a desk sergeant who seemed a little friendlier than the bobby on the beat.

"So what have you been up to young man?" he enquired.

"Loitering with intent," the constable answered. "I caught him thinking of breaking in to Ardwick barracks."

"I see," said the desk sergeant gravely but with a twinkle in his eye. "So what were you doing near the barracks at that time of night?" he demanded of Joe.

"I just fancied a walk in the park and I thought the building was very interesting. I meant no harm," he stammered.

"So," the Sergeant answered, "I have to know your full name and address before we go any further."

"My name is Joe Bergman," the young man replied, truthfully, "and I live at twenty seven Broadoak Street, Cheetham Hill."

The two policemen looked at each other in astonishment.

"Cheetham Hill," the desk sergeant gasped. "You are miles away from home. If you wanted to take a walk in the park, why come all this way?"

"I, I like to explore," Joe answered lamely. He pondered on telling the policemen the real reason why he was over in Ardwick but decided that his father would be angry if he caused any trouble for his cousin.

"Bergman, Bergman," the sergeant stroked his chin. "Cheetham Hill; you must be a Jewish boy. I have never heard of any of your people getting in to trouble."

He turned to the constable. "Did you actually see him committing a crime?"

"No Sergeant," the bobby answered, "but he was definitely loitering."

"Well Joe," the Sergeant demanded. "Were you loitering?"

"No, Sir," Joe answered quickly. "I had run all the way from Cheetham Hill. I saw the park and had a rest on a bench there. Then I saw the castle building and thought it looked very exciting. And that was all. I was just about to set off for home when this policeman came up to me. Please let me go, Sir, I meant no harm and will keep away from Ardwick in future."

"Do you know, young man that it is not always safe to knock about Manchester late at night, at your age? Maybe I should have a word with your dad about that."

Joe was almost in tears. If the policemen had swallowed his story, he knew his father would certainly not do so.

"There is no need to do that sir. I promise I will never do this again."

The sergeant gave a grin and said,

"Well then, off you go but if I catch you wandering around again late at night, you will have both your father and me to contend with."

Half an hour later Joe silently turned the key to open the front-door and crept up the stairs to his bed.

However, he slept not a wink as he worried over and over about what cousin Adolphus could have been up to that night.

Chapter Four

Manchester November 1912

Suspicions

All that Summer the newspapers had been full of reports about the Balkans War and its ramifications and many commentators feared that the imperial ambitions of the German Kaiser, both in Europe and elsewhere were placing their country on a collision course with the British Empire.

Jacob took a lively interest in international events but found that discussions were best avoided in front of his German nephew Adolphus. There had been one occasion when, soon after his nephew had arrived, he had voiced criticism of Kaiser Wilhelm during a family Sabbath meal. Adolphus, predictably, defended the German position and even saw fit to remind his uncle that he was a reserve officer himself, in the Kaiser's army.

Joe listened to this exchange and whenever he had the opportunity he poured over his father's Manchester Guardian. As a result he developed a good grasp of the situation in the Balkans and its likely effect.

After the Ardwick event, he began to wonder more and more about the real reasons for Adolphus' visit to Manchester. He also watched his sister Rachel forming an ever closer friendship with their cousin. Then there was the matter of the nocturnal absences of Adolphus and with the knowledge of the considerable interest taken by the German cousin in British military garrisons, or at least the one in Ardwick, Joe became more and more convinced that Adolphus was a spy sent by the Kaiser to obtain information about the British army.

He started to avoid Adolphus' company and eventually the cousin began to sense that Joe was less than friendly towards him.

"Ach, Joe," he said one day, when they came face to face in the hall. "Is everything alright? I hardly see you except at mealtimes."

"Yes," Joe answered somewhat coldly, "everything is fine thank you."

"You seem to be avoiding me. When I first came, all you wanted to do was to talk to me. Have I upset you in some way?"

"No!" Joe answered abruptly and marched off to his room.

Joe agonised long and hard about his suspicions; but he was in a dilemma, judging by the way his parents seemed to now treat Adolphus more as a prospective son-in-law than just a nephew. He knew that voicing what he suspected could earn him the disapproval of his parents. And, of course, the most vital piece of evidence, the Ardwick trip, could hardly be admitted without getting him into serious trouble.

However, he decided that something had to be said and one evening when he was alone with his father in the study he spoke out.

"Dad," he began. "There is something worrying me."

"Yes," his father replied. "Your mother had asked me to speak to you this evening as she was sure that you were not yourself.

What is the problem?" he continued kindly. "Is it something to do with your studies in school?"

"No dad," Joe replied. "It is cousin Adolphus."

"Well Joe," Jacob replied hesitantly, "we had decided to tell you about that. Your cousin Adolphus has asked to marry your sister Rachel and she will have to accompany him back to Berlin after the wedding. Isn't that wonderful! They really like each other and with the money their family have, she will live like a queen."

Joe sat back in the chair completely shocked by this intelligence. How now could he tell his father that the man they had obviously given their blessing to as a future son-in-law was, in his estimation, a spy?

"So, Joe," his father continued, "What was it you wanted to say about Adolphus? Had you overheard us discussing wedding arrangements with him?"

"Yes, dad," Joe replied lamely. "That was it."

"Well, aren't you going to wish me Mazeltov?" Jacob enquired grinning.

"Yes, yes, of course, Mazeltov Dad," Joe replied.

"You don't seem very excited," Jacob commented.

"Mazeltov!" Joe repeated, without enthusiasm. "Now I must go to my room to do my homework."

Chapter Five

Manchester December 1912

The Wedding

Jacob was not a wealthy man, but he had only one daughter and had saved for years so as to have the wherewithal to make her a wedding to remember. His first son Alfred had made a good match and, as was traditional when funds allowed, the bride's family had made a fairly lavish celebration party for the occasion. Jacob had vowed then, that when it was Rachel's turn, he would provide to a similar standard.

Rachel and Adolphus were to be married in the Great Synagogue on Cheetham Hill Road. This was usually the venue of marriages between members of the Jewish aristocracy, wealthy merchants' and the daughters of professional men and leaders of the community. The secretary of the Synagogue had been a little surprised to receive an application for a marriage ceremony from a man who had only arrived in the country some thirty years earlier as a penniless immigrant. However, Jacob had the funds and the arrangements were made.

A celebration dinner ball was to take place afterwards in the Cheetham Assembly Rooms immediately opposite the synagogue.

Rachel had originally protested at the idea of her father spending so much of his hard-earned money on her, but Jacob had explained that the money had been earmarked especially for her marriage and he would not consider any toning down of the event.

"In any case," he told her, "you are marrying into a wealthy family and I would not want my brother to think I was a poor relation when he arrives.

The date was set for Sunday the 14th December 1912 and the day arrived. It was cold, dry and sunny which was a great relief to all concerned as they all knew from bitter experience how dull, wet and miserable the Manchester climate could be at that time of the year.

Adolphus' parents had arrived at Exchange Station the previous Wednesday. Jacob and Leah had joined Adolphus on the platform as the huge train from the port of Hull puffed its way into the grimy station.

They had offered accommodation in their home but Karl had insisted on moving into the Midland Hotel to join their son who had taken up residence there the previous week. It was obviously not proper for a bride and a groom to remain under the same roof for the week before the wedding.

Jacob had been warned by Adolphus that Kalman was now known as Karl and his wife, Adolphus' mother Gittel, was now known as Greta.

"What will you do for the Sabbath?" Jacob had enquired but his brother just told him not to worry and they would make their own arrangements.

The two Bergmann brothers bore little or no physical resemblance to each other. Jacob was of average height and although no one could have called him obese, he had developed a middle-age spread. He had a well-trimmed beard as was the fashion among many Englishmen of the time, Jewish or Christian. Brother Karl, on the other hand, was tall and gaunt of countenance. He sported side whiskers and a droopy moustache in the fashion of the Austrian Emperor, Franz-Josef.

In personality too, the brothers were totally different. Jacob was always smiling, even in adversity, whereas Karl was serious and seemed to lack even the suggestion of a sense of humour.

Their two ladies, however, who previously had never met, established an immediate rapport. True Greta was dressed in the height of fashion whereas Leah, although smartly clad was obviously wearing day-clothes that looked and no doubt were, far less expensive. However, when the German Bergmanns had disembarked from the train Leah had welcomed Greta with traditional kisses which were smilingly reciprocated by her sister-in-law. The two women had then walked down the long platform arm-in-arm, chatting in Yiddish, ninety to the dozen as if they had been bosom friends for years.

Leah told Jacob that evening that she was happy that their daughter would be starting her married life with such a pleasant mother-in-law. It had worried her that Rachel knew no one in Berlin. At least with Greta, she felt that Rachel would soon settle in to life in the German capital.

The synagogue Rabbi and Cantor conducted the wedding service which culminated with the age-old Jewish custom of the Bridegroom stamping on a glass, to remind them, in the midst of so much joy, that they were still exiles from their own land of Israel.

The newly married couple and their parents then crossed the road to welcome their guests to the wedding celebration.

The whole event had proceeded in a flawless manner and even the groom's father had managed a few watery smiles to indicate his satisfaction.

There was only one person, a young man who had acted as an usher, who was far from happy with the marriage. Joe was deeply worried about what would happen to his sister. He was certain that his new brother-in-law was a spy and would no doubt be reporting to the German government when he arrived back in Berlin. But, with the other members of the family proud and happy that Rachel had made such a good match, his suspicions remained unvoiced.

Chapter Six

Manchester & Berlin August 1914

Hostilities

The summer of 1914 was a time of acute anxiety for the Manchester Bergmans. Jacob and Leah could see the European powers heading helter-skelter towards a full scale war. First there was the assassination of the Archduke Franz-Ferdinand of Austria by Gavrilo Princip. This was rumoured to be have been plotted by the Serbian army. Then Germany inevitably sided with Austria whereas Russia took the part of her Slavonic compatriots in Serbia. Next, Germany declared war on France and on the 4th August the Kaiser's army marched into Belgium. Britain had guaranteed Belgium independence and neutrality so, on that same day, Britain declared war on Germany. One by one most of the European nations came into the conflict. It was like a huge and tragic game of dominoes with countries choosing sides based on their ethnic and commercial preferences and imperial ambitions.

Until the outbreak of hostilities, mail between their daughter Rachel and her family in England had been frequent and her parents were relieved to learn that she was exceedingly happy with her husband Adolphus. Furthermore, her mother-in-law had taken her under her wing and introduced her to a wide circle of new friends. The final letter before the outbreak of war contained even more exciting news. Rachel was now pregnant and due to give birth in January 1915.

Jacob scanned the front page of The Manchester Evening News of August 4th with horror. Here in stark print was the information that he so feared, the information that Britain had declared war on Germany. Suddenly, their daughter Rachel was cut-off from them by conflict and just at a time when they should be happily anticipating the arrival of a new grandchild. A week later a letter came through their letterbox from Rachel, expressing deep concern about what would happen to her. Adolphus had been spending less and less time at home attending to his father's shoe business and more time away on military matters. He was no longer a reserve officer and was now known as Hauptmann (Captain) Bergmann of the German Imperial Army. He was attached to military intelligence so at least he would not be on the front-line. Her mother-in-law was deeply upset by the turn of events. She was worried about her son and terrified that he would be transferred to a fighting unit. She was sad for her daughter-in-law, now isolated from her own family as a result of the war and, although hardly her first concern, she was disappointed that her regular trips to Paris to purchase her fashionable attire would no longer be possible.

Rachel told them that her father-in-law Karl was very busy. He had secured a contract to supply boots to the German army and was the only member of the family who seemed to be pleased with the news of war.

In earlier letters, Rachel had told the Manchester family of how her husband had agreed to take her to synagogue every Sabbath which was a far cry from his previous attitude to religion. It was a reform service and very different to the synagogue in which she had grown-up in Manchester and much of the proceedings was in German.

She knew Yiddish which she had learned from her parents and quickly grasped the rudiments of the new and not dissimilar language. Her mother-in-law had helped her and within a few months she was speaking German fluently.

Adolphus had grown to enjoy the visits to synagogue in Manchester and was only too pleased to accompany his wife in Berlin and eventually he decided that they should transfer their allegiance to a more orthodox and traditional house of prayer.

Now, with the prolonged absence of Adolphus on army matters, Rachel was obliged to make the short walk every Saturday alone. Just occasionally her mother-in-law Greta would accompany her but neither she nor her husband had any feeling for their age-old faith or for any other religion, come to that. However, Rachel quickly made friends among other members of the congregation.

Back in Manchester Jacob and Leah were worried by the prospect of their two older sons, Alfred and Joe being called up in to the army. Alfred was now the father of two little boys and had been working for some years as the legal clerk to a firm of solicitors in Manchester. Although there had been no conscription in force for many years, the Bergmans were certain that their government, just like the German and French administrations, would start a compulsory call-up to arms. However, such was the horror felt by the loyal British population when the German army virtually routed a combined French and British force at Mons on 23rd August, that volunteering became the order of the day and three quarters of a million men rapidly joined up to fight for King and country.

Alfred caught up like most of his compatriots in the wave of patriotic fervour, joined large numbers of other city workers in signing up and because of his education was promised a commission, once his training was completed.

Jacob was a firm believer in a good education and, although far from wealthy, he had scrimped and saved to put all his children through school and in the case of Joe, he had shown such promise that he had been about to take up a place at Manchester University to read politics and economics. The new scholastic year began in September but in August, Joe told his shocked parents that he had already volunteered for the Royal Flying Corps and would be undergoing training in Preston before being shipped out to France.

Germany and its emperor, Kaiser Bill, as the British now called him, had become bywords for evil. The whole family were desperately worried about their daughter and sister but away from the family circle it was considered prudent not to mention that Rachel was married to a hated German or Hun, as the population now called their sworn enemy. Of course, all their friends who had attended the wedding of Rachel and Adolphus just two years earlier maintained a considerate silence on the subject.

Berlin

Over in Berlin life was even more difficult. At least the Manchester Bergmans were able to comfort each other. However, with Adolphus away, no doubt making a substantial contribution to the German war effort and her father-in-law, as incommunicative as ever, on the rare occasions he was home from touring his factories, Rachel's only truly loyal friend was her mother-in-law. All the other Berlin society friends who had so quickly sought her friendship were now nowhere to be found. The Englishwoman Frau Bergmann was being ostracised. True, she had her synagogue friends but they were busy with their own lives which were far from easy, with fathers, brothers and husbands now drafted into the Kaiser's army. As the days went by Rachel's longing to, somehow, get back to Manchester grew, almost in direct proportion to the size of her pregnant figure.

For Adolphus the outbreak of war was greeted with great enthusiasm. Although he now had an English wife and had developed a liking for England or at least the north-west corner of that country, he considered himself a loyal German. All his training in the imperial army was now to be put to good use for the benefit of his Kaiser and fatherland. As an intelligence officer with an excellent knowledge of the English language, one of his main duties was interrogating captured British army personnel.

In November Adolphus returned to Berlin where he was to interrogate a number of senior British army officers who had been captured at Mons. This enabled him to live at home for a short while and spend a little time with Rachel. He saw instantly how unhappy she was and he listened sympathetically to her tale of woe. Sadly he was soon ordered to return to Belgium where there were many more prisoners-of-war to be interrogated. He left his pregnant wife sad and lonely.

The family had lived for many years in a large house in a residential suburb of Berlin. To run this house effectively, Greta employed a number of servants. Soon after the outbreak of war this situation changed. Although young women were not drafted into the armed forces, they were required to undertake work that involved them taking over the jobs of men now in the army. And one by one the housemaids departed from the Bergmann household leaving just Ursula, the elderly housekeeper to run the house with Greta and Rachel. This hardworking woman, despite arthritic knees, insisted on cleaning the house from top to bottom and it was only on Greta's insistence that she was persuaded to allow Rachel to take over the food shopping duties. The local shops were only a short walk away and Rachel quite enjoyed her regular outings although she was aware of a developing coldness from the proprietors of a number of these establishments when they realised from her accent that she was English.

However it came as a great shock to discover that, apart from being dropped from the Berlin social scene, she was not only despised as an Englishwoman but was beginning to experience anti-Semitism. She was jeered at in the street by a group of young soldiers on leave from the front who called her the 'English Jewess Bitch.' Adolphus, by this time, was back in Belgium and she told her mother-in-law who was furious. *Why*, she brooded, *the most loyal Germans, including many of the middle ranking officers, are Jews and only too willing to fight for Kaiser and Fatherland. Was not her own son and Rachel's husband, Hauptmann Adolphus Bergman an officer in military intelligence?*

Greta resolved to complain to the officer in charge of the local garrison about the way his soldiers had catcalled across the street to Rachel. She made an appointment and, because both her husband and son were well known she was quickly granted an interview.

Greta was escorted into the office of Oberleutnant Ernst Wagner who immediately rose from his desk, clicked his heels, bowed and welcomed her.

"Ach! Frau Bergmann. It is an honour to welcome into our garrison the wife of Herr Karl Bergmann, whose factories are working so hard to keep our boys in the trenches well shod. Please be seated. Maybe the Frau would like a cup of fresh coffee?"

"No thank you," Greta replied, completely disarmed by the pleasant young man sitting opposite her.

"You are obviously here for a reason but before we discuss whatever has brought you here may I enquire about my good friend Adolphus? I gather he is now a Hauptmann and therefore my superior officer," the Oberleutnant commented with a slightly resentful smile.

"He is well, as far as I know, and busy with his work in the army," Greta replied. "What I came to speak to you about involves his wife, my daughter-in-law, who, incidentally, is pregnant."

"I see," replied the young officer, his curiosity thoroughly aroused. He had seen Adolphus with Rachel in a cafe some months before the outbreak of war and had been more than a little impressed by her good looks.

"She is of course English," he continued thoughtfully, "but, now she is married to Adolphus, I am sure she realises that our Imperial Majesty the Kaiser had no choice but to support our Austrian friends against the Slavs."

"It is true that many people in Berlin, considered as friends, no longer wish to associate with an Englishwoman, even one married into a family like ours," Greta continued, "but the problem goes deeper than that."

"How do you mean, deeper?" Wagner enquired.

Greta sighed and decided to explain.

"The reason for my visit today is to complain about a group of your soldiers who terrified her by shouting anti-Semitic slogans and mocking her as she returned from a short shopping trip."

"I see," the Oberleutnant replied, looking extremely uncomfortable. "I did not know you were Jews. I always looked upon Adolphus and his family as good Germans."

This was not the reaction she had expected.

"We are good Germans," she answered sharply. "Surely that is obvious. We are just as committed to Germany and winning this war as anyone else."

The officer knew he had made a mistake and before he could try to make amends his lady guest continued,

"The Jews of Germany are just as loyal to the Kaiser as the Protestant and Catholic members of this great nation. Many of your fellow soldiers are Jews. You should know that."

"I... I do," Wagner stammered, "and you can be sure I will find the young men who insulted your daughter-in-law and they will be disciplined".

Chapter Seven

Antwerp & Berlin-Late 1914-1915

Rudolph Arrives

Adolphus, after his all too brief return to Berlin, was ordered to take up a posting as an intelligence officer in the main German garrison on the outskirts of the Belgian city of Antwerp. This city, bravely defended by the Belgian army, had fallen to the invaders on the tenth of October 1914. To do them credit, the German Army had been ordered to treat the historic city with care and as a result damage from the conflict was minimal.

The Hauptmann was accommodated in the home of a German family by the name of Scholz. They had been residents of the Belgian city for some years and were very happy there. However, they were still loyal Germans and had quickly volunteered to offer hospitality to an officer in the Kaiser's army once the war had started. Herr Scholz was a Lutheran and never forgot that his family were of Prussian origin. As soon as he saw Adolphus he suspected that he was of Jewish origin but the Hauptmann was a German officer and, as such, he was to be offered the highest standard of hospitality that the Scholz home could muster.

Martin Scholz and his wife Elsa were in their sixties. They had two sons, both officers serving in Northern France, and the child of their middle age, a daughter, now twenty seven and unmarried, by the name of Romilda. She was an exceptionally good-looking young blonde with a slim but curvaceous figure. As the daughter of wealthy ex-patriots she had never worked. Until the war broke out she had spent her time indulging in social activities including theatre and opera visits and imbibing large amounts of coffee and cakes in the cafes of the city. She had a large circle of like-minded friends who, one after another, had married into the same rarefied strata of Antwerp life. Romilda had many chances to follow suit by accepting the proposals and courtship of handsome, well-to-do young men from her circle but these approaches were all rejected out-of-hand.

Herr and Frau Scholz, seeing their daughter expressing no interest in their own nominees for the enviable position of son-in-law, despaired and left her to her own devices.

Their guest arrived in early December and settled easily into the large, elegant home, so similar to the Berlin house where he had spent most of his childhood.

"We are honoured to have you, a German officer, as our guest," Herr Scholz told him, trying to push to the back of his mind the Jewish appearance of the officer. "I am too old to fight for the honour of our beloved Kaiser and country. Welcoming you to our humble home is my small contribution to the efforts of his Imperial Majesty to halt the aggression of the Slavs and their allies."

Deep down Martin Scholz resented the fact that their guest was a Jew and his position as an Intelligence Officer only served to confirm this. *Trust a member of that race to get himself into a comfortable billet in Antwerp while 'real' Germans are fighting and dying in the trenches of northern France.*

Every day, after eating a hearty breakfast, Adolphus repaired to the garrison and specifically to where the British and French senior ranks prisoners were securely housed. His task was to interrogate the officers and although most of these men were resistant to his persistent questioning, by a mixture charm and cunning he succeeded in obtaining much valuable information. He talked about his time in Manchester to the British and his mother's love of Paris fashion to the French and once he had their friendship, many of them unwittingly supplied titbits of information useful to the German war plans. That is not to say that most of these brave men were disloyal to their own countries but a charm offensive will often succeed where threats, torture and aggression will fail.

Adolphus was particularly instructed to gain information about the aerial war ability of the British with their newly formed regiment, the Royal Flying Corp. Their first airplane the BE2 and its various improvements was no problem when the new German fighter plane, the Fokker Eindecker, made its appearance. The result was that the German airmen named this primitive British plane *Kaltes Fleisch* (cold meat.) However, the Germans knew that this situation would not continue and it was an important part of interrogation, to discover what new planes were being planned and developed by the British.

It was with a heavy heart, in November 1914, that Adolphus had left his now heavily pregnant wife to be posted to Antwerp. The baby was due in January 1915 and Adolphus had requested a postponement but he was told in no uncertain terms that his first duty was to the fatherland and his parents could easily look after the requirements of the younger Frau Bergmann and her, soon to arrive, offspring.

Rachel and Adolphus corresponded frequently, and his new hostess Frau Scholz was always sympathetic to his anxiety and enquired frequently for news of his wife in far-away Berlin. His host, however, while always a model of courtesy, deep down resented the necessity to host this Jew-boy and always maintained a distance. This however, could not be said for the lovely Romilda. Just as Rachel his wife had quickly fallen in love with him when he had arrived at her parent's home in Manchester, Romilda had taken one look at Adolphus' dark good looks and was determined to entice him away from his wife and into her arms. The Hauptmann however seemed to be impervious to her charms and becoming aware of her interest, tried to avoid being alone with her. This was somewhat difficult as the only place he was really safe from her attentions was in his own room. Otherwise, if he tried to read in the library, relax in the lounge or dine alone, he could guarantee she would appear and try to engage him in conversation.

Romilda was exceedingly attractive and he was miles from home, involved in a stressful job and separated from his own dear wife. A lesser man might have been tempted to take what Romilda was offering but if ever Adolphus did let his imagination drift in the direction of this beautiful young lady, the thought of his pregnant wife always brought him back to his senses.

On January the twenty-first 1915, Rachel gave birth to a son. A telegram was quickly despatched to the child's father in Antwerp to acquaint him with the wonderful news. Adolphus was thrilled and applied for leave which was promptly refused. He tried to explain that the baby was to be circumcised in accordance with Jewish custom on the eighth day of his short life and it was usual for the father to be present.

"Herr Hauptmann," his commanding officer told him with a note of exasperation, "Are you aware that there is a war on? You are fortunate not to be at the front where other young German men are dying in the trenches. They can't just up and go home for babies or anything else and neither can you."

Adolphus sent off a telegram to Rachel explaining his enforced absence and suggesting that the baby be named Rudolph with the Hebrew name of Reuben.

Rachel was deeply disappointed but the baby was nevertheless brought into the covenant of Abraham on the appointed day, the ceremony being performed by a local elderly Rabbi. A number of her new Synagogue friends attended as did her father-in-law and mother-in-law, although the former let it be known that he did not approve of the practice.

By some miracle, letters between the warring nations were still being delivered and when the Manchester Bergmans received the news they were naturally delighted. This brought just a chink of light into the darkness of their lives at a time when they had just been informed that their oldest son Alfred had been killed in the bloodbath of the trenches in northern France. He had left behind a wife and two children and Jacob knew that without a bread winner, it would now be left to him to provide for his late son's family.

Chapter Eight

Berlin 1915

A Revelation

For the next two months Rachel was sustained in her happiness by spending every waking hour personally caring for her new baby son. That was until a letter arrived from Manchester telling her of the tragic loss of her oldest brother Alfred. She was broken-hearted. She loved her younger siblings but she and Alfred had grown up together. They had attended the local school and shared the same group of friends and now this wicked war had taken him away from her; from his wife, two young children and her beloved parents.

She wrote a tear-stained letter to her beloved husband Adolphus to acquaint him with her news.

Rachel's father-in-law had been away as usual, when the letter arrived and her mother-in-law Greta did her best to console the inconsolable young woman.

Rachel then decided to visit her Rabbi to enquire if there was any way she could observe a period of mourning for her brother, so long after the tragic event.

Rabbi Klein tried to comfort her by saying,

"All you can really do is to lavish all your love and attention on your new baby Reuben. He is the comfort the Lord has provided to help you in your loss."

Apart from caring for Reuben and a few household duties, Rachel spent most of her time corresponding with her husband in Belgium and her parents in England. The post to members of the armed forces was prioritised and arrived speedily with its intended recipient. How any letters found their way through to enemy territory was a miracle and most of her correspondence never arrived. However, she wrote daily and waited anxiously for replies that never appeared.

Rachel longed to see her husband who was still in Antwerp and in August of 1915 she could wait no longer. She went to see Oberleutnant Ernst Wagner at the local garrison. He had been more than helpful when her mother-in-law had visited him last year and had identified and disciplined the soldiers who had caused Rachel so much upset by shouting anti-Semitic remarks at her in the street.

"Ach! Frau Bergmann," he greeted her, delighted to be in the presence of such a beautiful young woman. "I hope you have had no more trouble with my men."

"Not at all," Rachel replied, smiling. "In fact two of your young men helped me with my perambulator in the grocery shop last week."

"Gut! Gut!" the Oberleutnant replied. "So my dear lady, how may I help you?"

"I want to visit Adolphus in Antwerp and I need a travel permit. I gather there are frequent trains and I will take my baby son Rudolph with me. Do you know that Adolphus has not yet seen him?"

"I am deeply sorry Frau Bergmann but I doubt that I can help you this time."

"Oh dear," Rachel answered, deeply disappointed. "I was sure that if anyone could help me it would be Oberleutnant Ernst Wagner."

"Frau Bergmann," the young officer replied. "I really wish I could make this happen for you, but civilian travel is only allowed for people involved with the war effort like your father-in-law Herr Karl Bergmann''.

Rachel could see that her request was well beyond the authority of the Oberleutnant and thanking him she warmly bade him farewell. She was, however, not about to give up on her plan to visit Antwerp. She knew that the area was some distance from the war zones and the German army was well in control of the city. She pondered on what other avenues were open to her to obtain the necessary travel authorisation. She visited the railway station where she was told that all trains were being used strictly for army and government personnel. Civilians, even the wives of officers, could not obtain tickets. While she was still agonising over the situation, her father-in-law Karl came home. Rachel was in awe of the stern man with his bristling moustache. However, she resolved to discuss her plan to visit Adolphus with him. So, after dinner, she sought him out in the library of their home and requested a conversation. Karl smiled, a fairly unusual occurrence, and asked her what he could do for her.

"I feel it is high time that your son was introduced to his grandson Rudolph," she began. "He is already seven months old."

Karl's smile vanished. "Do you think I can get leave for Adolphus just like that? I may have some influence with the High Command, but the army has its own rules that must be strictly obeyed, especially in wartime."

Rachel surveyed her father-in-law's angry face. "That is not what I meant. I am well aware there is a war on. Have I not already lost my beloved brother through this madness?"

Karl glared at her. "And who is responsible for this madness, as you call it? The British, trying to support the cursed Slavs and the tin-pot Belgians; it's about time they woke up to the realities of this war."

Rachel was always in fear of the senior Herr Bergmann but she was not to be deterred. "I want to take Rudolph to Antwerp to meet his father. All I need is a travel permit."

Karl was becoming increasingly agitated. "All you need is a travel permit; just a travel permit! Such a small thing when Germany is locked in a terrible war. That is impossible, and if you think I could or would use my influence with the High Command to get you one, forget it. They would laugh me out of their offices." Karl stopped his rant for a second and then continued. "You have a very comfortable life here in Berlin thanks to the German army buying my boots and shoes. Where do you think we would all be otherwise?"

Rachel could see that Karl would never help her. She rose from her chair and with as much dignity as she could muster she left the library.

The following morning at the breakfast table Herr Bergmann announced that he would be leaving later that day for his factory in East Prussia.

He gets all the travel permits he needs with no problem, Rachel pondered.

She plucked up courage to ask him, "So you have no difficulty getting travel permits, do you?"

Karl gave her an angry look which was observed by his wife Greta. She wondered why Rachel had made such a comment and she resolved to ask her what was behind it, after her husband had departed on his trip.

At first, Rachel tried to avoid answering her mother-in-law's question but then decided that she really should report the conversation in full to Greta. She listened carefully and a look of sadness swept over Greta's face. By the end, the older woman was fighting back tears and her reply came as something of a shock to Rachel.

"Now you know how he treats me," she said sobbing. "Since you have been in the house I have done my best to cover up my feelings. The only good thing about this wicked war is that it keeps him well away from me."

Rachel looked shocked. "I am so sorry," she murmured.

Greta regained her normally controlled facade and spoke again. "I gather that trains to German occupied Belgium, especially in the Antwerp area run easily and all the fighting is much further south," she said, looking sadly into Rachel's face. "Let me think what I could do to help you." Greta was very fond of her daughter-in-law and she considered it sad that her son Adolphus had still not seen his baby boy. She had endured years of verbal abuse from Karl, but without money of her own she was destined to remain locked in marriage to this man who she considered to be a monster.

Chapter Nine

Manchester & Belgium 1915

A Single-Handed Attack

The atmosphere in the Manchester home of Jacob and Leah Bergman was one of perpetual sadness. A year ago they had a son called Alfred who had married well and produced two fine little grandsons for them. Their beloved daughter Rachel had also found a fine husband and was living happily in distant Berlin, but with the prospect of visits always on the horizon. Their two younger sons were both living at home and the elder Joe had just started university. Now their whole world had all but collapsed. Alfred was dead, killed fighting the army of the Kaiser in northern France. His wife was a widow and the two little boys fatherless. Rachel was marooned in Berlin the capital city of their enemy, responsible for the death of poor Alfred. Her husband Adolphus was separated from her and their new baby son, as a member of the German army of occupation in Belgium. Joe had answered the call to arms and was an officer in the Royal Flying Corp and that sounded like a dangerous occupation even in peacetime. Only Ike remained at home and he was just sixteen.

Jacob was now working in a textile mill for a pittance when compared with the comfortable living he had made as a travelling jeweller. Most of the young men who had been his customers were away fighting in the trenches. The womenfolk left behind had no use for jewellery when it was enough of a struggle to put bread on the table for their hungry children.

Leah was working as a seamstress sewing army uniforms. She returned home every night exhausted and with her fingers raw and almost bleeding from working with the coarse thread in the machines.

For the first couple of months after the war broke out they received frequent letters from Rachel. She seemed to be coping well with her pregnancy and was fulsome in praise of her mother-in-law, who seemed intent on doing all in her power to stop Rachel fretting because of the absence of her husband in the army. The father-in-law Karl was never mentioned. This did not strike his brother Jacob as significant as he knew him to be a high-powered businessman, who spent most weeks travelling to supervise the running of his large chain of shoe shops. However, not surprisingly, the regular post ceased and it was something of a miracle that the letter telling of the birth of baby Rudolph did arrive in February 1915. After that there was silence.

Flight Lieutenant Joe Bergman was one of a totally new breed of fighting men. They were the cream of British universities and recruited, or in most cases, had volunteered to be pioneers in a totally new kind of warfare; war in and from the air. Once a very rudimentary training was completed, Joe and his small band of intrepid flyers were shipped over to Saint Omer in Northern France, the first British airbase on French soil. It was from here initially that The Royal Flying Corp was to make their ever increasing contribution to the war against Kaiser Bill and his Huns, as the British people called the enemy.

Joe's plane was at first the BE2 but by 1915 he was flying the improved BE2b. His main duties were surveillance and as a fighter aircraft. This meant dealing with German aircraft before they could inflict damage on the British and French armies, who were locked in trench combat with the enemy in northern France.

The BE2b also carried a number of 100 lb. bombs which could be dropped on any vulnerable enemy positions that he discovered on his forays. By this method Joe and his friends were managing to inflict a reasonable amount of damage on the German military infrastructure. However, their efforts were often thwarted by the German planes, many of which, in the first two years of the war, were superior in speed and fire-power to the allied aircraft.

It was in August 1915 that Joe was able to inflict a blow to Germany's war effort out of all proportion to anything he had previously achieved. Joe and his Observer Private Gareth Jones had been ordered to fly over southern Belgium to try and identify German troop concentrations, when they became aware that they had attracted the attention of two Fokker E fighter planes. The allied flyers had just been briefed about the fact that these planes were now fitted with a synchronised machine gun. Joe was flying the BE2b which everyone knew was no match for even earlier versions of the Fokker, let alone the E. He started to nudge his plane towards its maximum height of 10,000 feet, knowing full well that the Fokkers could still fly over him and attack them from above with their maximum height of 11,450 feet. Their top speed of 87mph was also superior to the BE2b, which could only attain 70 mph and that in optimum conditions. His only hope was to force the Fokkers to chase their plane and to frequently change altitude and speed. The one saving grace of the BE2b was its far greater range, and Joe hoped to be able to force the Germans to give up the pursuit and return to base or run out of fuel and crash. Joe kept his concentration firmly fixed on this option, as if his life and that of Gareth Jones depended on it, and in truth they both did. The tactic paid off with one of the Fokkers which suddenly turned tail and made off into the distance. The other must have become airborne later and quite obviously the pilot was still comfortable with what his fuel gauge was telling him. He was determined to get within range so that he could use his synchronised machine gun to literally blow the British aircraft out of the air. The Fokker pilot had been chasing the BE2b for some time when Joe noticed he was no longer behind them. He hoped that this meant that the Fokker had given up the chase as his companion had already done. And then he saw the German flying towards him. The Fokker fired its machine gun and a hail of bullets miraculously missed him or so he thought. However, one bullet had done its evil worst and tragically snuffed out the young life of his Observer Private Jones. Joe had waited until the enemy aircraft was almost in range with its machine gun and then nudged the BE2b into a dive. Joe thought that his tactics had worked as the second Fokker obviously realised that he was almost out of fuel and then flew off into the distance. When Joe discovered that poor Gareth was slumped in his seat, it took just a further moment to realise what had happened.

This game of cat and mouse, or rather two cats and a mouse, had lasted for some considerable time during which Joe had covered many miles and had little idea where he was. He pulled the plane out of its dive and started to study the ground below. He was sick with anger about what had happened to Gareth and determined to avenge the death. However, his first duty was to get himself and his aircraft back to base. He checked his compass and consulted his maps and then realised that he had flown many miles north of his original target area. Below him he saw rail tracks and then to his astonishment he saw a train approaching. He flew a little lower and was able to make out the markings that indicated that it was a German troop carrying train. This was indeed divine providence and flying as low as he dared he cut back the air speed to just over stalling speed and waited. Within a minute the engine of the train was immediately below him and he eased his first 100lb bomb out of the cockpit. *That is for poor Gareth,* he decided. Incredibly it was a direct hit. The engine tumbled off the line, a smoking wreck, dragging the first four carriages with it. Joe took one more look at the scene below and made off to the south-west in an endeavour to find his way back to Saint Omer. However, he was no more than a few miles from the scene of devastation that he had just personally created, when his engine began to cough and splutter and he realised that he himself was now out of fuel. Ahead was a clump of trees and the loss of altitude indicated that he would hit them unless he could bank off the machine to the right where the land was flat. He almost made it but his left wings just caught the outermost branches of the largest tree. The plane finished off on its side, uppermost wings caught in the tree and lower wings resting precariously on the ground.

Joe eased himself gingerly out of the cockpit clinging onto the lower side and jumped to the ground. First he had the heartbreaking task of easing the body of his comrade out of the cockpit and burying him. He waited for a few minutes to see if anyone had heard or seen the crash and as satisfied as he could be that he was not observed, he removed all identifying papers and objects from Gareth. Fortunately for Joe, if you could call this good fortune, Gareth was small and thin whereas Joe was tall and strong.

With superhuman strength he hoisted his dead companion on to his back and staggered to the next field. Then he saw there was a stream running alongside the western perimeter of this meadow and he dragged himself and his sad burden down to its bank. He placed his friend's body gently down and realised that he had no method of digging a grave. Then he saw that there were small rocks alongside the stream and using one of these that was almost the shape of a roofing slate he eventually managed to move enough of the soft damp soil to create a shallow indentation deep enough to contain his friends body. He then hastily covered the poor young airman with soil and rolled two of the larger rocks over the area. He had no idea of the Christian burial service and just repeated a few of the Jewish psalms common to both religions.

Exhausted and feeling guilty that this was the best he could do for his comrade, he returned to the plane. He suspected that he was in Germany and abandoning the wrecked aircraft he set out for the road bordering the field. He needed to find a finger-post that would tell where he really was and to do that he needed a road junction. He followed field after field alongside the narrow country road without seeing or meeting even one human being. Joe passed what looked like farm buildings but no sign of intelligent life, just occasional flocks of sheep.

He was now feeling hungry and thirsty and realised that it was six hours since he had left the airfield at Saint Omer. Then he saw that he was approaching a road junction. There was a sign on the corner and he quickly made his way to it. *Antwerpen* he read was just thirteen kilometres to the left. There was also mention of a place called *Anvers* in the same direction but Joe had no idea that these names represented the Flemish and French descriptions of the same town. He suspected that *Antwerpen* was Antwerp and he knew from briefings that this city was the headquarters of the German army in that part of Belgium. Somehow it was a relief to be in Belgium rather than Germany although he realised that with the occupation now almost a year old, it might just as well be Germany itself where he was stranded.

He never heard the person approaching but suddenly there was a tap on his shoulder which made him jump. He looked round to gaze into the face of the prettiest young girl he had ever seen.

She spoke to him in a language he did not understand although he thought it had a vague resemblance to German or Yiddish.

Rather stupidly, he was still wearing his flying helmet and leather jacket with its British army insignia, so there was no point in denying his origin. Then she spoke again.

"You hat better kom met me," she said in recognisable English.

The girl seems charming and certainly good looking but is she about to hand me over to the Germans? He wondered.

Chapter Ten

Berlin & Antwerp 1915

A Nightmare Journey

It was the height of summer and Rachel had not seen her beloved Adolphus for eight months. Nor, for that matter, had Adolphus met his new son and heir. He was now a bonny baby boy with a smile that would melt the hardest heart. This was a fact, as on his rare visits to the family home even Grandfather Karl's hard heart melted and he was fascinated and delighted to be in the company of his first grandson.

How Greta had managed to obtain the ticket and travel permit for her daughter-in-law and young Rudolph was nothing short of miraculous. She had called in favours from senior government figures that were in her pre-war social diary and even a junior member of the Kaiser's extended family had been used in her quest.

Rachel was ecstatic when the August day arrived for her and dear little Rudi, as she called him, to take a taxi to the Berlin Hauptbahnhof. The Antwerp train was leaving at 10am and a porter carried all their baggage and Rudi's Moses-basket. Rachel wheeled her young son in his perambulator to the position on the platform where the first-class carriages would stop.

When the train pulled into the station Rachel was somewhat concerned to see that the second and third class carriages were clearly designated as troop-carrying and were consequently already full of soldiers. Even the first class compartments seemed to be occupied by officers. She was both pleasantly surprised and very relieved to discover that whoever her mother-in-law had persuaded to book the trip had ensured she had a compartment entirely to herself. She decided that this was an impressive achievement, especially in war time, and wondered how she could ever repay Greta's kindness in making such excellent travel arrangements.

A train guard had escorted her to her compartment and once inside had drawn the curtains to the corridor leaving her protected from prying eyes. He had offered to close over the drapes on the outer side but Rachel wished to watch the countryside as the train sped on its way towards Belgium and Adolphus.

Rachel knew little of the countryside of Germany and was surprised how beautiful and peaceful it was especially when a bitter war was being fought just outside its borders. She pondered on the rights and wrongs of the conflict that she knew was claiming the lives of countless young Germans and no doubt similar numbers of British and French young men. The news of the death some months previously of her beloved brother Alfred still weighed heavily on her mind. *What are they fighting for?* She brooded, her eyes brimming with tears. *What cause is so great as to justify the loss of so many young men on both sides?*

Little Rudi had been very good on the journey and after his feed had settled into a contented sleep. Then the train slowed down and Rachel could hear shouting coming from the corridor. She peeped through the curtains to see that a long line of soldiers had formed waiting for the train to come to a halt, when she suspected they would disembark. Turning to the other window she could see that they were in a semi-built up area and the train was now almost stationary. Then, with a shudder it stopped and she could clearly hear the soldiers chatting and laughing as they made their way onto the platform. *What are they so happy about,* she pondered. *They must know that many of them are on their way to certain death.*

Then she heard other voices some speaking German and a few speaking a similar guttural language but one that she could not understand. She was sure that she also heard some French which she had learned at school in Manchester. Then there was a loud knock on the door of her compartment and this was swiftly followed by it being flung open, even before she had had the time to respond.

Two men entered. One of them was wearing the familiar field-grey uniform of the German army while the other was dressed in a totally different uniform, replete with brass badges which no doubt indicated his rank.

The foreign man spoke first and asked her in bad German for her tickets and travel documents. He was courteous enough and his German companion was nodding and smiling which was re-assuring.

The German now spoke. "We are at the border between Germany and Belgium and this man is a customs officer. Please answer his requests and questions as best you can and we will then be able to leave you and your little one in peace to continue your journey." When he had finished this speech he clicked his heels and bowed.

The Belgian peered closely at the tickets and travel permit as if expecting them to be forgeries and after what seemed to be an eternity he nodded his head and returned them to Rachel. He then bowed and with a quick "Merci, Madame," the two men departed.

Rachel knew that customs officers usually asked a myriad of questions and she was relieved that the travel documents had been enough to satisfy the Belgian.

The noise of conversation in the room had awakened Rudi who needed a feed and some other attention before settling back to sleep.

The train was stationary for a good two hours while all the immigration and customs checks were completed. Eventually Rachel decided to have the packed lunch she had been given by her mother-in-law and it was while finishing this that the train once again started to move forward.

Rachel was delighted with the way that Rudi was coping with the journey and she settled down to read in the knowledge that within an hour or so they should be in Antwerp. Two or three minutes after opening her book, however, there was a tap on the door of the compartment. The men at the border had certainly not tapped; they had knocked hard and then opened the door without being given permission to enter. This was a tap and when she ignored it, suspecting it was her imagination playing tricks it came again. She closed her book which was an English story and slid it back into a bag. Anything associated with England or the English was not likely to endear her to a German national. She once again peeped through the curtain and could make out the figure of a young man in civilian clothing standing outside her compartment. There were still plenty soldiers on the train so she quickly opened the door.

"What do you want?" she demanded in German of the man.

The man looked at her in astonishment and said, "Are you English?"

"I am the wife of a German army officer," she replied. "Who are you and what do you want?"

"I am a mechanic working for the Belgium Railway Company," he replied in accentless German. "I can tell by your accent that you are English." He dropped his voice to a conspiratorial whisper. "I need to speak to you, can I come into the compartment."

"Absolutely not," Rachel replied. "Just state your business and leave."

Just at that moment she heard a shout from further down the corridor and two military policemen came running up to her compartment door.

"Is this man disturbing you?" they enquired.

Rachel, although she had been less than welcoming to the man at the door, had no desire to get him into trouble with the two tough, humourless looking men.

"No, its fine," she explained. "I was just enquiring what time the train arrived in Antwerp."

And then all hell let loose. There was a huge explosion from the front of the train which came to a grinding and juddering halt with the carriages before hers and those behind ricocheting into each other. The three men in the corridor were hurled to the ground as Rachel staggered back into the compartment and fell heavily on the upholstered seat. Poor little Rudi had awakened from the shock and the noise, and was crying bitterly.

It seemed like a few minutes before she could stand again although it was probably less than sixty seconds. Each time she made to go over to Rudi's Moses-basket there was another shock and another bang to shake the entire carriage. She realised, as these reduced in intensity that they were the result of carriages further behind on the long train, banging into each other. *Thank heavens*, she thought, *I put the basket on the ground not on the other seat or it would have been thrown off by the impact* and she shuddered as she thought of the consequences for her darling baby son if that had happened.

At last she managed to pick up Rudi who was unhurt but shocked by the impacts and commotion and holding him close to her for comfort she peered through the window.

Outside there was the noise of shouting and running, mainly from the rear of the train and looking out, she was horrified to see the engine and four front carriages all lying at crazy angles alongside the track. There was smoke everywhere.

Then she remembered the three men who had been standing at the door of her compartment when the initial explosion occurred. The door was still open but the two policemen and the civilian had all disappeared from view. She peered down the corridor and was horrified to see that only the first and unwelcome visitor appeared to be conscious while the other two were spread-eagled on the floor. Then the doors of the other first-class compartments started to open and an array of somewhat groggy looking army officers began to appear. Many of them looked as if they had been sleeping and were jacketless. Just two older men were fully dressed and one of them made his way, stepping over the bodies of the two unconscious policemen, towards Rachel.

"Ach!" he began. "Frau Bergmann. We have a serious problem here. I take it that you and your baby are alright, Ja?"

Rachel nodded and even tried to form a sad little smile.

"This carriage, the one in front and all the ones behind are safe but there is no way we can move. It appears that a cursed English plane dropped a bomb onto our engine. There are many dead and injured. Do you have food for yourself and the baby?"

Again Rachel nodded, wondering, gratefully how this senior officer had time to worry about her in the midst of so much devastation.

"Your father-in-law Herr Karl Bergmann is a good friend of mine," he explained, as if reading her thoughts. "I promised Frau Bergmann to keep an eye on you during the journey. As you know, the German army marches in Bergmann boots."

Rachel looked at the man in astonishment. *His own men are dead and dying out there and he is worrying about Bergmann's boots.*

"Thank you," Rachel answered. "May I know your name?"

"Ach! Forgive me. I am Oberst (Colonel) Otto von Lubeck," he replied clicking his heels. "Now, if you're sure you are alright I will go and see what needs to be done in all this mess."

Rachel looked around for the civilian who had tapped on her door just before the bomb, if that is what it was, exploded but he had disappeared. She was relieved to see that the two military policemen had now regained consciousness and were gingerly getting to their feet. She re-entered her compartment and closed the door. All this time baby Rudi had been gurgling happily in her arms but now he began to grumble. *Thank heaven, I came with plenty supplies for him,* she pondered, *but they won't last forever.*

Chapter Eleven

Belgium 1915

Wreckage and Reconciliation

Adolphus arrived at the train station in Antwerp half an hour before Rachel's train was due to arrive. He paced up and down the platform unaware of the amusement he was causing as a result of passers-by seeing a German army officer clutching a large teddy-bear as he waited for the first glimpse of his son.

Then he heard the announcement in Flemish, French and German that the Berlin train was delayed and people meeting it should wait for further announcements. Even in wartime German trains were famed for their punctuality and Adolphus was concerned enough to march over to the Station-Masters office to ask for an explanation.

When the railway clerk saw the Hauptmann at the enquiry window he immediately went to find a more senior person to deal with the German officer's demand for information. Two minutes later Adolphus was ushered into the office of the Station-Master himself.

"Please be seated, dear sir," the obsequious official said. "What can I do for you?"

"What has happened to the Berlin train that not only is it late but you don't know when it will arrive?" Adolphus queried.

The Railway official squirmed and said, "It appears there has been some sort of incident or accident. I've just received this telegram," and he handed the paper to the Hauptmann.

Adolphus felt sick. What if something had happened to his wife and child? If that was so, he could never forgive these idiot Belgians. Then he enquired, "Where is this place? Where did this so-called accident occur?"

"It is just over half an hour from here by train, but the line will be blocked by the Berlin train. However, your army are sending over some men now to see what the problem is."

"Where are they leaving from?" Adolphus demanded and a few minutes later he was sitting in an open truck with a motley group of Belgian railwaymen and German Soldaten (private soldiers) on the way to the stricken train. The German troops looked extremely uncomfortable to have an officer on board and after he had literally jumped onto the truck as it sped off, they tried to give him as much room and as wide a berth as possible.

Thirty five minutes later the men on the back of the rickety truck could see the giant railway engine lying on its side like a dying prehistoric monster. Behind it lay the derailed carriages. *Oh my God,* Adolphus agonised, *if Rachel and Rudolph were in one of those, I don't give them much chance of survival.*

The truck pulled alongside the first derailed carriage and Adolphus jumped to the ground. There were bodies lying all over the field, many obviously dead and the rest injured. All the casualties wore the field-grey uniform of the Kaiser's army. Other Soldaten were trying to help their wounded comrades but no medical assistance had yet arrived. Then he saw her! She was kneeling down by one of the injured men trying to help him, but where was his son? He started to run towards her, nearly tripping over bodies in his haste and finally he saw the Moses-Basket lying on the ground beside her.

"Thank God you are alright," he sobbed.

Rachel had been too engrossed in helping the wounded man to see him approaching, and suddenly being aware of his presence she looked up and simultaneously jumped to her feet.

"Oh, my God, Adolphus, where did you come from?" she cried, with tears running down her face. "Were you on the train?"

Adolphus pulled her into his arms kissing her face feverishly.

"No my dear girl, I just arrived from Antwerp on that truck," he explained pointing to where the contraption stood, just some two hundred metres away. "Now where is my son?"

Bending over the Moses-Basket he tenderly lifted the baby out and looked searchingly into his face. "He looks just like you," he said. "What a beautiful baby!"

Suddenly Rachel remembered the injured soldier propped up on his elbow. He had been watching the reconciliation with a little smile. "I must give this poor man some water," she explained.

By now two truck-loads of nurses and doctors had arrived from the garrison and were busily making their way around the injured men to ascertain who needed the most urgent help.

"I think we can now leave this to the professionals," Adolphus said.

With baby Rudi safely returned to the Moses-basket and carried by the proud father, they set off in search of Rachel's belongings. On the way they met Oberst Otto von Lubeck.

"Ach! Adolphus, my dear fellow, I see you have found your family; a little dusty but thankfully nothing worse. Get your things together and you can get a lift back to Antwerp."

Two hours later Hauptmann Bergmann, his wife and son were safely installed in the home of the Scholz family.

Chapter Twelve

Belgium 1915

Joe the Farmer

As Joe walked down the country lane with the girl, he wondered if he should make a run for it. She seemed friendly and sympathetic to his plight, but she was leading him further and further away from both his wrecked plane and from Antwerp. *How do I know I can trust her?* He agonised. *She is probably leading me to some German garrison and I will soon be a prisoner-of-war.* On the other hand, he considered, *why take me further into the countryside when the German army will be concentrated in towns like Antwerp?*

"Ve vill soon be home," she told him in her guttural accent. "It is a... farm yes that is the word, like French Ferme. Ve hab Koei, Ja?"

"Do you mean you live on a farm where there are cows?" Joe ventured.

"Ja! Dat is eet," the girl agreed.

Joe was beginning to think that he had little sensible alternative to accompanying the pretty young lady. "What is your name?" He enquired.

"Vat ees nem?" she answered.

"My name is Joseph," he ventured, "what is your name."

"Ahh! Yosef." she exclaimed. "Me Magda, Magda de Vries."

And so the stunted conversation continued until they turned down a narrow, unmade lane at the end of which Joe could see a farmhouse. As they approached he could see cattle standing contentedly in the warm late afternoon sun.

Magda escorted him into the house and pointed to a large armchair.

"Seet," she murmured, "Kaffee?"

Joe nodded enthusiastically and she went into what was obviously the kitchen to prepare a cup for him. It was hours since anything had passed his lips. *It seems just like Yom Kippur in Manchester,* he decided.

In five minutes she returned with a large mug of the steaming liquid. Then he had a sudden thought, *what if it is drugged?* And then he thought again, *what the hell? There is no way I can escape from here without finding myself even worse off.*

So, desperately thirsty, he gulped down the coffee and thanked Magda for her kindness.

She was indeed a very pretty girl, he decided as she sat in silence watching him enjoy the drink.

Joe had just finished the coffee when the door of the house opened again to admit a middle-aged man with white hair and a ruddy complexion. He had piercing blue eyes and they surveyed Joe in surprise and then turned accusingly to Magda.

"This is an English flyer. What is he doing here?" he enquired in Flemish.

Joe, of course had no idea of what the man was saying and watched with some surprise as Magda launched into a long and excited speech, the subject of which seemed to be him.

When Magda finished the man turned to Joe and said in passable English, "Welcome. We will try our best to help you."

"Thank you," Joe replied. "Magda has already been more than kind. If the Germans find me here you will both be in big trouble. If you will tell me how to get back to Saint Omer in northern France, I will set off now."

"There is no way you can leave here," the man said."I am Kurt de Vries by the way," and he held out his hand to Joe who shook it warmly and gratefully.

"My name is Joe Bergman," the Englishman explained.

"Bergman is a German name, not an English one," Kurt replied suspiciously.

Joe decided to explain.

"My parents are Jewish and the family came over to England from Lithuania before I was born."

Kurt stared deeply into Joe's face for a few moments which was long enough for Joe to worry if that piece of information would help him or throw him onto the mercies of the German occupation.

Eventually Kurt replied, "In that case you are doubly welcome; first as a Jew and secondly as an Englishman. Throughout my life I have only been blessed by my association with the two nations you embody."

Joe felt a little unworthy of all the praise being lavished on his origins and then realised that Kurt was once again peering at him thoughtfully.

"So would you be the brave English airman who bombed the Berlin to Antwerp train today?"

It suddenly occurred to Joe that he was giving away far too much information to this stranger. But what could he do? He could try to run but to where, and how? *He knows I'm an airman, I'm wearing all the kit,* he decided. *He knows my name; like an idiot I told him. If I admit the truth he will either try to help me or report me so, what the hell, I may as well tell him the rest of the story, I can't be any worse off than I already am.*

Joe nodded. "Yes that was me. I was being chased by two Fokkers and was completely lost." Joe's eyes filled with tears as he continued the story. "My Observer was killed by a stray bullet and then I saw the troop train and I decided I would have a go at stopping it; so I did."

"Well done," Kurt replied. "These bastards have been occupying my country for nearly a year now and what did poor little Belgium do to deserve such treatment? Nothing!"

"All I can ask of you is to forget I was ever here. I'm not going to cause you and your charming daughter any more trouble by outstaying my welcome."

"My friend," the farmer replied. "You are not going anywhere. You can stay here until this horrible war is finished. It is already almost a year. I am sure it will all be over soon enough." He turned to his daughter and said in Flemish, "Magda, let him have Henryk's room. Take him there now and let him see if he can use any of Henryk's clothes."

"I'm afraid I don't understand what you just told your daughter," Joe apologised.

"Of course," Kurt replied, "You must teach Magda English while you are here. What I said was to give you the room of my son Henryk who is a prisoner-of-war of the Germans. He is about your size and you can borrow some of his clothes while you are here. Now Joe, no more talk of trying to get away on your own. You would be picked up by a German patrol within an hour or two. When they guess who you are, the train bomber, you will be in front of a firing squad in double quick time."

Joe nodded gratefully. "What you say makes sense and you have my word that I will always be in your debt."

"Go now and settle in," Kurt replied. "We eat at seven and I know you don't eat pork. All I want from you in return for all this is a little help around the farm."

So Joe Bergman, British student and flyer became a Belgian farm worker, at least until some other even more remarkable events occurred.

Chapter Thirteen

Manchester & Antwerp 1915

More Bad News

When Alfred died, his parents learned of his death by means of a telegram from the war office. The stark news that he had been killed in action was heart-breaking enough and for it to be received in this inhuman way was all the more distressing. They observed the traditional first seven days of intense mourning and were grateful that, as the parents of a war hero, they were allowed this short period of time to grieve. They were also deeply worried about their daughter Rachel in Berlin and their new grandson and the total lack of news about them fuelled an imagination which was becoming increasingly despondent. Then another blow arrived.

Joe was an officer in the Royal Flying Corps and they prided themselves on looking after their own. As a result when Joe failed to return to Saint Omer from his mission a signal was sent to London to arrange a personal visit to his parents by an RFC officer.

The Officer sat in the Bergman's front room in Manchester and explained that their son's plane had failed to return to base. At that stage they had no idea if he had crashed or been shot down by the enemy.

"As soon as we have further news, we will be in touch," the officer gently told the couple, now in a state of virtual collapse. "We must always hope for the best."

Just two weeks later the same officer returned to tell them that the Germans had discovered Joe's plane had crashed in a clump of trees in a remote country area of

Belgium. There was no sign of the pilot or his one-man crew.

"So there is still hope. How do you know all this anyway? Surely the Germans didn't tell you," Jacob commented.

The officer nodded and explained that they had many friends in Belgium who were able to pass on this type of information. Then he went on his way.

After seeing the officer out of the house Leah collapsed in tears.

The Bergmans had just one remaining son at home, Ike. He was now seventeen and if the war had not ended by then, he would be called up into the army on his eighteenth birthday. Quite understandably they anticipated the arrival of that day with little short of terror.

Antwerp

Rachel settled well into the Scholz family household. She was back at last with her beloved Adolphus and with baby Rudi they made a fine family unit, even if in someone else's home. Elsa Scholz was very welcoming and doted on her youngest guest. It was many years since there had been a baby in her home. Her older sons were army officers but her third child, Romilda had graduated from a spoilt child into a petulant, selfish young woman. With a plentiful supply of handsome young army officers in town, she had long ago betrayed her strict Lutheran moral upbringing in favour of pleasures of the flesh. As for Elsa's husband Martin, he certainly did not mellow with age. He became an increasingly bad-tempered and demanding head of the household and his gentle wife was terrified of his frequent outbursts. It took Rachel just a few hours to pick up on the undercurrents in the home and she too tried to give Martin

Scholz a wide berth. In addition, Romilda worried her. It was not that she was in any way discourteous to Rachel but she quickly noticed the way that Romilda's entire demeanour changed when Adolphus was present. She became quite coquettish and giggled like a schoolgirl as soon as he appeared. To his credit, Adolphus treated the young woman with a mixture of cold courtesy and disdain. This was all re-assuring for Rachel who initially wondered if Romilda could be capable of snaring her husband or indeed had done so before she arrived to resume her wifely duties.

It was then that a strange and unsettling event occurred. Adolphus had a new batch of prisoners-of-war to interrogate. As usual they were officers and Adolphus spent the first few days after the arrival of his wife and baby son in Antwerp, interviewing the British soldiers. On the fourth day the second man was a junior officer in the Royal Flying Corps. He was a dark haired, young man who had just one minor imperfection or he would have been described as very handsome. He had a long scar on the left cheek.

"Please be seated," Adolphus addressed the young officer. "What are your name, rank and serial number?"

The young British prisoner proceeded to supply the required information in accordance with international protocol for prisoners-of-war. "My name is David Goldberg, I am a Second-Lieutenant in the Royal Flying Corps and my serial number is 2364379."

"May I call you David?" Adolphus started his usual charm offensive.

"My name is David Goldberg, I am a Second-Lieutenant in the Royal Flying Corps and my serial number is 2364379."

"Come, come," Adolphus replied. "I am just a humble Hauptmann myself; there is no need to be so unfriendly."

The young British officer sat opposite Adolphus glaring at him.

Adolphus tried again. "Where do you come from in England?"

"My name is David Goldberg, I am a Second-Lieutenant in the Royal Flying Corps and my serial number is 2364379."

Adolphus gave him a big smile. "Look David, this is all rather silly. We are both about the same age and I am sure that if not for this war we would be good friends."

"Herr Hauptmann, you know as well as I do that all I need to provide is my name, rank and serial number and you have these. May I please be returned to my comrades in the Prisoner-of-War camp?"

Adolphus gazed at the Englishman with a look of disappointment. "I am not asking you to betray your country, just for us to be friends."

"My name is David Goldberg, I am a Second-Lieutenant in the Royal Flying Corps and my serial number is 2364379."

Goldberg, Goldberg, he pondered. *That is usually a Jewish name. Yes, I am sure he could be Jewish. I will try something else.*

"Oy, Dovidle, Dovidle, you are giving me plenty Tzoros, (aggravation)" he ventured.

"Look Herr Hauptmann, I thought you were Jewish the minute I saw you but you are still an enemy officer and I have no information for you other than my name, rank and serial number," the Lieutenant confirmed.

Adolphus was a very patient man and his kind of interrogation usually produced some results. Time was on his side. He went home at night to his family while men like

David Goldberg were locked up in the primitive conditions of the camp.

Adolphus stood up. "Thank you Lieutenant, you can go now."

When Adolphus returned home that evening he related to his wife, after dinner, the episode with the British Second-Lieutenant.

"I was sure he was Jewish," Adolphus told her. "Apart from his name, I could just tell somehow. He didn't have any strongly Jewish facial characteristics, but how many of us do?"

"So what was his name?" Rachel enquired.

"David Goldberg," Adolphus answered.

"Surely you know that is always a Jewish name in England?" Rachel suggested.

"I don't know English names like you do and in Berlin we never socialised much with other Jews, so I wasn't sure," Adolphus explained.

"David Goldberg is a very common Jewish name in England. I used to know three young men myself in Manchester with exactly that name."

"So, maybe this is one of them," Adolphus replied. "This man was about my age, tall, dark haired and fairly dark skinned."

"That sounds like half the young Jewish men of England," Rachel grinned.

"Ah, but my man had a long scar on his left cheek," Adolphus added triumphantly.

Suddenly Rachel went white. "Oh, my gosh!" she exclaimed. "I do know him. He lived around the corner from us and was a good friend of my poor brother Alfred."

"Well, he is an RFC officer just like the man who bombed your train. For all I know, he might be the flyer who did the deed and nearly killed you and baby Rudi."

"Don't forget all the awful things your army is doing to them," she retorted.

"Well as far as I know we haven't resorted to bombing trains with women and children on them," Adolphus answered testily.

"Come on, Adolphus," Rachel replied, "it was obviously an army train; how could the flyer know that there were civilians on board?"

What followed was their first serious row. Only the knowledge that they were guests in another family's home kept them from shouting, but Rachel had never seen Adolphus in such a rage and eventually she went off to bed trembling with indignation. Much later she heard her husband slide between the sheets but not a word passed between them that night or across the breakfast table in the morning.

"I want to interview Second-Lieutenant Goldberg again," he barked when he arrived at the camp.

Half an hour later the British flyer was marched into his office.

Adolphus glared at him. Goldberg was somewhat surprised by the Hauptmann's demeanour. He had decided that the German officer would give him an easy time, if only because they were co-religionists.

The previous day Adolphus had been genial, friendly and had invited him to sit opposite him at his desk. Today, he simply barked, "Stand to attention."

The prisoner-of-war regarded his inquisitor with surprise.

"Ach," Adolphus began, "I know all about you now. You are from Manchester and I even know where you lived, in Jackson Street, Cheetham Hill. I also suspect that you may be the criminal who bombed the train and nearly killed my wife and son."

David Goldberg was shocked. How could this German officer know where he came from? And what was all this talk about him being responsible for a train bombing?

Once again, trying to disguise his anxiety, David repeated, "My name is David Goldberg, I am a Second-Lieutenant in the Royal Flying Corps and my serial number is 2364379."

This seemed to enrage the Hauptmann even more.

"Enough of this rubbish," he shouted. "I want to know why you bombed a train."

The British officer was in no position to lose his temper much as he resented being accused of something that he could not possibly have done. With icy calm he replied, "I was not even in France when the plane that bombed your train took off. And," he continued, "You should not be questioning me about operational matters. Do you want my name rank and serial number again? That is all I have to tell you."

Adolphus began to calm down and reclined comfortably in his high-backed leather chair to survey the prisoner. He stayed gazing into David Goldberg's face for what, to the British officer, seemed like an eternity. The latter decided to break the silence. Curiosity had gained the upper hand over discretion – the silence was achieving for Adolphus what bullying accusations had failed to produce.

"Sir, can I ask you a question?"

"I am the interrogator here," Adolphus answered. "However, what do you want to know from me?"

"How do you know I am from Manchester?"

"Ach," Herr Lieutenant, "we have our sources," Adolphus replied mysteriously."

"We are ordered to leave all personal information, including letters from home, in our barracks when we go into action and I follow my orders in this respect with great care. The only information you should have about me is from my Identity Card and that certainly does not contain any personal information."

Adolphus felt that he was now making progress. "Do you know a British officer in the infantry by the name of Alfred Bergman?"

The Second-Lieutenant nodded sadly. "I did, he was my boyhood friend; you people shot him in the trenches in France early this year."

Suddenly Adolphus felt pity for Goldberg. He could see his eyes had filled with tears at the mention of Alfred's death. Also, Alfred was, after all, the Hauptmann's first cousin and brother-in-law.

"Look," he said, "Lieutenant, please sit down."

David Goldberg was confused. Yesterday, the German interrogating officer had been all charm and this morning an arrogant bully. Now, he seemed to be reverting to the demeanour of the previous day.

David carefully and a little gratefully sat down. Then suddenly the entire situation began to make sense. The name of the German was Hauptmann Bergmann; he had seen that on the door of his office. Was not the surname of his poor lost friend Bergman? He began to suspect that they must be related, and then he remembered something else. Alfred's sister had married her cousin, an army officer, from Berlin. This must be the man, he decided. This must be Rachel's husband. He had been invited to the wedding but had been away at university at the time, otherwise he would have recognised the Hauptmann instantly.

Suddenly the German officer spoke again. "Why are you staring at me?" he demanded.

"You may know who I am," David explained, "but I now know who you are. You married Rachel Bergman and took her back to Berlin."

Adolphus surveyed the prisoner and remembered his comments from the previous interview, *we are both about the same age and I am sure that if not for this war we would be good friends.*

The Hauptmann nodded. "Ja! You have guessed. I didn't know if you were aware of the death of Alfred Bergman but you obviously had heard."

David nodded sadly. "I suppose you know that Joe, his younger brother is missing."

Adolphus looked at him in shock. There had been no communications for some time now and how was he to tell Rachel that another of her brothers could be lying dead on some muddy, cold French field.

"Mein Gott!" he exclaimed. "What happened to young Joe?"

David looked carefully into the face of the man who was his interrogating officer and realised that the small amount of information he had about Joe would hardly aid the German war effort.

"Joe Bergman is or was a flyer in the RFC, just like me," he explained.

"Ach! So," Adolphus nodded agonising on how he was to tell his dear wife Rachel the terrible news. "Do you have any more details?"

"No," David replied. "All we know is that he never returned from a mission last month and we believe that your people discovered his empty plane after it crashed in a field not far from here."

Adolphus looked a little shocked and rose to his feet gesturing to David to remain seated. "I will return in just a few moments," he explained. "You must stay here and do not try to leave this room or you will be in trouble with the guards outside."

The few moments extended to about fifteen minutes during which time David became more and more curious as to why his interrogating officer should suddenly leave him alone. He was after all a prisoner and this seemed a strange way to treat him.

Then Adolphus returned. "It is perfectly true that the plane that Joe Bergman was flying crashed," he told David. "There was, however, no sign of his body or that of the other crew member and the way that the aircraft crashed was a 'soft' landing in a clump of trees. Now you might ask how we knew that the pilots name was Joseph Bergman? This is how," the Hauptmann finished, brandishing an empty envelope addressed to Second Lieutenant Joseph Bergman that had been found in the cockpit of the BE2b.

"Thank you for telling me this," Goldberg replied. "So there is room for some hope then, that Joe is still alive."

Then David once again sensed a mood change in the attitude of the German officer.

"I don't know if 'hope' is the right word. I have just been told that it was almost certainly your friend Joe and my accursed brother-in-law who bombed the train which nearly killed my dear Rachel. If our people find him, and believe me they are looking hard, I do not fancy his chances. So," the Hauptmann continued, "you had better be returned to your camp now and I will consider if it is wise for me to talk to you again."

Adolphus opened the office door, to summon a guard to return David Goldberg to the prisoner-of-war camp and both men brooded on the positions in which they now found themselves from their widely differing perspectives.

However, neither of them could have anticipated in their wildest dreams or nightmares what would happen next.

Chapter Fourteen

Somewhere in Belgium 1915

Down on the Farm

Joe had been living on the de Vries family farm for some five months. During that time he had learned from his host Kurt the rudiments of farming. He worked hard and initially was happy to be away from the war. His thoughts on fighting the enemy veered between satisfaction at the huge blow he had single-handedly achieved in bombing the train and sadness about the loss of human life that his action had caused. It was one thing to shoot someone before they could shoot you and another to release such destruction on those below who were blissfully unaware of his existence.

He worried incessantly about his parents and youngest brother. Did they know he was alive or did they consider him as dead as his poor oldest brother Alfred and his comrade Gareth Jones? As for Rachel, she was stuck in Berlin, as far as he knew, with her German husband. *How right I was about him*, he pondered. *I knew he was up to no good in Manchester. He was a spy and we now know what they do with spies; shoot them!*

And then there was the matter of Magda; Magda, the pretty, shapely young farm girl who had crept into his room and into his bed just two weeks after he had accepted the hospitality of her father. The situation with Magda worried him on many counts. He was sure that if Kurt discovered that he had taken his daughter's virginity, he would either shoot him on the spot or tell the Germans to come and arrest him. Then he felt guilty from a religious point of view. His parents had expected him to settle down with a nice Jewish girl and provide them with grandchildren that they would be proud of. And then the inevitable happened and Magda told him that she was pregnant.

They discussed the situations interminably in whispered conversations as she curled her young body around his in the warmth of his bed. Curiously, Magda seemed almost happy with the situation and when a bulge started to show beneath her clothes Joe decided that he must secretly plan to leave the comfortable security of the farm, if he was not to bring disaster upon her as much as upon him.

On Thursdays Karl always took the farm's produce to market and Joe told Magda to prepare to leave with him the following week. The idea of abandoning the girl to the inevitable anger of her father seemed the lesser of the two evils, although he knew that what he was planning would involve Magda and their unborn child in great danger, as the companion of an allied officer on the run.

On the Wednesday evening before their intended departure the trio sat down to their supper together as usual.

"We are getting a very good yield of milk from those new Friesians," Kurt commented with a broad smile on his face. "I hope our little lady here will also produce good milk for her little offspring when it arrives."

"W'what did you just say Kurt," Joe stammered.

"I said I hope our little lady Magda will feed her new baby as well as our new cows are feeding theirs."

Joe looked across the table at Magda who responded with a big smile.

"Poppa has known I was pregnant for a few weeks now and he thoroughly approves of the father of his future grandchild."

Joe was astonished. "Why then did you listen to all my plans to leave here and take you with me?" he demanded.

"Once I knew you would not leave me behind, I knew you really loved me, although you would have been taking me into danger if the Germans had caught us."

"Well that is settled then," Kurt pronounced. "I am very happy that you have given my daughter a baby. When the war is over you can marry her."

Two members of the trio finished their meal in a contented silence; the other in the dazed recognition that he was probably destined to spend the rest of his life as a Belgian famer. This was not the future that he and his parents had dreamed of but at least he was alive and he realised that this was a far more comfortable prison than the one the Germans would have provided for him.

Chapter Fifteen

Antwerp 1915

Separation

Adolphus returned home in the evening after his second interview with David Goldberg. As far as his superior officers were concerned his interrogation methods worked. They were aware of no difference in the way he had ultimately interrogated the Second-Lieutenant, from his usual probing for military information.

His first task was another potentially difficult interview; this time with his wife Rachel. After the bitter argument that they had the previous night they had ignored each other at breakfast. Adolphus, as was his custom, went up to baby Rudi's room to say goodbye to him but not a word was exchanged with his wife.

Rachel was chatting to Elsa, the lady of the house, when her husband returned from the barracks. He marched into the room and voiced a friendly "Guten Abend," into the air without looking at either lady. He then seated himself in an armchair. Rachel continued with her conversation and ignored him. Elsa quickly picked up on the atmosphere and glanced swiftly from one to the other. She then resumed her conversation with Rachel while Adolphus sat quietly, unable to join in the discussion about the effect that the war was having on the prices of vegetables. After a further fifteen minutes, during which time Adolphus had been gazing into space, Elsa rose and after giving him a watery smile, she left the room.

Adolphus sat in silence with Rachel for a further two minutes and then ventured, "I have some news for you."

"Are you talking to me?" Rachel enquired.

"Well, I don't see anyone else in the room now that Elsa has left," he retorted.

"Sarcasm is often called the lowest form of wit," she announced as if the room was full of people.

"I have some news for you," Adolphus repeated.

"Well, if you have some news you had better tell me what it is. It is no good just sitting there announcing you have news and not telling me what it is."

"Your brother Joe is missing after his plane crashed just outside Antwerp," he explained trying to master his anger in the knowledge that his wife would need all of his support now another brother was a possible casualty of the war.

"Oh, no," Rachel whispered bursting into tears.

Adolphus rose from the chair and crossed the room to put his arm round his wife. "The plane was found by our people in a clump of trees with no sign of the two-man crew so it sounds as if he is alright. He is probably on the run somewhere in Belgium."

Rachel was understandably heart-broken to hear the news. She was also angry and felt that her husband somehow represented the entire German nation and all that it was inflicting on her family.

"Get away from me," she muttered and ran out of the room sobbing.

Adolphus rose to follow her but when he caught up with her on the stairs she told him, "Just keep away from me. I want nothing more to do with you, your army and your entire nation."

He returned sadly to the lounge and seated himself in the same recently vacated armchair to consider how he could be reconciled with his wife. After half an hour, he heard her return downstairs to have a lengthy conversation with Elsa.

He strained his ears as he tried to hear what was being said. *Obviously,* he decided, *Rachel is telling Elsa about Joe but why is she blaming me.*

He resolved to stay in the lounge and see if Rachel had calmed down after talking to Elsa. Eventually he heard footsteps approaching the lounge door and assumed this would be Rachel. However, it was Elsa who entered the room.

"Your wife is very unhappy and broken-hearted about her brother. She blames you for all her misfortunes and longs to return to her family in Manchester. That, of course, is impossible so she is returning to Berlin tomorrow with baby Rudi. All she wants from you at the moment is the necessary travel documents. She asks that you sleep in another room tonight and she does not want to see you at all before she leaves." Then Elsa dropped her voice to little more than a whisper. "She is not being entirely reasonable or logical at the moment but maybe that is not so surprising in her condition."

Adolphus was deeply upset to hear the news. He adored his wife and just thirty six hours ago the three of them seemed to be an ideal family unit. Then he started to absorb the last part of what Elsa had said; the whispered comment. "What do you mean 'in her condition'?" he enquired.

"Did you not know she is three months pregnant?" Elsa replied in surprise.

Adolphus had been a spoilt young man who had inherited a strong streak of arrogance from his father. However, unlike his sire, he had mellowed as he approached his third decade. He deeply loved his wife and son. All the emotion of the last day suddenly engulfed him and he burst into tears.

Elsa also had a hard arrogant husband and she had no idea how to comfort an officer in the Kaiser's army who had been reduced to tears. "Please, Adolphus," she said, "restrain yourself."

"I am going out now," he explained sadly, dabbing his eyes with a handkerchief. "I will return with the travelling permits and tickets in about an hour. Please acquaint my wife with this information. I am deeply sorry about her brother but there is nothing more I can do if she blames me. Just tell her I love her and I will come to visit her in Berlin as soon as I have leave. By then, I trust, she will be in a better frame of mind."

And so Adolphus was again divided from his family; much to the satisfaction of one particular young lady.

Chapter Sixteen

Bradford & Antwerp 1915

Feldwebel Erich Braun

Eric Brown was born in Bradford Yorkshire in 1891. Like many of his fellow-countrymen his father had left Germany and settled in England to gain employment in the woollen industry. Günter Braun was an intelligent and ambitious young man. He married Jean Roberts, a local lass who worked in the mill where he was now a manager and they lived on the edge of the area known as Little Germany.

Eric was their second child, the first being a girl who died in an epidemic of measles in 1890. He was a bright boy and his father was able to have him educated at the best schools in the area. This enabled Eric to win a scholarship to Leeds University to study textile engineering. However, when the time came for him to seek employment the mill owners of Bradford, one by one, rejected his applications for a position in management. They were all most impressed with his education but on interview he was found to be arrogant and aggressive. A number of these mill owners were German Jews and Eric had expected that as he was of German descent himself, they would be lining up to employ him. He quickly decided that Jews did not like him and his hatred for them was kindled.

His father Günter had been more than happy to settle in England, marry an Englishwoman and by dint of hard work and ability, provide well for his family, out of his employment. However, although his physical life may have been largely spent in the country in which he now resided, his heart was still at home in Saxony. As a consequence he was determined that young Eric should be completely fluent in the German language and should inherit the same love of his father's native land as he had retained.

At twenty two years of age, and unable to find a suitable position in Bradford, Eric resolved to visit Germany and discover his father's old haunts from his boyhood. Günter was delighted by the suggestion and financed the trip enthusiastically. It was just a few months before the outbreak of the war and whatever loyalty Eric had for England quickly dissipated as he became more and more enchanted with the land ruled by the Kaiser. Realising that he could be very useful to Germany he approached an army base and asked to speak to a senior officer. Being completely bi-lingual his value to the Kaiser's army was incalculable. After a series of meetings it was agreed that his name would be changed to Erich Braun and that he would be trained in military intelligence. It was there that he encountered Adolphus who was at that time, before the outbreak of war, training other and younger men. Erich instantly decided that he disliked the soon-to-be Hauptmann and lost no opportunity to speak of him in a derogatory way to others. He always described him as the Jüdisch Offizier (The Jewish Officer.)

When his period of training was over, he was promoted to the rank of Feldwebel (Sergeant.) Many of his colleagues on the courses achieved higher ranks but his arrogance and resentful attitude towards authority, as in Bradford, dissuaded his senior officers from giving him too much responsibility too soon. Erich, of course, was convinced that Adolphus was responsible for him being passed over for a commission and when he heard that Adolphus had been promoted to Hauptmann his hatred knew no bounds.

He had seen the prisoner-of-war David Goldberg entering Adolphus' office on two consecutive days and he was certain that the British Second-Lieutenant was a Jew. *I have a nose for these people,* he told himself.

There was nothing unusual in intelligence officers having frequent meetings with senior prisoners. However, Erich was suspicious that Adolphus was about to betray his country, just because the British officer was also a Jew. He tried to listen to the second conversation outside the door of the Hauptmann's office until he was disturbed by approaching footsteps. However, he had heard what he considered enough to make trouble for Adolphus. As a result he asked for a meeting with one of Adolphus' senior officers, Major Rolf Werner and voiced his suspicions.

"What makes you think that Hauptmann Bergmann is acting against the interests of Germany?" the officer demanded.

"Well," Erich answered, "I was passing the Hauptmann's office where he was interrogating a British Lieutenant when I caught the words *it was almost certainly your friend Joe and my accursed brother-in-law who bombed the train....*

The Major was furious. "You have been trained in Military Intelligence; you must know how important it is to try and make friends with prisoners. That way they will trust us and give away secrets. That is how Hauptmann Bergmann operates and it works. In any case, how dare you go eavesdropping outside the office of a senior officer? Do you have any other grounds to suspect the Hauptmann?" the officer finally enquired.

"Only that they are both Jews and I know how dishonest they can be."

"That will be quite enough of that. Many of our finest soldiers are Jews," the officer told him, angrily. "You are

English, are you not? How do we know we can trust you? I suggest that you get out of my office before I have you brought up on a charge."

Erich was shocked. This was not at all the reaction he expected. Of course there were many men in the German army who shared his obnoxious views about Jews but he had certainly picked the wrong one on this occasion. What he did not know, however, was that Major Rolf Werner's paternal grandfather had been of Jewish origin and this was information that the Major had no intention of giving to the lowly Feldwebel.

However, the delicate flower of trust can easily be damaged by the waters of discontent and once Braun had been dismissed from his presence, the Major started to ponder on the snatches of conversation that Feldwebel Braun had overheard. The words *it was almost certainly your friend Joe and my accursed brother-in-law who bombed the train....* did seem strange and overly-friendly to have been expressed to an enemy officer and Major Werner decided to try and ascertain the veracity of the report. He approached Adolphus in the officer's mess.

"Ach, my dear fellow Adolphus," he started. "How are things with you and your family?"

"Fine, Sir," the Hauptmann answered, feeling anything but fine. His wife had just returned to Berlin taking his baby son Rudi with her and this after two days of angry exchanges between the pair.

"Gut! Gut!" the Major muttered. "How are your interrogations going?"

"Herr Major, you know I report all important information to the Oberst-Leutnant (Lieutenant Colonel.)" Adolphus responded, allowing a slight indication of an uncharacteristic irritation that a superior officer should be asking such a question.

"Ja! Ja!" the Major replied patiently, "but I was just interested in how you were progressing with the British flyer we captured last week. "I believe that this war will be won in the air and not in the trenches."

"I think you are right," Adolphus responded slowly. "I take it you mean the British Second-Lieutenant from the RFC."

"Ja!" the Major confirmed. "I heard you had two meetings with him on consecutive days."

"Well, Herr Major, you are well informed," the Hauptmann replied. "I doubt that I will see him again. He talked a lot but said nothing of any value."

"I see," the Major tried again. "I thought that maybe he had some information about the train bombing."

"Nein! Nein!" Adolphus answered, feeling increasingly uncomfortable.

"So you could not get out of him the name of the British flyer that was responsible?"

"Nein! Nein!" the Hauptmann repeated trembling. He was in a highly vulnerable state after his bitter altercations with Rachel and just wanted to get away from the Major.

"Are you alright?" the Major enquired, surveying him, as if for the first time. "You don't look well to me."

Adolphus clicked his heels. "Herr Major, I am fine. Thank you for asking and if you have finished I will now get back to work."

"Ja! Ja!" the Major repeated thoughtfully. "Ja! You get back to work." He watched as the Hauptmann left the officers mess. *That horrible little man Feldwebel Braun seems to be on to something, but what? I would stake my life on*

Hauptmann Adolphus Bergmann being a good loyal German officer but something is wrong.

Adolphus, apart from being heart-broken as a result of Rachel's departure, was now a very worried man.

Major Werner was also a worried man. Why was a fine young officer like Hauptmann Bergmann lying to him?

Feldwebel Braun was disgusted. All his dreams about Germany lay in ruins. How dare the Major question his loyalty. Well, to hell with them he decided in his paranoia. *I was born an Englishman and however much the Jews try to stop me, I will find a way of returning to my own country.*

Chapter Seventeen

Antwerp 1915

A Job Interview

Erich Braun brooded on how he could have revenge on
Germany for the atrocious way that he believed the army
had treated him. He needed a plan and the answer to his
prayers appeared before him on the following day. A
confidential letter was delivered to selected members of the
interrogation unit inviting applications for a special task
force of intelligence officers to go into enemy territory in
France. All applicants must be fluent English speakers. He
could hardly wait. This was just what he wanted and he
made straight for the designated office to register. A shock
awaited him there however. The officer in charge of the
project was none other than Hauptmann Adolphus
Bergmann.

After Rachel had deserted him (as he described her
departure to himself) and the uncomfortable conversation
with Major Werner, Adolphus was desperate to leave
Antwerp. He had been made aware of the formation of the
task force the previous day and had lost no time in being
interviewed to be the leader. Fortunately for the
Hauptmann, Major Werner was not a man who acted
without considering the consequences and he had so far
kept the strange behaviour of Adolphus to himself. Another
Major, Heinrich Becker, was in charge of recruitment and he
had already been ordered to appoint Adolphus to lead the
expedition, subject to interview.

When Adolphus entered his office he greeted him
warmly. "Ach," Major Becker began, smiling. It had been

the Oberst (Colonel) Otto von Lubeck who had ordered him to interview Adolphus. "What can I do for you Hauptmann Bergmann?"

"I am very interested in leading the group you are forming to go behind enemy lines," Adolphus explained.

"Your qualifications are excellent except for one thing. How good is your English?"

"I have been married to an English woman for three years," Adolphus explained, "and we often discoursed in that language. Also, I have studied hard to be an Interrogation officer and I always conduct my interviews in English."

"Yes," the Major answered, "but we Germans never really lose our accents unless we have spent years of early childhood in England. I don't think that's the case with you, is it?"

"Nein," Adolphus shook his head. "However there are plenty of Flemish speaking soldiers fighting with the British and their accent sounds quite similar to ours."

The Major looked at Adolphus gravely. "You realise that you will be acting as spies. You will be wearing British uniforms and if you are caught, you will be shot."

"Ja! Ja!" Adolphus nodded. "They treat us exactly the same way as we treat them."

The Major sat back in his chair considering the situation. "Ach, So," he eventually said, "you will be Lieutenant Martijn Heijman."

Adolphus nodded. "That sounds good and I think Heijman is sometimes a Jewish name which will fit well, because I am a Jew."

"Ja!" Major Becker replied grinning. "I thought you would like that name. Now you must get used to it. I know you did some wonderful work in England and gave our people some invaluable information about the British army strength in the Manchester area in 1912. Later this afternoon I will give you your orders and tomorrow you can start recruiting your men. This is not a fighting force. Your job will be to infiltrate the enemy lines and obtain information about their air capabilities. The area to which you will be sent is Saint Omer. Do you know it?"

Adolphus nodded. "I know the country around Saint Omer very well. My father used to take a house there in the summer and we used to have trips to many of the small towns and villages in the area."

"Well, that is another reason why you will be the ideal man to lead this expedition," Major Becker added. "I can tell you now that the group will consist of only four men. I can also tell you that the first requirement of the other three will be to speak with English accents. You will be the only Belgian," he added smiling again. "Well that is all for now. You will be briefed in more detail later on and tomorrow you must choose your team as you need to start training urgently."

Chapter Eighteen

Berlin & Antwerp 1915

Seduction?

Greta had been shopping. The war had not curbed her desire to be the most fashionably dressed woman in Berlin. The difference now was that she had to be content with German designers who she considered to be dull and unimaginative. How she longed to be able to walk along the Champs Elysées in Paris dressed in the latest fashions of that elegant city. Now she had to be content with the fashions of the Schloßstraße and its surrounding streets.

She returned home at five o'clock and was shocked to hear the sounds of a baby crying emanating from upstairs. She called one of the maids who informed her that the younger Frau Bergmann had returned just an hour ago from Belgium. Greta dropped her purchases on the hall rug and quickly ran upstairs. She entered the room that had become Rudi's nursery to find her grandson sitting in a high-chair and being fed by his mother Rachel.

"What are you doing here?" Elsa demanded. "Is Adolphus with you?"

Rachel promptly burst into tears and flung herself into the arms of her mother-in-law.

"I've left him," she sobbed. "We had a terrible row...and...and...my brother Alfred is dead...and my other brother Joe is missing...and I am pregnant. I could not bear to stay in Antwerp another minute. What I really wanted was to go back to Manchester but that is impossible. I know Adolphus is your son but he really shouted at me and I could not take it. So, here I am. Please can I stay?"

Elsa surveyed the grief-stricken young woman.

"Of course you can stay. This is your home and the home of my grandson Rudi, and you say there is another baby on the way?"

Rachel began to calm down. With her own mother, Leah, far away in Manchester she looked upon Elsa as a substitute mother. She was very different in appearance from Leah who had neither the time nor the money to take much interest in fashion, but deep down Rachel knew that despite the elegant facade, Elsa was just another Yiddisher mother at heart.

The younger Frau Bergmann was far from being a 'silly' woman herself. She had held down a good job in Manchester before her marriage and had been involved in the Votes for Women movement until her father had persuaded her to give up this activity. However, the avalanche of terrible news about her brothers and the row with Adolphus, when she was in a highly emotional state from her pregnancy, had overwhelmed her.

The following day Elsa secretly sent off a telegram to her son;

What have you done to your darling wife...stop...you should ask for leave to come back to Berlin to sort this out...stop...I am really surprised at you...Mamma

However, when Adolphus returned from the garrison to the Scholz home that evening, the plans had already been finalised for him to be flown deep into France the following night. Rightly or wrongly he decided to leave the telegram unanswered. He was still angry with Rachel and now his mother was included as she was taking his wife's part.

He spent the evening on his own in the Scholz' lounge drinking Kirschwasser, a cherry based brandy. Having downed most of the bottle, he had just decided to stagger up the stairs to bed when the daughter of the house Romilda arrived home after an evening dinner date with two girl friends.

Romilda was an exceptionally good looking girl but, try as she may she had never managed to tempt Adolphus to take any interest in her.

"Ach! Adolphus," she said as she entered the room. "And where is dear Rachel?"

Adolphus surveyed her and thought she had never looked so attractive. Obviously the Kirschwasser was responsible for that thought and here he was, somewhat drunk, off on a dangerous mission the following day and separated from his wife.

"She had to return to Berlin," he explained.

Romilda sat down in an armchair opposite him and crossed her legs under her long tight skirt so that Adolphus could see the shapely contours through the thin fabric.

"I see you have a bottle of Kirschwasser on the go. Can you spare a little for me?" she enquired, giving him a seductive smile.

"Of course," Adolphus replied and pulled himself out of the armchair to find another glass.

"It is ok," she said. "I can drink out of your glass; I am sure it will not poison me."

Adolphus filled his glass and delivered it to Romilda.

"Ach, that is very good," she told him after downing the liquor. "Here I have left a little for you. Come sit on the arm and we can drink together."

Very soon the bottle was empty and Adolphus, now very much the worse for the alcohol, announced, "I think I must go upstairs to bed."

Romilda rose and announced that she too would now retire.

They left the lounge arm in arm which was probably for the best, as certainly Adolphus was in no condition to walk upstairs unaided.

Fortunately the staircase was wide enough to take two abreast and indeed Romilda contrived to make her generous breasts brush against Adolphus tantalisingly as they ascended. Arriving at the top, with a liberal amount of giggling, Romilda thought to enquire of the whereabouts of her parents.

"Oh they are away visiting friends in the country", Adolphus airily explained.

"So, we have the house to ourselves," Romilda commented.

"Yes, I suppose we have," said the very drunk Adolphus, once again giggling.

"You do know you have had far too much to drink tonight, don't you?" Romilda suggested. "Anyway, I think I had better get you into your room and ready for bed."

Adolphus flung an arm around her shoulders and said, "Oh, yes please."

However, once in the bedroom he simply collapsed onto the bed fully clothed. Romilda, however, had other ideas and quickly undressed the sleeping man. He was quite heavy but she was a strong young woman and managed to roll him over until he was between the sheets. Then she quickly stripped off her own clothes and climbed into bed alongside him. She snuggled up to his sleeping form and quickly fell into a deep sleep.

At six o'clock the following morning they were both awakened by the housemaid knocking loudly on the bedroom door to bring Adolphus his usual cup of strong, hot coffee.

Adolphus awoke with a start, was shocked to see Romilda's long blonde hair besides him on the pillow and jumped out of bed.

He pulled on a dressing-gown, opened the door just enough to accept the drink, without the girl being able to see who his companion was. Then he returned to sit on the edge of the bed.

Romilda sat up pulling the sheet over her breasts but only after ensuring that Adolphus had had a good look at the twin promontories.

"Ah, Liebling," she told him. "You were wonderful last night; what a lover."

Adolphus was horrified. He had been in such a deep state of inebriation, that his last memory of the previous night was Romilda entering the lounge and asking to share his drink.

"Mein Gott," he said. "I do not know how to apologise. I am a married man and not in the habit of plying women with drink to take advantage of them."

"Darling," she began. "You did not take advantage of me. Surely you remember our romantic night together. We were both aching for each other and you certainly did not disappoint me."

Adolphus was heart-broken. Not only had he driven his wife back to Berlin with his aggressive behaviour; now he had slept with another woman and one he had been resisting all the time he had been in Antwerp.

He bathed and dressed quickly ignoring Romilda who had curled up again in his bed.

A quick breakfast and he was on his way to start interviewing volunteers for the Saint Omer expedition.

Chapter Nineteen

Antwerp 1915

A Three Man Team

Only four men had volunteered to accompany Adolphus to the secret destination of Saint Omer and he quickly started the interviews. His head was aching from the previous night's over-indulgence and he was overwhelmed with guilt about what had apparently transpired with Romilda. He had now also recognised that going into such a dangerous project as Saint Omer without making peace with his wife was a terrible mistake. However, the interviews were of paramount importance. He must be able to rely completely on the three men who were to accompany him.

The first man was Gefreiter (Corporal) Hans Bach, who had been born and educated until the age of twelve in Birmingham. He was possibly a little unimaginative but his English was excellent if tinged with a Black Country accent. He had worked as an aircraft engineer before joining the army. In addition, he appeared a straight-forward, well disciplined young man and Adolphus was more than happy to tell him that his application to take part in the dangerous mission had been successful.

The next two applicants both had the rank of Feldwebel (Sergeant) and were very similar in attitude. He was sure they would work well with him but Adolphus had sensed an animosity between them when he addressed all four applicants before the individual interviews and felt they may not be good team players.

The fourth volunteer was another Gefreiter and he was a pleasant young man with a good attitude. However,

Adolphus thought him to be a fairly poor specimen physically and he eventually admitted to having recently developed attacks of asthma. *Probably caused by stress,* Adolphus suspected and much as he had taken a liking to the young man, he had to be eliminated.

So as things stood there were just the two of them, Adolphus and Gefreiter Hans Bach and the Hauptmann was tempted to interview the two men with the rank of Feldwebel again, when there was a knock on his door.

"Come in," he called and another Feldwebel entered. Adolphus recognised him immediately as he had been a member of a group who he had trained in interrogation methods. He even remembered his name, Erich Braun. He had been an enthusiastic student.

"Please sit down, Herr Feldwebel," Adolphus instructed him.

"Thank you, Sir," Braun replied.

"Are you here about the expedition inside enemy territory?" Adolphus enquired.

Erich had been shocked to discover the identity of the leader of the expedition but he was determined to make his way to the British and to achieve that, he was happy to appear as a loyal German, a disciplined member of the Kaiser's army and even to flatter a Jewish officer although that really stuck in his throat.

"Yes, Herr Hauptmann," Erich said. "I was really interested to read about it. I was born and educated in Bradford but my father is German and he instilled into me his love for our fatherland. The British have had their own way in building an empire for far too long. It is about time we Germans took the upper hand."

"Herr Feldwebel," Adolphus explained, "this is a very dangerous project. We will be spies and if caught can expect no mercy; just the firing squad. All I can tell you is that we will be flown, under cover of darkness, to an area in northern France. Do you know Gefreiter Hans Bach? He is already confirmed as part of the mission. Then there will be our pilot whose name I do not yet know. If I decide to accept you, you will be the fourth member of the team. Do you still wish to volunteer?"

"Yes, Herr Hauptmann," Braun replied. "I have met Gefreiter Hans Bach and know him to be a good soldier. I think, like me he is English speaking although his Brummy accent is a little strange. I would really welcome the opportunity to serve our beloved Kaiser under such a distinguished officer as you."

The words were almost choking Erich but this was his chance, maybe his only chance to desert the German army and fight for his native land. He could not imagine what his father would think of him, but then his father had deserted Germany many years ago to live and work in Bradford. Maybe he would approve?

Chapter Twenty

Antwerp 1915

Briefing

The expedition had been planned by a senior officer, Oberst (Colonel) Otto von Lubeck. He was a close friend of Adolphus' father, Karl Bergmann, the shoe manufacturer. It was he who had organised Rachel's rail journey to Antwerp and then ensured she was safe and well after the train was bombed. It was the Oberst who had suggested that Adolphus should lead the expedition. He knew much of the Hauptmann's background; of his diligent intelligence gathering work in Manchester. He also knew of the German Jews total loyalty to their country of birth and residence.

A final briefing before departure was scheduled for six o'clock in the evening. The three men were ordered to report to the Oberst himself and they assembled in the corridor outside his office a few minutes earlier. At exactly six pm Adolphus knocked on the door and marched the two lower rank men into the office. They all came smartly to attention before von Lubeck's desk.

"Stand easy men," the senior officer told them. "Pull up those three chairs and be seated. I must tell you that you three have the opportunity to substantially contribute to our victory in this war. Please remember that your success will win the undying gratitude of His Imperial Majesty the Kaiser and the entire German nation. Now listen carefully to your orders..."

When the Oberst had finished he waited for a reaction from the three men who were about to depart on this most dangerous mission.

"Sir," Adolphus began. "I have just one or two questions."

"Quite so, Herr Hauptmann," the Oberst replied. "I would expect you to have."

"You have told us we will be wearing the uniform of the Royal Flying Corp in British ranks appropriate to our ranks in the German army. If we feel we are suspected by the British, is there any way we can try to save our lives and return here?"

"Yes," the Oberst explained. "Immediately on arrival you will be told the name of a British army officer who, in fact, is also one of our men. He was planted in England before the war as a University Lecturer and signed up as a Major in the British Army Medical Corp. You will establish contact with him as soon as you arrive and he will be able to help you in many ways, including escape. However, if you compromise him you can be sure the British will not hesitate to shoot the four of you and the Major."

"Sir," Adolphus queried, "I understand that I will be arriving by air in Saint Omer first with the Gefreiter and the Feldwebel will be following. Is there a reason why we cannot all arrive together?"

"Yes," von Lubeck replied. "There are two reasons. Firstly the aircraft we will use to take you is only a three-seater and secondly it will be much easier to slip you into the British camp in twos. Hauptmann," the Oberst continued, "you will go tonight with the Gefreiter. Your pilot will then return for the Feldwebel and they will join you the following night. Is that all clear?"

"Sir," Adolphus asked, "just one more question. How can we be sure that the enemy will allow a German plane into their airspace?"

"Gut!" the Oberst replied. "I have been waiting for that question."

"You will be flown out in a British plane. We recently captured one and it is now repaired from a little damage and ready to fly. It was a two-seater and has been modified to carry the pilot and two passengers. Our engineers were a little concerned that the weight of an extra person might reduce fuel consumption but that is considered to be a very small risk. Obviously the plane will be tanked up again with British fuel at Saint Omer before returning here. Your pilot will be Leutnant Franz Schmidt; he was educated in Scotland and should have no problem in passing as a British pilot. Herr Hauptmann and Gefreiter Bach, please report to the number three hangar at nine o'clock tonight for final briefing and for your departure."

Chapter Twenty-One

Somewhere in Belgium 1915

On the Run

Life as a farmer did not suit Joe. Whatever Magda thought of him he now enjoyed neither stimulation nor pleasure from her company. She was pretty enough but as her girth increased in response to the baby growing inside her, so did Joe's longing to escape. Kurt was a hard task master and although capable of original thought, the only subject he ever wanted to discuss was plans for the farm's future when the three of them spent time relaxing in the farmhouse. Joe also felt as if he was a deserter from his regiment. He had signed up, learned to fly and intended to devote himself to the British war effort, not to the production of milk for the good people of Belgium. Eventually he could stand it no longer. He had to go and this time he planned to make the trip alone.

Magda deliberately became pregnant, he had long since realised, *and with the approval, nay the encouragement, of her father. If he thought he was going to get a farm-hand/son-in-law that way, he had another think coming.*

Kurt had made certain that the worst of the unsociable hours for work were allocated to Joe, once he had settled in. In the summer, he was responsible for milking the cattle and then ensuring they arrived safely at the grazing grounds. This entailed him rising at four thirty in the morning, a routine he had solidly cursed, until the day he prepared to leave. Then suddenly it was a blessing. He could slide out of bed early in the morning without having to explain to Magda what he was doing. He had secretly packed food and water for the long walk and hidden the bags in the largest of the cow-sheds. Also there were trousers and jackets belonging to Henryk, the son of Kurt de Vries, mercifully an almost perfect fit. He would look exactly the part he wished to portray – a Belgian farm-worker.

The day dawned and Joe's plan went exactly accordingly to plan. That was despite the cows already beginning to complain vociferously that they had not yet been milked by the time he had changed his clothing and left. He had been studying maps in the farm house and with his air navigation training he knew that the farm house was some miles to the north-west of St Niklaas in central Belgium. He also knew that his destination, Saint Omer, was roughly one hundred and fifty miles away. He had decided that he would try to cover at least thirty miles each day and he had to take care to keep to the fields to avoid German patrols. He might look like a Belgian farm worker but the moment he spoke they would realise that his linguistic skills in Flemish were severely limited. It was vital to avoid the large towns, Ghent, Bruges and the costal resorts of Knokke and Oostende which would be swarming with Germans.

It was the evening of the third day and he had made very good time. As a result he had found a deserted barn south of Oostende and near the coast. He had just settled down to eat the remains of the food he had brought with him from the de Vries farm and then curl up on the dry hay for a good night's sleep. He reckoned he was only about fifty miles from Saint Omer and he hoped to complete the long trek the following day.

It was then that he heard the sound of an aircraft approaching, flying very low. He could tell by the sound of the engine what type of plane it was. It was definitely not a

Fokker or any of the other German aircraft. In fact it sounded very much like a BE2b, the aircraft he had been piloting when he crashed all those months ago. However, as the sound came nearer he could hear the engine coughing and spluttering just as it had for him when he had run out of fuel and crash landed in the trees. He decided that he just had to take a look and he crept out of the barn to see the BE2b. Yes it actually was a BE2b, coming to rest in the next field. Something however, was troubling Joe. What was a British plane doing coming from the north-east? This was still German occupied Belgium and he himself would never have been so far north if not for the Fokkers. So, what was this British plane doing? Maybe it too had been pursued by Fokkers. Anyway, he quickly decided, it was a British plane and the pilot probably needed help.

Joe ran across the field, through a gap in the hedge and saw the plane standing safely at the other end of the adjoining area. The engine had stopped completely and as he approached he was surprised to see three men clamber onto the wing and jump to the ground. The BE2b he had flown had been strictly a two-seater but this model had provision for a pilot and two passengers. Other than that it looked exactly the same, exactly the same as the plane in which he had crashed! *Well*, he considered, *they all look pretty similar and this one is a three seater so it couldn't be mine.*

He could now see by their uniform that the three men were all members of the Royal Flying Corp. He thought that if they were returning to Saint Omer he would probably know them and, yes, the tall one certainly looked familiar, very familiar. Joe broke into a trot and started to wave as he approached the three stationary figures. Then one of them produced a pistol which he levelled at him. This brought Joe to a halt.

Of course, they don't know who I am, he realised. *All they can see is a Belgian farm worker yelling and running towards them. They certainly wouldn't even guess that I am English. After all, this is still German occupied Belgium.*

"It is alright," Joe shouted with his arms raised above his head. "I am British."

And then another shot rang out.

Chapter Twenty-three

Southern Belgium 1915

A Night of Surprises

Adolphus had never before met Leutnant Franz Schmidt. This was hardly surprising as he had only just been transferred to Antwerp from an aerodrome in the south of occupied Belgium where both Fokkers and the giant Zeppelin Airship were located. He was an intelligent and charming young man and the pair forged an instant rapport.

The Hauptmann was surprised to discover that the only occupant of number three hangar was covered over with white sheeting. The Leutnant pointed to the object in the far corner of the large building. It looked, in the distance, like a huge white ghost but Adolphus quickly recognised the aircraft shape under the voluminous cover.

"There she is," Schmidt whispered. "That is the baby that is going to take us to Saint Omer. She is a BE2b and no match for our Fokkers. We have shot down large numbers of them."

"How then can we be sure that our own people will not shoot us down when they see a British aircraft in our airspace?" Adolphus asked.

"At eleven o'clock tonight, we take off and all German airfields have been warned to give us clearance," the Leutnant explained.

Adolphus had learned a considerable amount about British and French aircraft. He had gained this information when questioning prisoners-of-war from the allied flying services. At a quarter to eleven the wraps were taken off the

BE2b ready for their journey. It was then that Adolphus realised that this was a two seater plane that had been converted by German engineers to accommodate both a pilot and two passengers.

"Our boys did a good job," Leutnant Schmidt commented. "This was the only intact British plane we had captured and of course it was a two seater. Now, thanks to our clever German engineers it is perfect for me to fly you and another member of the team over to Saint Omer."

"Have you ever flown one of these before?" Adolphus asked, trying to make the question sound casual although he was somewhat nervous about the imminent flight.

"Oh Ja," the Major replied reassuringly. "I was in England in 1913 and I managed to persuade a friend to let me try flying the first version, the BE2. So don't worry, you are in safe hands."

Gefreiter Hans Bach (Corporal Harold Bailey) had been waiting patiently during the conversation between the two officers. He was now wearing the uniform of a British Corporal-Mechanic. The two officers had British Army identity documents in the respective names of Lieutenant Frank Smith (the pilot Schmidt) and Captain Martijn Heijman, (Adolphus) both of the RFC. Lieutenant Smith clambered quickly into the cockpit and the two passengers settled themselves into the respective spaces they were to occupy for the flight.

The plane had now been pushed out of the hangar, the propeller swung to start the engine, chocks were removed and the tiny plane quickly ascended.

With the smell of aviation fuel, the cold night air and the restricted space, this was hardly a pleasure flight. The German engineers had done an excellent job in converting the plane to take two passengers and had carefully calculated the extra fuel that the additional weight would necessitate. What they had however completely failed to allow for was the weight of the extra fuel itself in the enlarged tank. It was only some sixty miles from their destination that Leutnant Schmidt glanced at the fuel gauge and realised in horror that there was no way they could reach Saint Omer. The noise of the engines and the wind precluded any kind of voice communication with his passengers and he began to look for a suitable place to land. They were still over German occupied Belgium which normally would have been some comfort but no ground forces had been warned to suddenly expect three 'British' airmen to land on their territory. The **Die Fliegertruppen des Deutschen Kaiserreiches** (World War One German Air force) may have been told to allow the BE2b safe passage but ground troops were not expecting visitors.

Leutnant Schmidt decided to fly as low and as slow as he dared without risking stalling the engine. Adolphus quickly noticed they were losing altitude and blissfully unaware that there was a problem was expecting to see the Air Field and hangars of Saint Omer appearing imminently. Finally the Leutnant spotted a flat area of grassland and decided to put down there. However, now the engine was in its death throes of coughing and spluttering and both Adolphus and Gefreiter Hans Bach knew that they were in deep trouble.

Franz Schmidt was an experienced flyer and expertly landed the plane in the field he had selected. The long grass slowed down the aircraft which came to a standstill with at least another twenty metres to spare before it would have hit a border fence.

The three men clambered out and jumped gratefully to terra firma.

Leutnant Schmidt was furious. "What have our engineers been thinking of? This should have been an easy flight but someone has miscalculated the amount of fuel required."

Adolphus was more concerned about where they might be and, with his usual dedication, how they were to get to Saint Omer and proceed with their mission. "Where do you think we are?" he demanded of Franz Schmidt. "Are we still in Belgium or is this northern France?"

The Leutnant explained that according to the plane's instruments they should still be in Belgium.

"Well I think we had better take off everything that can identify us as British," he said. "Otherwise we will finish off being attacked by our own army."

It was just at that moment that he saw a figure making its way towards them from across the meadow.

"It looks as if we have company and neither German nor British. He looks like a farmer but he might have friends waiting behind that hedge. He could be anybody."

Adolphus drew his service pistol pointed towards the approaching man and pulled the trigger. He knew that he was out of range but being fired upon should discourage the man from approaching.

The man stopped approaching them and put his arms up in the air.

Then he called out, "It is alright I am British."

Adolphus squeezed the trigger again. However, he knew they needed help and if this man was indeed British he might be able to help them to get to Saint Omer.

He turned to Leutnant Schmidt and said, "Did you hear what he said? He said he was British. Let's keep our RFC uniforms on and cover him with our pistols. We can tell him to approach slowly. You call to him. You have no German accent so he will be more likely to trust you than me."

The Leutnant nodded.

"Come towards us slowly," he called in English. "Keep your hands over your head."

Adolphus watched the approaching figure. *Somehow I feel as if I know this man. But how could that be?* He conjectured.

Not surprisingly the Belgian farm worker, if such he was, was having exactly the same thoughts as Adolphus. *Somehow I feel as if I know this man. But how could that be?*

They were just fifteen metres apart when they both gasped,

"Joe!" said Adolphus.

"Adolphus!" said Joe.

Chapter Twenty-Four

Antwerp 1915

Major Concerns

It was another two days before Major Werner decided to share with another officer the information given to him by Feldwebel Erich Braun. He had agonised on what the correct course of action should be. He was somewhat irritated by the way that Hauptmann Bergmann had responded to his own enquiry about the interview with the British Second-Lieutenant. On the other hand he considered Adolphus to be a friend and was sure he would never act in any way prejudicial to the interests of Germany.

Major Werner had no idea that the Hauptmann was no longer in the Garrison. There were hundreds of German soldiers in the Antwerp base and it was quite possible to go several weeks without seeing a colleague unless one deliberately went out of one's way to find him. In fact, the contact between the Major and the Hauptmann was often through written weekly interrogation reports rather than face to face. However, he needed to discuss Feldwebel Braun's information or at least share it with another officer and he chose an old friend, Major Becker, assistant to the Oberst, with whom to talk over the matter.

Major Werner looked out for his colleague in the officer's mess for a further three days until he saw him and then, finding him eating alone, he decided to join him for lunch.

"Ach! My dear Rolf," Becker greeted him. "How are things going in the interrogation section?"

"Fine, fine," Werner replied. "It is a tough job trying to get information from the British and French but we keep up the pressure and one way or another, we try to get them to spill. Sometimes just a random word is enough to give us a lead."

"Of course, you have now lost one of your best men; that will not help," Becker commented.

"I was not aware of that," Rolf Werner answered with a frown. "Who are you referring to?"

"Hauptmann Adolphus Bergmann," Heinrich Becker replied warily. "Surely you know he has been transferred to other duties. The order came from the Oberst von Lubeck himself."

"I had no idea and I must say that when the weekly reports are submitted I always look for Bergmann's first," Rolf Werner answered. "His technique in interrogation often leads to successful information. I am sorry to lose him and between you and me, my dear fellow, I do think I should have been told he was leaving my section."

"He has been seconded to an important top secret mission," Heinrich Becker explained.

"Then what I have to discuss with you becomes even more vital," Major Werner commented and proceeded to tell Major Becker about his conversation with Feldwebel Braun."

Major Becker listened attentively until the name of the informant Feldwebel Braun was mentioned. "Did you say Feldwebel Braun, Erich Braun?" he enquired, suddenly looking worried.

"Yes," he replied. "Why? Do you know him?"

"I certainly do," Becker answered. "He was due to join Adolphus Bergmann in France last night. However, the aircraft piloted by Leutnant Franz Schmidt failed to return from taking Bergmann and another member of the mission and we are very worried by this. I may as well tell you,"

Major Becker continued, "that they were in a captured British aircraft and all three men are wearing the uniform of the RFC. If the British catch them and are not convinced that they are genuine, they will be shot as spies and if our men see them they will shoot on sight."

"Of course," Werner replied thoughtfully. "Now tell me how did this Feldwebel Braun respond to being on a mission behind enemy lines with the Hauptmann he had tried to denounce only a couple of days earlier?"

"Absolutely fine," Werner answered. "Adolphus Bergmann did the initial interview and I saw him on his own for a final briefing."

"So, are you saying that this Braun, who tried to insinuate that Hauptmann Bergmann had questionable loyalties, was totally relaxed about going on a dangerous mission with a senior officer he did not trust?" Becker enquired.

"Something is very wrong here," Werner commented. "What I did not tell you before was that Braun is also a rabid anti-Semite. And he knows that the Hauptmann is a Jew."

"So I think we need to talk to this Feldwebel Braun," Becker suggested, "as a matter of urgency."

"Absolutely," Werner replied.

Chapter Twenty-Five

Southern Belgium 1915

Bluff and Double-Bluff

The cousins surveyed each other in astonishment. The fact that they had come across each other in the middle of a field in northern Belgium when their two countries were at war with each other, was enough of a shock.

What was Adolphus doing in German occupied territory dressed as an officer in the Royal Flying Corp? Joe was mystified. *Who were his two companions from the British BE2b plane that looked so much like the aircraft he had crashed, miles to the north?*

What, Adolphus puzzled, was Joseph Bergman, his British cousin and brother-in-law, doing in southern Belgium dressed as a farm worker?

Not only did the two men need answers, they also needed to give each other credible explanations even if they consisted of a pack of lies.

Adolphus had a slight advantage. Thanks to the British prisoner David Goldberg he knew that Joe was in the RFC and had crashed his plane well to the north of where they now were. However, what had happened to him since the crash and how he had arrived here, south of Oostende, were questions for which he needed answers.

For Joe the overriding question was, had Adolphus seen the light and joined the RFC to fight the Kaiser or was he a spy?

Then there were the two strangers. Judging by their uniforms they were definitely British flyers.

All these questions were buzzing around in their heads as the cousins now stood face to face.

"Hello Adolphus," Joe began and in a failed bid to say something sensible, continued, "What are you doing here?"

Adolphus, of course made no attempt to answer this somewhat ridiculous question. However, being equally at a loss, after a short pause, he repeated the same formula, "Hello Joe, what are you doing here?"

It must be remembered that Adolphus and Joe were not the only ones present who were looking for answers.

Leutnant Schmidt was equally mystified. Adolphus and Joe had addressed each other in English and both he and Corporal Harold Bailey (Hans Bach) were very much at home in the language of their enemy. The Leutnant decided to enter the conversation.

"Hello," he began in his educated Edinburgh accent. "I gather you are called Joe but Adolphus does not seem to be in any hurry to introduce us, so I will tell you my name is Lieutenant Frank Smith of the Royal Flying Corp. I am sorry we shot at you but we had no idea who you were." *Not that we do now,* he thought to himself.

Joe returned the greeting carefully. "I am pleased to meet you, Sir." He was highly suspicious of the three men and that definitely included his cousin Adolphus.

Then the Corporal stepped forward. "My name is Corporal Harold Bailey, Sir," he intoned in his strong Birmingham accent.

Joe surveyed the three men. *The Lieutenant and the Corporal seem genuine enough but what is Adolphus doing with them? What right does he have to wear the uniform of the RFC? If he was their prisoner he would not be wearing British uniform,* he agonised.

"What happened to the plane," he asked in an attempt to appear friendly while considering his next move.

"We ran out of fuel," Adolphus explained which was true. "We were chased by Fokkers and burned up everything in our tank trying to avoid them," which was definitely not true but totally credible.

Joe decided to try a new tack. "The last time we saw each other was in Manchester, when you were married to my sister. At that time you were a reserve officer in the German army. How come you are now a Captain in the British Army Royal Flying Corp?"

Adolphus had to make a decision. The moment for truth, or rather lies had arrived.

"I was unhappy with the way that Germany invaded Belgium last year and I felt it to be my duty to change sides and fight for what I considered to be right."

"And where was my sister while all this has been going on?" Joe demanded.

"She is stuck in Berlin with our baby son Rudi," Adolphus replied. "The family spread the story that I had been taken prisoner so that there would be no trouble for them as a result of me changing sides."

So this is the line, Adolphus decided. *If we stick to it maybe Joe will help us to get to Saint Omer.*

Adolphus' two comrades had been listening to this exchange with fascination. This man Joe was some sort of English relative of Adolphus and if they all stuck to the story, maybe he could help them. If and when they did reach Saint Omer, he could add credibility to their arrival there.

As they talked Joe kept glancing at the plane.

"Are you sure it ran out of fuel?" he asked Lieutenant Smith. "I am a mechanic – maybe it was an engine failure and there is still plenty of fuel in the tank."

"Firstly," the Lieutenant suggested, "before we discuss the plane, we have told you who we are. I gather you are some kind of long-lost relative of the Captain but who are you and what are you doing here? You sound like an educated Englishman but you look like a Belgian peasant."

Joe needed to think on his feet and to do so very quickly. "As you realise I am Adolphus' cousin and I was taken prisoner by the Germans when my plane came down just a few miles from here. I am also an officer in the RFC and I was lucky enough to be able to escape."

That was almost the truth and it was a truth that suited the three Germans very well. However, Joe was still very suspicious and longed to take a closer look at the plane.

"So," he began, "Shall I take a look at the plane for you?"

"No, that will not be necessary," Adolphus said quickly. *If he looks closely at the BE2b he might recognise it as his old plane,* he realised. Adolphus was fairly certain that it was Joe's plane after his conversation with David Goldberg. "We have Corporal Bailey here and he is a mechanic."

"Do you have plenty food?" Joe enquired. "Mine is in the next field. I will go and get my things."

"I could do with a walk," Adolphus replied. "I will go with you."

How could they be certain that Joe was really alone, he conjectured? There may be more British soldiers hiding in the next field. He patted the pistol in his holster. *I'd better keep an eye on him,* he decided.

As they strode along Joe asked Adolphus about the family but the latter seemed disinclined to talk about Rachel and even little Rudi.

"It is hard for me," Adolphus explained. "They are over in Berlin and I cannot communicate with them."

On the way, Joe managed to walk as near as possible, to the plane without alerting Adolphus to his suspicions. The Corporal had now gone back to the plane and opened the engine cover. Joe waved to him as they passed by. This gave him the chance to take a long hard look. Some time ago he had painted a picture of the British lion inside the cover and Joe could easily see the bright colours. *So, just as I thought, that is definitely my plane,* he decided. *That proves without a shadow of a doubt that the three of them are German soldiers. They must have been on the way to a spying mission when the fuel ran out. I must let them think I have swallowed their story. So I will do my best to get them to Saint Omer and then they will be in for a big surprise.*

The dangerous one is Adolphus, Joe realised. *He must never know that I recognised the plane or that will be the end of me.*

Chapter Twenty-Six

Antwerp 1915

Reduced to the Ranks

"Do you know where we will find Feldwebel Braun," Major Becker enquired.

"Ja, as it happens I know exactly where he will be," Major Werner explained. "He has been ordered to stay near Hangar number Three. There is a Sergeant's mess in the area and he has been told to wait there for the plane to return from Saint Omer. He cannot wander about as he is dressed in a British Sergeant's uniform."

"Right," Becker replied, "can we go to see him now? I am becoming increasingly worried by what you have told me. Something is wrong here."

The Sergeant's mess alongside Hangar number Three consisted of one large dining room with a bar and some temporary accommodation for non-commissioned officers in transit. Feldwebel Braun was sitting in one of these smaller rooms reading when the two majors entered. He quickly stood up and saluted.

He looked at Major Becker enquiringly. "Has the plane returned at last, Sir?"

"Nein," the Major replied. "I think you know Major Werner. We want to ask you a few questions."

Braun looked at the two officers and could see by their expression that something was wrong.

"Can you get us two more chairs Braun?" Werner demanded.

A few moments later the Feldwebel was seated opposite the two majors.

"Herr Feldwebel," Major Werner began. "I think you had better start by repeating to Major Becker what you told me you had heard as a result of your eavesdropping activity outside the office door of Hauptmann Bergmann."

For Erich Braun however, the situation had changed. Hauptmann Bergmann was his ticket back to England or at least to the British army. Any trouble he caused Adolphus could easily rebound on him and his plans.

"Oh Sir," he began, "do you mean the conversation I accidently overheard between the Hauptmann and a British prisoner?"

"Yes. That is precisely what I mean," Major Werner answered. "Now get on with it man. Tell Major Becker about the conversation."

"I, I don't really remember," Braun stammered.

"Well, you remembered well enough just the other day," Werner responded angrily.

"I've been thinking about it and it is quite possible I misheard," Braun replied.

"I see," Major Werner replied angrily. "And your comments about Jews not being trustworthy German soldiers; you made that comment yourself or did I also mishear that?"

"I, I was upset about what I thought I had heard. I am sorry I made that remark," Braun said.

Major Becker had not so far joined in the conversation. He sat there considering what should be done with the Feldwebel. The man was obviously lying. Whether he had heard something incriminating about the Hauptmann or not troubled him. However, what troubled him even more was the fact they had been on the point of sending an unreliable, lying soldier on a delicate mission under the command of an officer with an impeccable record. *Why did he want to make trouble for Adolphus Bergmann and why, suddenly had he changed his tune.* One thing was certain and that was the fact that this man was neither fit to go on such a mission or to have the rank of Feldwebel.

Major Becker spoke. "I am reporting this entire matter to Oberst Otto von Lubeck, with my strong recommendation that you should be stripped of the rank of Feldwebel and posted to a front line division in the trenches in France."

Braun was beside himself with rage. "I am English speaking and an invaluable member of the Intelligence and Interrogation unit. I am about to depart to France to undertake under-cover work for Germany. You cannot do this to me."

It was now the turn of Major Werner. "How dare you argue with Major Becker? You are no longer involved in this mission. You are dismissed."

Braun stood up angrily banging his chair back against the wall. "You cannot speak to me like this. Don't think I don't know why you are treating me like this. You are both Jews just like Hauptmann Bergmann and you people always stick together."

The two Majors rose to their feet.

Major Becker walked over to the door of the Sergeant's Mess and called for two of the guards on duty in the Hangar to take Braun to the lock-up.

And that was the last that was seen of Erich Braun (Eric Brown) for many a long day.

Chapter Twenty-Seven

The Road to Nieuwpoort 1915

A Bumpy Ride

Major Heinrich Becker had a far greater problem than Erich Braun. His project was now one man down on the mission but more importantly, what had happened to the first phase with its leader Adolphus?

There was no sign of the BE2b returning and that on its own posed a problem. The aircraft had been given clearance to return the previous day, and it could not fly back now without Die Fliegertruppen des Deutschen Kaiserreiches (German Air Force) being alerted to allow the British registered war plane safe passage. Otherwise, their own Fokkers would, almost certainly, make short work of shooting it out of the sky.

Where were they, Becker agonised? There had been no signal from their man previously planted in the British camp in Saint Omer and he had been told to only break radio silence to let them know the time that the BE2b would return. Use of radio was extremely dangerous as transmission was made by a chain of portable radio stations stretching between the two points that needed to communicate. The enemy was just as likely to pick up the signals as the intended recipient of the information.

Adolphus was still determined to get to Saint Omer. The plane was useless without fuel and the decision was taken to proceed on foot. Joe, of course was just as anxious to finish his journey back to the air base as were the three Germans in British uniform. He was now certain that they were intent on spying once they entered British controlled territory. The fact that the BE2b was his old plane had confirmed that. He knew, without a doubt, what his three companions were up to but he had the same agenda as them, at least until they all reached the destination of Saint Omer. Then the situation would be very different.

They had covered another twenty-five miles when they discovered an abandoned Minerva Belgium Armoured Car behind the hedges adjoining the rough roads. The occupants of the vehicle must have been taken prisoner when the Germans overran the country some months earlier. The question was would the vehicle start and did it have any fuel left in the tank? The Minerva could be a godsend Adolphus decided and ordered **Corporal Harold Bailey to see if it could be made to work.** Eventually after cleaning the points and repeatedly cranking the engine it spluttered into life. They all piled in and the Minerva bumped and rattled as it made its way over the cart tracks. This was still faster than walking but potentially extremely dangerous if they were spotted by a German patrol. Here were three 'British' soldiers and a Belgian civilian in a Belgium armoured car.

Adolphus found it strange that this road, so near the coast, should be so quiet. Ten months ago it would have been packed with German soldiers marching towards the French border. Where were they all now? He wondered. And then he noticed that, despite the dry late summer weather, the road was becoming increasingly wet.

A few moments later he could hardly believe his eyes. Ahead of them was what looked like a huge inland lake! Of course, the intention had always been to fly to Saint Omer and there should have been no necessity to be briefed or reminded that...

After the first battle for Ypres in mid October 1914 the Belgians had opened the sluice gates at Nieuwpoort so that all the re-claimed land to the east of the river Yser in this low-lying part of Flanders, up to and over the French border, was flooded, thus keeping the German army away from the channel ports.

A fat lot of use an armoured car will be now. What we need is a boat! Adolphus told himself.

Adolphus stopped the car and the four men disembarked from the ramshackle vehicle. "We will have to head for the coast and commandeer a sea-worthy ship when we get to Nieuwpoort," he announced. There was however, one monumental problem with that idea. Only Joe was dressed as a civilian who might have some slight chance of getting near the German lines. Adolphus, Schmidt and Bach were all dressed as British soldiers. As soon as the Germans saw them they would probably open fire.

Adolphus started the car again and the long torturous journey resumed but this time driving due west. He stopped the car a safe distance from the small port of Nieuwpoort and told the men of the plan that he had hatched as they drove along.

"Joe," he began. "Do you speak German?"

"Well, yes I do. I learned at school but it will all be mixed up with Yiddish which my parents often spoke at home."

"Well Joe," Adolphus continued, "the only way we are going to get to Saint Omer is this. The Germans will be suspicious of you if you approach them but they will not just open fire. If they see us however, they will shoot first and ask questions afterwards.

"This is the story Joe. I want you to go up to the first German soldier you see and ask to be taken to an officer. Then I want you to tell the officer that you are travelling with three **German** soldiers but they are dressed in British uniform as they were supposed to be working behind enemy lines in Saint Omer. As you know, this is not true. We are British soldiers but I am German and was until last year an officer in the army of the Kaiser."

He then turned to Schmidt and Bach and asked them if they spoke German. Schmidt instantly realised the double bluff to keep up the charade because of Joe, and Bach looked at Adolphus as if he had gone crazy.

"I speak quite good German," Schmidt told Adolphus. "In fact I went to Heidelberg University for three years before the war."

Adolphus was only concerned what Bach would say. He need not have worried as the Gefreiter had now realised what the plan was.

"Yes," he assured Adolphus in his strong Birmingham accent, "I speak a little German."

"So," Adolphus turned to Joe again. "Can you do this?"

"I really have no choice, do I?" Joe replied.

Of course, Joe fully recognised the double bluff that was being staged for his benefit. But Adolphus was confident that Joe was blissfully unaware that his three companions really were German soldiers. How wrong the Hauptmann was.

Chapter Twenty-Eight

Antwerp 1915

A High-Level Conference

Three days had now elapsed since the BE2b with Adolphus, Schmidt and Gefreiter Bach had left for what should have been a three or four hour flight. Major Becker was seriously concerned. Had they crashed in some remote country area; possible, but in a country the size of Belgium, somewhat unlikely? Had they wandered off course and been shot down by one of their own planes; unlikely, with a highly experienced flyer like Leutnant Schmidt. Then there was the third and almost unthinkable option; that Hauptmann Adolphus Bergmann was a traitor. Major Becker remembered very well, the details of the conversation between Adolphus and the British prisoner David Goldberg reported by Erich Braun. He decided it would do no harm to interrogate Goldberg himself.

The British second-lieutenant was in the nearby prisoner-of-war camp and was quickly escorted under guard to the office of Major Becker.

"You may sit down, Lieutenant," Becker told him.

"Thank you, Sir," Goldberg answered, sitting down rather stiffly on the hard wooden chair facing the Major.

"I know you have been interviewed by a number of officers," the Major began. "However, one of our men reported certain irregularities in the interrogation by the last one and I would just like to clarify one or two facts."

"My name is David Goldberg, I am a Second-Lieutenant in the Royal Flying Corps and my serial number is 2364379.

That is all I need to tell you and that is exactly the same as I told Hauptmann Bergmann."

"So you remember his name," the Major commented. "You must have had a number of interviews, how come you remember this one?"

"It was the last one and still fresh in my mind," Goldberg explained. "Sir, the only information I need to give you is my name, rank and serial number. Shall I repeat them for you again?"

"Nein, Nein, that will not be necessary," Becker replied quickly. "I am going to tell you what was reported to me about your last interview and then you can comment."

"Sir, I am under no obligation to give you information. If you want to check what was said, why not ask Hauptmann Bergmann himself?"

"I cannot do that at the moment as he is away on army business," the Major explained. "Lieutenant, I understand from the report I received that you have a friend in the RFC called Joe or Joseph Bergman and that Hauptmann Bergmann is married to his sister. We all know the Hauptmann's wife is originally English so, a simple question for you; your friend Joe, is he the one who bombed the train?"

"Would you like my name and...?" Goldberg started.

"Lieutenant, don't start that again. I think by your reaction that we can take it that what I said is correct. Before you go back to the prisoner-of-war camp I think you might like to know that we know for a fact that it was your Joe, the Hauptmann's brother-in-law who bombed the train and nearly killed his own sister."

The Second Lieutenant was well aware of this but feigned surprise.

"So do you have anything to add to all this? If not I will call the guard and you can get out of my office."

Once he was on his own, Major Becker began to consider the situation. The Hauptmann had disappeared along with two other German soldiers. He had a brother-in-law in the cursed RFC who had almost certainly bombed the train, causing many casualties and disrupting supplies between Antwerp and Germany for many days. This brother-in-law, British Second Lieutenant Joseph Bergman had also vanished. After his plane was found the army had scoured the surrounding countryside to find him and the British soldier who was with him in the plane. They had drawn a complete blank.

I would have trusted Adolphus as a loyal German and a good friend and now I don't know what to think. Could a superb officer like him turn out to be a traitor? He agonised.

Major Becker contacted Major Werner and they discussed the situation but could come up with no explanations.

The following morning they went to see the Oberst von Lubeck and reported the entire matter to him.

He listened intently. "So, we have a missing plane, a British plane which we had captured, or rather found in a Belgium clump of trees. Your plan," he said addressing Major Werner, "was to use it to deliver a senior intelligence officer, Hauptmann Bergmann and three other good German soldiers dressed in British uniform behind enemy lines, to evaluate the strength of their air force; an excellent plan that I approved. We now find that the plane and three of the men on this mission, including Hauptmann Bergmann have disappeared. Then we discover that the British air man who bombed the train was the brother-in-law of the Hauptmann and a Second Lieutenant in the RFC. And all this information comes together as the result of eavesdropping by a Feldwebel who had his own agenda for causing trouble for the Hauptmann."

The Oberst sat back in his chair and looked deeply into the faces of the two Majors. "What did you two gentlemen do with the Feldwebel who had alerted you to the possible disloyalty to his Imperial Majesty the Kaiser by Hauptmann Bergman? Why, you locked him up! An excellent way to reward a soldier for caring about his country, don't you think?"

The two Majors looked at each other and Major Werner spoke. "Sir, don't you think that it was somewhat strange that Feldwebel Braun after reporting his suspicions about the Hauptmann then volunteered to accompany him on a secret and dangerous mission behind enemy lines?"

The Oberst looked startled. "Jawohl! You are right. Something does not add up here. I wish to see this man myself tomorrow. Major Becker, have him in my office at 8 o'clock in the morning. As for the rest of this story, I want to know every development however small, is that clear?"

The two Majors rose to their feet, clicked their heels as they saluted the Oberst and left his office.

Chapter Twenty-Nine

Nieuwpoort 1915

Hospitality

After the Belgians had flooded the adjacent area, the port of Nieuwpoort ceased to have serious strategic significance for the Germans. They posted sentries on the roads leading into the town. These positions went to older foot-soldiers and a pair of them was on duty when they were approached by a young, unarmed Belgian farmer who addressed them in halting German.

"I have some important information for your senior officer. Can you take me to him?"

The senior of the two soldiers, a Gefreiter, replied. "Why would you wish to speak to an officer?"

"It is a matter of great importance to your army," the Belgian replied. "I have a message from a Hauptmann in the interrogation unit."

The soldiers then had an animated discussion which resulted in them agreeing that the Gefreiter would escort the man to their Feldwebel back in a small garrison, nearer to the town centre. This non-commissioned officer listened to Joe's request and agreed that he should be escorted to the German headquarters in Kaaistraat. Eventually he was taken to a Major who listened with suspicion to what Joe had to say.

"So, you are saying that there are three German soldiers just outside the town, dressed in British uniform and on the way to Saint Omer on a special mission when their plane crashed?"

"Yes," Joe replied with relief. "That is exactly what I am saying. The senior officer is a Hauptmann, Adolphus Bergmann."

The Major was in a quandary. He was in his fifties and posted here as a soft option. He had been wounded years earlier in the Southwest Africa campaign and since that time he had served his country in an administrative rather than a fighting capacity. He decided to despatch ten soldiers to escort the three 'British' soldiers into town.

Joe however had another problem. If his companions were successful in persuading the German garrison commander to supply or commandeer a small ship to complete their journey, how could Adolphus allow him to accompany them when he was sure that Joe would immediately denounce them as spies to the British?

Joe realised that the moment Adolphus convinced the Major in Nieuwpoort that the three of them were genuine German soldiers he would also denounce Joe as a British flyer on the run. He may have had no choice but what he had done was to make matters worse. He was facilitating the insertion into the main allied airfield in France of three German spies. Furthermore, he now realised that Adolphus and his friends could never assist in his repatriation. They may be cousins but they were definitely enemies.

Joe was now desperate to make his own way back to Saint Omer but he could not give Adolphus and his men or the German escort party the slightest indication that he suspected the men in British uniform were not working for the British forces.

It was three hours since Joe had left the others to go in to Nieuwpoort and Adolphus was becoming anxious. Then they heard the sound of marching and the ten-man German escort party came into view. Adolphus was relieved to see

Joe was still with them and was apparently still satisfied that they were really working for the British. Hopefully, he mused, he had been able to convince the German garrison of exactly the opposite.

Adolphus was deeply uncomfortable about the situation with Joe. He was his cousin and brother-in-law but he could not allow him to accompany them to Saint Omer where the Hauptmann's mission would come to an abrupt end before it had even started. On the other hand to report him to the authorities in Nieuwpoort as an allied airman on the run was something he would find very hard to do. He turned over the options in his mind but with so many conflicts of interest he was unable to come up with a solution.

The group had now reached the German army HQ in Kaaistraat. Belgians and off-duty German soldiers stared with curiosity as the group marched by and wondered how the occupying forces had managed to arrest three British soldiers so far from their own territory.

Adolphus asked the senior member of the escorting party to take him to see the Major who was in charge of the garrison.

When Adolphus entered his office, still dressed in the uniform of a British First-Lieutenant, Major Bruno Feldheim gazed at him in some wonder. He had not seen active service for years and had no idea in any case of the appearance of a 'modern' British officer.

Adolphus clicked his heels and saluted and the Major told him to be seated.

"Are you really a German officer?" the Major enquired, smiling.

"Yes, of course. I am Hauptmann Adolphus Bergmann and by now I should be involved in undercover operations inside a British air base in France."

The Major was a cautious man, unused to making difficult decisions. He needed to ask a superior officer to deal with this situation but in Nieuwpoort there was no superior officer.

"I can make you no promises but what is it you want from me?" the Major enquired.

"I need a small ship, a fishing boat or similar to take me and my men down the coast so that we may land on a deserted beach once we are over the French border. From there we should be able to use British or French personnel to organise transport to Saint Omer."

"How do I know you are really who you say you are?" the Major asked.

"You had better ask me some questions and then interview my two men and ask them some similar questions," Adolphus suggested.

The Hauptmann was less than impressed with the questions that followed. This was not the way he would have conducted such an interrogation, but this was probably not a skill that was taught in the old German army. The one thing the Major now knew was that the three soldiers had all started their disastrous journey from Antwerp."

"And who is this Belgian farmer. Is he also a German soldier in disguise?" the Major eventually enquired with a touch of irony.

"I will discuss him with you later," the Hauptmann replied, with something of a heavy heart.

"Well Herr Hauptmann, I will allocate a room to you where you can all wait until I have contacted the Area Commandant to receive instructions. Please understand that this Belgian and his conduct are entirely your responsibility," the Major told him.

"Of course and thank you Major," Adolphus answered.

"Oh, Herr Hauptmann, write down for me the names and ranks of your two military companions and the name of your Belgian on this form. On no account may any of you leave this building. Should you do so, you will be arrested. Do I make myself clear?"

So the man is not a complete idiot, Adolphus decided. However, after giving full details of his two comrades and himself he concocted a Flemish sounding Belgian name for Joe which he hoped would satisfy the Major.

A further two days were to pass during which they were well fed and warm and able to sleep. And then the news was received that Adolphus had suspected might be the case.

Chapter Thirty

Antwerp 1915

The Oberst takes a Close Interest

At 8 am precisely Major Werner and a military policeman marched Feldwebel Erich Braun into the office of the Oberst Otto von Lubeck.

All three men clicked their heels and stood to attention.

"Here is the prisoner Erich Braun in accordance with your orders, Sir," Major Werner announced.

"Ach, Gut," the Oberst replied. "Major Werner, please be seated over there by the wall." He then turned to the military policeman. "You can wait outside until the Major calls you back in."

Otto von Lubeck was forty-two years old, the latest in a long line of Prussian army officers. He was almost six foot tall with iron-grey hair and a moustache to match. He regarded Erich Braun with piercing blue eyes.

"So, Braun, what are you up to?"

"Up to, Sir?" Braun replied. "I am a loyal German soldier and I fail to understand why I have been treated like a criminal."

"There is something very strange about you, Braun. You were born in England with a father who deserted his ancestral home in Saxony and I gather your mother is English."

Erich nodded wondering what was coming next.

"You came here just before the war and volunteered to fight for us and use your linguistic skill for the benefit of His Imperial Majesty the Kaiser and our Fatherland."

Erich nodded again.

"You took a strong personal dislike to one of the officers who had trained you in interrogation techniques, mainly it seems because he is a Jew. I do not number myself among them but there are people in this country who do not like Jews. You however, took your hatred a step further and tried to make trouble for this officer, Hauptmann Adolphus Bergmann." The Oberst looked down at the notes he had prepared before the interview. "It now looks as if your suspicions regarding the Hauptmann just may have some foundation."

Braun thought this was his chance to turn the tables. "Why then am I in the lock-up? If I have alerted you to treason I would have thought I should be rewarded not punished."

"Silence," the Oberst shouted."How dare you interrupt me? You are forgetting one thing. When the opportunity came to be enrolled on a mission under the command of the Hauptmann, which involved going behind the British lines, you jumped at it. How do you explain that?"

Erich Braun was speechless.

"Well man," the Oberst repeated. "Explain yourself."

"I thought that the opportunity to help Germany by going on the mission more than compensated for having to work with Bergmann."

"Bergmann, Bergmann," the Oberst repeated. "You are talking about a serving officer in the Kaiser's army. You do not refer to him as Bergmann. He is Hauptmann Bergmann to you, unless and until he is found guilty of the crime that you accuse him of."

Erich Braun's natural arrogance came to the fore. "I will not refer to that Jew as Hauptmann. It is people like him who are ruining Germany."

"And you still wanted to entrust your life to him as the leader of a dangerous expedition. Something is wrong here. Do I get an explanation before I return you to the lock-up?" the Oberst replied.

Braun was now completely out of control. "This country is doomed. You will lose this war and you can thank yourself and your Jew officers for that."

Major Werner sitting at the back of the room had listened to this exchange with astonishment.

The Oberst turned to him. "Major Werner, tell the guards to throw this man back in lock-up. He is stripped of his rank and when you next have troops being sent to the trenches in northern France, make sure he is among them. His commanding officers are to be made aware that he is a trouble maker and is only fit for cannon-fodder."

Oberst Otto von Lubeck surveyed his now empty office. On the wall behind him was the portrait of the Kaiser Wilhelm II. In front of him was a huge question mark. Was Adolphus a traitor or not? His gut feeling was that the Hauptmann was as loyal an officer as any in the Kaiser's army, but there still were disturbing facts to face up to, and he wished that the Hauptmann was sitting in front of him now and could settle the whole matter.

Sometimes wishes do come true.

Chapter Thirty-One

Antwerp 1915

Pillow Talk

The Oberst Otto von Lubeck decided that he should become personally involved in investigating the matter of the missing Hauptmann. This was quite an unusual step as the normal procedure would have been to instruct other more junior officers, possibly the two Majors, Werner and Becker, to undertake a thorough investigation and report back to him. However, Adolphus' father was a personal friend and the principal supplier of boots to the German army and the Oberst had a special penchant for pretty young Jewesses. He had been more than a little impressed when he had met Frau Rachel Bergmann at the scene of the train bombing.

He decided to personally visit Rachel later that day and knew that the Bergmanns were billeted at the home of Herr Scholz. His driver was instructed to take him to the address and he himself rang the bell to gain entrance. The door was opened by a well-endowed young blonde lady in her mid twenties whom he surmised to be a daughter of the house.

"Guten Abend, Fraulein," he said having quickly checked that there was no wedding ring on the young woman's finger. You must be the charming daughter of Herr Scholz."

Romilda was more than a little impressed to find a tall, good-looking senior officer on the doorstep and immediately invited him in.

She escorted him into the library and said, "I assume you are here to see my father."

"Nein," the Oberst replied, "it was Frau Bergmann who I believe is staying by you, who I wish to see. Is she in?"

"Nein," Romilda replied, "and neither are my parents. Frau Bergmann returned to Berlin last week and I do not know if and when she has any plans to return. However, my father should be home in the next quarter of an hour. Please be seated and I will ask the maid to make a cup of coffee for you."

The Oberst was now even more concerned about Adolphus. *I am sure she knew her husband was away on a mission but surely she would have preferred to wait in Antwerp to greet him on his return. Why go back to Berlin now?*

"A cup of coffee would be most welcome," he said and eyeing the young lady up and down, his normal response to the presence of an attractive young woman, he continued, "And how do you like living in Antwerp"?

"It is dull, very dull and provincial," Romilda replied. "I just wish I could go back to Frankfurt and to all my friends".

"Why do you think Frau Bergmann decided now to return to Berlin," the Oberst enquired.

"I have no idea," Romilda answered. "You would think she would have wanted to stay here to see her husband as soon as he returned; but then I do not think she realises how lucky she is to be married to a man like Hauptmann Bergmann."

"Why do you say that?" the Oberst probed.

"I think they had a row the day before she left," the Fraulein answered. "If he was my husband I would treat him very differently."

Von Lubeck looked closely at her expression. *She seems to be very smitten with our friend Bergmann*, he decided. *Of course before his wife arrived, I would not be surprised if something had been going on and who could blame him. She is a very attractive young woman.*

"So," the Oberst continued. "Tell me about yourself."

He had been sitting chatting to the young lady for half an hour and there was still no sign of her father returning.

"Look, my dear young lady, I will have to leave. Duty calls but I have very much enjoyed our conversation. Maybe we could have dinner together one evening?" von Lubeck suggested.

Romilda was delighted. To be taken out to dinner by a senior officer in the army of the Kaiser was a great honour. He was somewhat older than Adolphus, but he took notice of her and made her feel like a real woman, whereas the Hauptmann tried hard to avoid her except on the one occasion when he was drunk.

The Oberst Otto von Lubeck had been married for some fifteen years to Elfriede (nee von Neustrelitz) the daughter of a respected Prussian family. She was tall and thin and austere both of appearance and character. She had produced two sons for Otto before deciding that the process that led to their conception was something she could no longer tolerate. The Oberst did not argue with her decision and felt that this gave him the licence to disseminate his sperm where it was more welcome. In truth, even when 'making babies' with Elfriede he still had no resistance to the smiles and wiles of pretty young ladies, be they dark haired, Mediterranean or blonde Germanic goddesses.

The Kursaal Hotel had a first class restaurant and was frequently patronised by German Army officers and their friends. It was decided that the Oberst would collect Romilda from her home the following evening and they would dine there. Her mother however, knowing the reputation of the womanising Otto von Lubeck saw fit to try and warn her daughter off. Romilda, however, was far from the innocent angel that her mother blissfully assumed her to be.

"Don't worry, Mutti, I can take care of myself," she assured her. "It is a great honour to be the guest of an Oberst of his distinction."

"Well, you must be careful; even being seen dining with a man like that can harm your reputation."

"What do you mean, 'a man like that'; Otto von Lubeck is a distinguished officer in the Kaiser's army. I am delighted to be seen dining with him."

"You do know he is married, I presume?" the mother continued.

"Yes of course and don't worry Mutti, there is nothing to be concerned about." Romilda replied.

It has to be said that Romilda was far from the shrinking violet that her parents assumed her to be. She had lost her virginity at university at the age of eighteen and by twenty-one had secretly disposed of an unwanted pregnancy. So, having shared his table for a delicious dinner accompanied by the best champagne, the Oberst had little difficulty in persuading Romilda to share his bed.

Afterwards, lying comfortably in the Oberst's arms he decided to once again visit the matter of Hauptmann and Frau Bergmann.

"Do you not think it is strange that Rachel Bergmann should return to Berlin when she and her baby son were so comfortable in your home?" the Oberst enquired.

"Yes I do," Romilda replied. "I know they had a terrible row but surely they could have recovered from that, particularly when Adolphus was being posted away on special duties."

"How well do you know Adolphus?" Otto now enquired.

Romilda was not about to admit that Adolphus had gone to great pains to avoid being alone with her but she could truthfully add one piece of information.

"If you must know, one evening after Rachel left and we were both drunk, we slept together and I must tell you Otto, he did not compare with you as a lover, not for one minute." It was, of course true that they had 'slept together' and slept was the operative word.

The Oberst was, of course, flattered and at the same time he was desperate for information about the Hauptmann.

"Tell me, my dear, what is your real opinion of friend Adolphus?" he enquired, gently stroking her long blonde hair.

Romilda could never forgive Adolphus for failing to fall for her repeated attempts to entice him away from Rachel. Now was her chance to repay him for scorning her advances.

"Do you really want to know?" she replied. "You might not like what I have to say."

"All I want is the truth," the Oberst answered. "I am only asking your opinion."

"Very well," Romilda began. "He is unreliable and arrogant. Because he is a Jew and his father is such a powerful businessman, he thinks he is superior to us Germans."

This was interesting for the Oberst but he wanted more.

"Do you think then that deep down he despises us Germans and Germany?" he ventured.

"Look I do not want to get him into trouble but I would be very careful about how much trust you give him." Romilda decided she had now said more than enough. The poison had been dripped in and she could sit (or lie) back and watch how events developed.

Chapter Thirty-Two

Antwerp & Nieuwpoort 1915

The Problem of Cousin Joe

The Oberst was completely smitten with Romilda. She was a charming and elegant companion on his arm and a young woman who really knew how to give and receive pleasure in the bedroom. Because of her upbringing and background he could introduce her to his friends and that was more than he could say about his other female bedroom companions. In addition, she had helped him to decide what should be done about Adolphus, assuming he was eventually found and brought back to Antwerp.

Otto was sitting back in his chair, behind his large desk, stroking his moustache as he contemplated his next meeting with the delectable Romilda, when there was a knock on his door.

"Come," he called and Major Becker entered.

"Ah, Becker," the Oberst intoned, smiling. He was in an exceptionally good mood that morning as a result of the previous night's activities. "What can I do for you?"

"Sir," the Major replied. "We have news."

"So sit down and tell me about it," he replied.

"Bergmann and his two comrades have been found," Becker explained. "They are in a small town in the North of Belgium called Nieuwpoort."

"Excellent," the Oberst replied, "well get them back here. I want to have a serious talk with our friend the Hauptmann."

"There is just one other thing," Becker continued. "There is a Belgium peasant with them. Should we bring him back as well?"

"A Belgium peasant, did you say? That sounds somewhat curious. Where does this information come from?" the Oberst demanded.

"A Major Bruno Feldheim, an old boy, a relic of the Africa wars, who had been put out to pasture in sleepy little Nieuwpoort. He is the garrison commander."

"Well, tell him we want the Belgian sending back with our own three men. It seems there are always mysteries surrounding our friend Adolphus," the Oberst commented wryly.

Nieuwpoort

"It seems that the authorities in Antwerp want you all to return and that includes your friendly Belgian, whoever he is," Major Feldheim was informing his guests some hours later, after a telegram arrived with the orders. "Because you are dressed in British uniform I am to release ten men from my platoon to escort you."

Adolphus was far from surprised to be recalled to Antwerp. The mission was a disaster and if re-activated would need either another British plane or the recovery of the BE2b. He realised that Joe would be a most unwilling passenger on such a return trip. He was really struggling with what would be the best solution for his cousin and brother-in-law and one that would not compromise him and his two companions. It was not just Adolphus who knew the real identity of Joe, they all did. Adolphus decided to speak to Leutnant Schmidt and Hans Bach separately.

"I have a difficult personal problem with our friend Joe," he explained to Schmidt. "We would probably have finished up being shot by our own army if not for him. And as you know he is a close relative."

"I realise that," the Leutnant replied. "I wondered what you wanted to do about him."

"I wish I knew," Adolphus replied. "I know my first loyalty is to Germany and the Kaiser but Joe has really helped us here in Nieuwpoort and I think he deserves some consideration for that. When you consider it, he has saved the lives of three German soldiers."

Schmidt nodded sympathetically.

"Well, I will give the matter a little more thought," Adolphus decided. "I must make a decision before tomorrow morning when we set off for Antwerp."

Adolphus then had the same conversation with Bach who also seemed to be sympathetic to the quandary.

I am fortunate to have men of this calibre with me, Adolphus decided gratefully.

Joe was now very worried for his own safety. He knew of the fanatical loyalty that Adolphus had shown for the Kaiser and his country. Joe could cast his mind back to Adolphus' stay in Manchester in 1912 and how he, Joe, had observed him spying on British army garrisons at that time. *On the other hand,* he agonised, *I probably saved his life and that of the other two and do my strong family links with Adolphus count for nothing?*

The four men had been accommodated overnight in a dormitory and at quarter past three in the morning, Adolphus came to a decision. He must facilitate Joe's escape from there. He crept over to Joe's bed and tapped him gently on the shoulder. Joe, of course was wide awake and quickly turned to find Adolphus standing over him.

"Get dressed and come with me," Adolphus whispered.

While waiting for Joe, he packed up some food and drink for him and then the two of them crept out of the unguarded building.

He told Joe to wait in the doorway while he went to speak to the lone sentry on the corner.

"When you see I have engaged him in conversation you must cross the street and make for the open countryside," Adolphus instructed him.

"Thank you, thank you," Joe said, "almost in tears."

"Never mind that," Adolphus replied. "I am letting you escape but not to return to Saint Omer where you can again start bombing trains and our poor soldiers fighting for their lives in the trenches. You must stay in Belgium."

"I cannot promise that," Joe replied. "Just as you want to fight for your country, I am committed to fighting for mine. You must accept that."

Adolphus ignored Joe's reply. *He will find it almost impossible to get back to France on his own,* he decided.

Adolphus was wearing just a shirt and trousers and these were not easily identifiable as British army issue without the officer's jacket. He told Joe to wait in the doorway of the building and he approached the sentry on the corner.

The sentry was a middle-aged man with two or three day's stubble on his face. He was hardly the smart German soldier of whom the Kaiser and his officers were so proud.

The sentry had been leaning back against the wall of the building smoking and only heard Adolphus' approach on the last minute.

"Is this how you perform your duties?" Adolphus demanded. "I could have killed you before you even knew I was upon you. God help us if we have to rely on men like you. Stand to attention when I address you. Do you know who I am? I am Hauptmann Bergmann and I return to

Antwerp tomorrow morning. Otherwise I would report your slovenly appearance and inability to carry out your orders to Major Feldheim."

The sentry clicked his heels, saluted and said, "Jawohl, Herr Hauptmann."

Adolphus turned on his heels and walked smartly back to the doorway of the building where he found, much to his relief, that Joe had made good his escape and would soon be well away from the small town of Nieuwpoort. Where Joe would go from there was Joe's problem, Adolphus realised, as long as it did not become his problem.

Chapter Thirty-Three

Antwerp 1915

The Interrogator is Interrogated

At six o'clock in the morning after a sleepless night, the three remaining men packed their few belongings in preparation for departure. They were enjoying a quick breakfast when Major Feldheim came into their dormitory.

"So, are you all ready to go?" he enquired.

"Yes, Sir," Adolphus replied.

"And where is the Belgian civilian?" Feldheim demanded, looking round the room.

"He must have left on his own in the night," Adolphus replied, with a quick glance at Schmidt and Bach. "As a Belgian he probably prefers to stay around here than go to Antwerp. After all he was not our prisoner. He just joined us on our way here."

"Well I do not know what the Oberst in Antwerp will have to say about that. He is expecting four men, not three. Very well, you had better prepare to leave."

Adolphus and his two remaining companions climbed into a converted, troop-carrying truck to return from Nieuwpoort. Adolphus sat in the one passenger seat, alongside the driver and a far from happy Leutnant Schmidt in the cramped conditions of the back of the open vehicle. Not only did this mean that he would be uncomfortable; it also meant that he, an officer, would be transported, like a common soldier, along with Bach and the other nine members of the escort group.

It took most of the day to travel back to Antwerp. As soon as the truck had been checked by the sentries guarding the gates of the large garrison, Adolphus asked the driver to leave him, together with Schmidt, at the officer's mess where they could have a meal.

"You can then take the rest of the party including Gefreiter Bach to the canteen," Adolphus explained. "Then you will need to set off back to Nieuwpoort while it is still light."

The driver, a Feldwebel, looked at Adolphus. "Those are not my instructions, Sir."

Adolphus surveyed the driver with a look of irritation. "What then are your instructions?"

"You are to report personally to the Oberst von Lubeck who has been alerted by the gate sentries to your arrival. The Leutnant and the Gefreiter are to proceed to the office of Major Becker."

It was certainly not his fault that the doctored British plane, the BE2b, had let them down. The only thing he could feel mildly guilty about was helping Joe to escape and he had done that with the acquiescence of Schmidt and Bach. He was certain they were both awake when he quietly saw his cousin out of the building. Why then did the Oberst want to see him the minute he returned? He could not possibly know that Adolphus had helped his cousin to slip away in the dead of night.

Adolphus knocked on the door of von Lubeck's office and opened the door, on hearing the response to enter.

The Oberst was sitting at his desk with the huge picture of the Kaiser immediately behind him on the wall.

"Ach, Hauptmann," he said, in an icy voice, "come in and sit down."

Adolphus approached the desk, clicked his heels, saluted, said, "thank you Sir," and sat down.

The eyes of the Kaiser in the portrait seemed to be boring in to him and so did the blue eyes of the Oberst.

The Oberst looked grave. "Herr Hauptmann, we have some questions for you."

Something was wrong, terribly wrong, but what could it be?

"Herr Hauptmann," the Oberst began. "Are you a loyal officer in this army; are you loyal to his Imperial Majesty the Kaiser and our country, or not?"

"Of course I am, Sir," Adolphus answered quickly. "I swore allegiance many years ago as a reserve officer before visiting England to obtain information about the British army at that time."

"Ah, yes, the visit to England," the Oberst repeated with heavy irony. "And what else did you get up to while you were in England?"

"Get up to, Sir?" Adolphus replied.

"Jawohl! What else did you get up to in England?"

"I met and stayed with my English relatives."

"Ja, and then what?" the Oberst prompted him sternly.

"I met the lady who became my wife," Adolphus replied. "Everyone knows that my wife is English. Has that suddenly become a problem?"

"Herr Hauptmann, it is I who asks the questions but the fact that your wife is English should not have been a problem."

"So, Sir, may I ask what is the problem?"

"Herr Hauptmann, I have just told you that it is I who ask the questions, not you," the Oberst replied angrily.

Adolphus sat quietly as the Oberst consulted his notes.

"Firstly I have to return to the matter of Feldwebel Braun and his attempt to discredit you, which at the time looked like personal prejudice."

Adolphus nodded being aware that he must not interrupt the Oberst by asking any more questions.

"You conducted two interviews with a British Lieutenant called David Goldberg which had some strange content. You seemed to have talked to him as an old friend even when it became obvious that his real friend was your own brother-in-law, Joseph Bergman of the RFC, who bombed the Berlin train and nearly killed your wife."

"Sir, can I answer that?"

"Jawohl! I would love you to explain that to me."

"Sir, my job as an officer in the interrogation unit was to obtain information about allied air power. To do that I needed to get the confidence of the prisoners I was questioning. On that occasion I discovered that Lieutenant Goldberg was an old friend of my wife's family and I thought I could use that to advantage."

"So what did you learn from this RFC man?"

"I was able confirm that it was Lieutenant Bergman who bombed the train."

"Now I want to ask you about your wife. I understand that as a good loyal army wife she came with your baby son to share your billet here in Antwerp."

Adolphus nodded once again and the Oberst continued, "So why did she return home after what I gather was a terrible row between you?"

"How do you know about that?" Adolphus gasped.

"Silence," the Oberst shouted, thumping the table. "How many times must I tell you that it is I who asks the questions?"

"Can I now reply to your question, sir?" Adolphus enquired quietly although inside he was seething.

"Ja! Ja!" von Lubeck replied.

"My oldest brother-in-law, Alfred Bergman, had been killed in the trenches and then I learned that Lieutenant Joseph Bergman was missing after the train bombing. When I told my wife, she was very upset and tried to blame me for what was happening to her family. We rowed and she returned to Berlin to my mother whom she considered more sympathetic than me."

"And was there not another reason why your wife left; something to do with your affair with the daughter of the family Scholz, where you were living?"

Adolphus was horrified. Rachel knew nothing of his one night of drunken passion, if such it was, with Romilda. It was certainly no affair. He had gone to great pains to avoid the advances of the young lady. How could the Oberst have all this information? He agonised.

Eventually Adolphus realised that the Oberst was waiting for a reply.

"Sir, there was no affair with Fraulein Scholz."

"Well, we may come back to that later," von Lubeck continued. "We still have to deal with what happened on the way to Saint Omer."

"That is quite simple. Our engineers had converted a British two-seater plane, the BE2b, into a three-seater. They thought they had allowed enough extra fuel storage for the heavier weight of the additional passenger, but they had obviously miscalculated and we ran out of fuel in southern Belgium."

"I see," the Oberst replied. "Then tell me finally about the mysterious Belgium civilian that you discovered in the middle of nowhere and who has now conveniently disappeared."

"Sir, you know as much as me. He helped us to establish contact with the German garrison in Nieuwpoort for which we are eternally grateful. We could not have approached as we were all dressed in British uniform."

"That was a very convenient meeting for you, was it not? There seem to have been a number of convenient and coincidental happenings in your life lately, Hauptmann Bergmann. I must tell you that you are confined to barracks and suspended from all duties. If you make any attempt to leave you will be placed in the lock-up. I will be continuing this investigation personally with the assistance of Major Becker."

Adolphus sat there stunned until the Oberst spoke again.

"That will be all, Hauptmann Bergmann. You are dismissed."

Adolphus clicked his heels, saluted. He left the office of the Oberst feeling deeply shocked. How could this happen to him? What had he done to deserve such treatment? He had always been loyal to his Imperial Majesty the Kaiser.

In the knowledge that he was confined to barracks he went to recover his German uniform from the officer's mess and to arrange his sleeping accommodation in the garrison.

When he arrived in Antwerp he had been ravenously hungry. Now all he could manage was a little soup before settling down for a second sleepless night. Little did he know that worse was to follow!

Chapter Thirty-Four

Antwerp 1915

An Unwelcome Revelation

Rachel was sad. Her marriage appeared to be in ruins. Her oldest brother was dead and her middle brother missing. The only bright star in her dark night was little Rudi and she spent many long hours looking after him and playing with him. She knew that the amount of attention he was receiving would ultimately rebound on her as, during the day, she hardly left him, even for a minute. Her mother-in-law was as supportive as ever and without her, Rachel felt she could not have carried on at all. Greta worried incessantly about Rachel. She was hardly eating and although pregnant was losing weight at an alarming rate. And then matters went from bad to worse.

Karl Bergmann had a meeting with the officer in charge of purchasing footwear for the German army in Belgium and he was based at the Antwerp garrison. After the meeting and feeling very happy with the huge order for boots that he had just received, Karl decided to try and contact his son, and if he could be excused from his duties for an hour or two, to take him out for lunch. As he was already in the garrison, he made his way over to the Interrogation unit and asked for Adolphus. The Feldwebel on the desk asked Karl for identification.

"I am Karl Bergmann," the visitor replied. "It is my son Hauptmann Adolphus Bergmann that I hope to be able to see. Is he in the garrison?"

The Feldwebel looked most uncomfortable, asked to be excused and explained that he would go and discover where the Hauptmann was.

A few minutes later the Feldwebel returned in the company of an officer.

"Herr Bergmann," Major Becker introduced himself and explained. "I am afraid you cannot see your son at the moment."

"Is he out?" Karl enquired.

The Major looked most embarrassed and said, "No, he is not out but he is not available."

"Well then I can wait," Karl replied.

"I am afraid that it will not be possible for you to see him at all, today," Becker answered.

"If he is in the garrison, surely I can see him if I wait," Karl suggested.

"Herr Bergmann," the Major replied. "I think you had better sit down and I will see if the Oberst can have a word with you."

"Is Adolphus ill?" Karl enquired, suddenly quite worried.

"No, he is not ill, but please wait and I will go and tell the Oberst that you are here."

What on earth is going on? Karl pondered. *If he is not ill, why not just tell me he is very busy? That I can understand. But there seems to be some sort of mystery.*

Karl Bergmann was not used to being left in a draughty corridor and was becoming increasingly annoyed. He had to keep reminding himself that this was the Imperial German Army and even he, Karl Bergmann, had to do as he was told. He also reminded himself, they were his largest single customer. He did not dare to protest about the treatment he was receiving *and, of course, there is a war on*, he remembered, as if he could forget.

After nearly an hour of sitting fuming, Major Becker returned to Karl. "I am sorry to keep you waiting. The Oberst Otto von Lubeck can see you now."

"Ach," said Karl, slapping his thigh. "My old friend Otto; I am sure he can arrange for me to see my son."

The Major escorted Karl to the office of the Oberst and announced him.

"Karl my old friend, how are you?" the Oberst greeted him.

"I am very well," Karl replied. "I have been over to the purchasing offices and thought I should look up my son Adolphus while I am here."

The Oberst suddenly looked serious. "I am afraid that will not be possible," he explained.

"I know Adolphus is involved in very important work but I did think that maybe, if he is so busy, I could just see him for a minute," Karl suggested.

"I am afraid not," von Lubeck replied. "He is well and he is on site but I am afraid you cannot see him."

"If I was to stay over until tomorrow, maybe I could see him then," Karl suggested.

The Oberst decided that he must give his old friend some explanation.

"I am afraid there is a disciplinary problem and the Hauptmann is confined to barracks until after the investigation is completed."

"Adolphus, in trouble," Karl gasped. "Not because he is my son but I cannot believe he would in any way break army rules. He loves the army and is a loyal follower of his Imperial Majesty the Kaiser. He is a German through and through."

"I must say that is the way I always saw him but certain things have been brought to our attention which cannot be ignored. I could not have been more shocked if he was my son, but these matters have to be thoroughly investigated. We are at war and cannot take any chances," the Oberst explained.

"Can you at least tell him that I was here and asked about him," Karl replied.

The Oberst nodded and gave Karl a watery smile. "Now Major Becker will see you out of the building and please give my warmest greetings to your charming wife Greta. I gather that your daughter-in-law is back in Berlin. Please also give her my best wishes. I may need to travel over to Berlin to interview her as part of our investigations but please keep that to yourself, at least for now."

A deeply shocked Herr Karl Bergmann left the garrison and walked down the street to the Railway Station. The Berlin train was scheduled to leave at 3.30pm and he climbed aboard to make his way to his reserved seat in the first-class carriage. He had a large order for the supply of boots in his pocket but it gave him no pleasure. He had always been so proud of Adolphus and now, suddenly, he felt as if his son was going to turn into a major embarrassment for him.

Karl Bergmann was a man who thrived on pride. He was proud to be the owner of the largest chain of shoe shops in Germany. He was proud to be the largest supplier of boots to the German army. And he had been proud of his only son who had reached the rank of Hauptmann at such a young age. Now he was beginning to become angry with Adolphus. How dare the boy embarrass him in this way?

Chapter Thirty-Five

Berlin 1915

Reporting to the Ladies

Rachel had always had a difficult relationship with her father-in-law. If the truth be known he terrified her. Greta's confession about how Karl verbally abused her had done nothing to improve matters and Rachel did her best to avoid being in his company. It was strange therefore that on this particular evening she was waiting anxiously for Karl to come back from Antwerp. She was sure that he would have seen Adolphus and she hoped that he would return with some good news from that quarter, *maybe he is to be allowed to spend a leave in Berlin*, she dared to hope.

It was late evening when Karl arrived. As soon as he entered the house he bellowed, "Greta, where are you?"

Rachel, from her listening post in the study heard her mother-in-law reply, "coming dear. Is everything alright?"

"No it is far from alright," she heard him shout. "For goodness sake woman, come downstairs and hear what your son has been up to."

Rachel then heard Greta descending the stairs and enquiring, "Would you like something to eat?"

Then she heard the two of them making their way to the dining-room while Karl was muttering, "how embarrassing! Whatever the devil Adolphus has done, it must be serious."

Rachel felt sick. True they were estranged but she still loved him and if he was in trouble she needed to know what kind of trouble it was. Did she dare to go and find her father-in-law in the dining-room or should she wait for Elsa to tell her what had transpired in Antwerp?

After just a few moments she decided she must be brave and she knocked timidly on the door.

"Come in," Karl bellowed. Then he saw it was Rachel not the servant bringing him a little late supper.

"What do you want?" he challenged her.

"I knew you were in Antwerp today and I thought you would return with news of my husband," she ventured.

Karl was red in the face and frowning. "Yes, you are his wife so I suppose you had better hear this as well," he said. "Well ladies, I called to see your dear son and your dear husband today while in Antwerp and discovered to my embarrassment and horror that he is under some sort of house arrest – 'confined to barracks' they call it. What the devil he has done, I do not know, but I had to put up with that sanctimonious Oberst of his, Otto von Lubeck, telling me that Adolphus is in trouble, but what kind of trouble he would not say?"

Karl had entered the house furious but now he seemed to be intent on winding himself up even more. He stood up, pushing his chair noisily away from the table where he had just sat down and started pacing up and down.

"Do you realise how embarrassing this is for me. I am by far and away, the largest supplier of boots to the German army. My son has done me untold harm and I will probably lose all this business." He turned towards his quaking wife. "We will be ruined after all my years of hard work making us into a family to be reckoned with in this town. What a disgrace! You can forget all your fashionable clothes and smart aristocratic friends."

Rachel knew these rages were a frequent occurrence between Karl and Greta. She also knew that Greta had learned to let the worst of the invective flow over her but this time she burst into tears.

"It is no good you blubbing, woman," Karl shouted. "Your son has ruined us. I will never be able to hold my head up in Berlin again."

"But what has he done?" Greta sobbed.

"I keep telling you woman, I have no idea. Otto wouldn't tell me anything other than the fact that Adolphus was under investigation, but what for, I have no idea?"

Rachel sat there listening to the row. She didn't care about Karl's reputation. She thoroughly detested the man even if he was her husband's father. However, she cared deeply about Adolphus. Karl only cares about himself and his reputation, she realised. He had not shown the slightest concern for his son and what agonies he would be suffering.

Rachel decided she must now speak out. "I must go to Antwerp and be there for him when all this comes to a head," she announced.

Karl surveyed her dismissively. "What good can you do?" he sniffed.

"I may not be able to do anything for him with the army authorities, but he will need to know that I am there for him and that Rudi and I are close by, while he has this trouble proceeding," she said.

Karl looked at her, pregnant and looking far from well. "You are crazy to even think of it. Look at yourself, woman, you are in no condition to travel."

"Apart from getting a message to Adolphus that I am back in Antwerp, I will ask to see the Oberst Otto von Lubeck," Rachel continued. "I met him before and he is a charming gentleman."

Karl began laughing. "You, what could you do with Otto von Lubeck? Do you really think he would listen to you?"

Then suddenly Karl remembered that the Oberst had said that he wished to interview Rachel. He was not however about to admit that. "I will contact the Oberst tomorrow and see what he has to say about you going back to Antwerp. It is a crazy idea and I am sure his answer will be 'no.'" Karl then realised that this was an opportunity to play the man of importance and influence to his family. "However, I will do my best to persuade him."

Chapter Thirty-Six

Antwerp 1915

The Schmidt Interview

The Oberst Otto von Lubeck sat at his desk considering the various possible crimes of Hauptmann Adolphus Bergmann. The fact that he had recognised in Adolphus an officer with a glittering future in the the German army, only made him more determined to get to the bottom of the entire matter.

The first crime was supplying information to the enemy in the person of Lieutenant David Goldberg of the Royal Flying Corp. There could be little doubt that, at the second interview, the Hauptmann had told the enemy flyer that the German Intelligence Services were well aware of the identity of the train bomber in the person of the Hauptmann's own brother-in-law, Joseph Bergman. Goldberg was, of course, a prisoner-of war but he might escape or be part of some future prisoner exchange, if such ever happened. There was also the problem as to why Adolphus had lied when questioned on the matter by Major Werner. That looked very suspicious.

The Oberst had suggested to Major Becker that he should interview the Hauptmann first for the position of leader of the mission to Saint Omer. It seemed very strange that Adolphus should volunteer for this job before being told that he was the Oberst's preferred candidate. Such enthusiasm to wear British uniform and to be flown to Saint Omer did have the whiff of a suggestion that he would have transferred his allegiance after landing there.

And then there was the mystery Belgian. Why had he helped them without any persuasion? Most Belgians, quite understandably, were not particularly well disposed to the German army of occupation. This, now vanished man, had gone out of his way to help Adolphus and his two comrades. Why? The Belgian had then, very conveniently disapeared from the same room where Adolphus and his two comrades were sleeping. This needed further investigation.

He quickly decided that his formal investigation would start there. He sent for Major Becker and told him to have Leutnant Franz Schmidt ready for an interview at ten o'clock that morning.

The Leutnant arrived exactly on time, saluted and clicked his heels in front of his commanding officer.

"Please be seated, Leutnant," the Oberst began. "This is a preliminary hearing into various aspects of the conduct of Hauptmann Adolphus Bergmann. You are not under oath, but if it transpires that you have been less than truthful or even withheld information, you can expect to finish up being subject to disciplinary proceedings yourself. Do I make myself clear?"

Franz Schmidt was beginning to feel very uncomfortable and that was before a single question had been asked. He wanted to protect the Hauptmann who he now regarded as a friend, but not at the expense of his own life and career. All he could do was to try and show Adolphus' actions in as good a light as possible but without lying.

"So, Leutnant Schmidt, tell me about the aborted trip to Saint Omer," the Oberst ordered.

"First, Sir, I would like to tell you about the aircraft, the British BE2b. This plane is slow and has a disappointing altitude limit."

"Yes, yes, I know all that," the Oberst replied impatiently.

"If I may continue Sir, it is normally a two-seater providing for the pilot and one passenger-observer. However, this particular plane had been converted into a three-seater by our German engineers, especially for this mission."

"Yes, yes, I know all that too," the Oberst again interrupted. "But what happened?"

"Well Sir, the engineers had miscalculated how much fuel would be needed to get us to Saint Omer and I was obliged to make a forced-landing in northern Belgium."

"Yes, I also know all that and well done that you managed to land the plane without injury to the three men on board."

"Thank you Sir," Schmidt replied.

"So, man, then what happened?" the Oberst demanded.

"We met up with a man who was apparently a Belgian farm worker," Schmidt continued.

"And did any of you know this man?" von Lubeck asked.

Schmidt knew that all the prevarication about the plane was not going to stop him from arriving at this point. He had no choice but to tell the truth.

"Yes Sir," the Leutnant continued. "Hauptmann Bergmann knew the man and they recognised each other instantly."

"And did you discover who this man really was?" the Oberst demanded.

"Yes, he was an English flyer from the RFC, and he was on the run."

"So what did you do, arrest him?"

"No Sir, we thought we could use him to get us to Saint Omer and we told him that we had all defected to the British, hence the RFC uniforms."

"And did this man believe you?" the Oberst asked.

"He seemed to," Schmidt replied.

"So then what happened?" von Lubeck demanded.

"We all set out together for Saint Omer and then we found an abandoned Minerva Belgium Armoured Car and Hans Bach, our mechanic, got it going. We then travelled a lot quicker until we came to the flooded area. Do you know that the Belgians flooded...?"

"Yes of course I do," the Oberst replied testily.

"We then made our way on foot to the outskirts of the town of Nieuwpoort, however," the Leutnant continued, having no problem in relating this part of the story, "because we were in British uniforms we realised that the vigilant German soldiers of Nieuwpoort would shoot at us as soon as we appeared. For this reason we asked the British flyer, disguised as a Belgian farm worker, to enter the town and explain to the Garrison commander that we three really were German soldiers. That worked well with us being allocated temporary accommodation in the German HQ."

"So far this all makes sense," the Oberst commented. "So then what happened?"

"The Garrison commander contacted you and orders were received to return here," the Leutnant explained hoping that the most obvious question about the true identity and present whereabouts of the British flyer would not be asked.

And then the question came that Franz Schmidt had been dreading. "So, who was the mysterious Belgian farm worker or British flyer to give him his correct description? And where is he now?"

"Sir, he was the cousin and brother-in-law of Hauptmann Bergmann and he left on his own on the night before we were to return here."

"How did he manage to leave the German HQ in Nieuwpoort in the middle of the night without help?"

They were now at the crux of the matter. If Adolphus had helped an allied officer to escape he would be guilty of treason against the Imperial Majesty of Germany as embodied in the person of Kaiser Wilhelm the Second.

"I do not know," Franz replied aware that this was one step too far in protecting the Hauptmann. "I went to sleep the night before and when I awoke he had gone."

"How many people were sleeping in that room," the Oberst asked quietly.

"Just the Hauptmann, Gefreiter Hans Bach, the British officer and me," Schmidt replied equally quietly.

"I have to tell you that I find it incredible that a man would be able to arise, get dressed and leave the main German garrison in the town in the middle of the night without anyone being aware of it," the Oberst replied coldly. "You have not heard the last of this matter, Herr Leutnant."

Chapter Thirty-Seven

Antwerp 1915

A Chat with a Lady

A good night's sleep did nothing for the temper of Karl Bergmann. He was still furious that his son the Hauptmann Adolphus Bergmann should be embarrassing him. However, getting Rachel back to Antwerp would be a good move and he sent off a telegram to his son's commanding officer, the Oberst Otto von Lubeck.

```
I have persuaded my daughter-in-law Rachel
Bergmann  to   return   to  Antwerp  to  be
interviewed - stop - Please arrange travel -
stop  -  I  hope  this  will  help  to  prove
innocence  of  my  son  -  stop  -  best  wishes
Karl Bergmann
```

The Oberst was pleased but did not share Karl's apparent optimism that this would somehow prove Adolphus innocent.

The Scholz family was notified of her imminent return and Frau Scholz, Elsa, was looking forward to having the young woman and her baby son Rudi in her house again. Martin, often absent, had only one opinion on the matter – if it helped him to stay in the good books of the army, so be it. He, of course, at that stage had no idea of the trouble that his young female guest's husband was in.

As for Romilda, she could not understand it. Why was Rachel coming back when she had only just deserted her husband to return to Berlin? However, she was still enjoying the company of the Oberst and with the little English Jewess pregnant, she saw her as no threat to that relationship. It came as profound shock to her, therefore, to discover the driver of the Oberst's car at the front-door just one day after Rachel's return from Berlin and there to collect not Romilda, but Rachel.

A guard escorted Rachel to the office of Otto von Lubeck and she knocked gently on the door. Being invited to enter, she did so and was warmly greeted by the Oberst who rose to his feet to welcome her.

"My dear Frau Bergmann, how nice to see you again," he ventured. "Please be seated."

The welcome re-assured Rachel who had been very worried since she had heard the news, from her father-in-law, of Adolphus being confined to barracks.

"I am trying to understand your husband's recent behaviour and I thought you could possibly help me," he began.

Rachel nodded and waited for the Oberst to continue.

"I need to ask you one or two fairly personal questions about your relationship with Adolphus. Please understand that I do this to try and ascertain why he took certain actions which do not appear to be in the best interests of the Imperial German Army and our beloved Kaiser."

Rachel again nodded and wondered how embarrassing these personal questions might be.

"Rachel, if I may call you that?" again Rachel nodded. "I believe you had a bitter argument with Adolphus which resulted in you taking your baby son back to Berlin."

"Yes, that is true," Rachel replied hesitantly, "but I returned as soon as I heard he was in some kind of trouble. I love my husband and I wish to support him especially if he has a problem."

"Rachel," the Oberst continued, "can I ask you how you feel about the war and the conflict of interests within your family unit."

"I feel it is a tragedy and particularly for those of us who have lost near and dear ones as a result," Rachel explained, her eyes filling with tears. "My brother Alfred was killed in the trenches in the first weeks of the war fighting for the British. My parents, who I have not seen for over a year now and my brother's wife and children, must be broken-hearted. We are not the only ones! All over Britain, France and Germany, in fact all over Europe there are probably millions of families in the same situation."

"Does your husband share your view that this war is a tragedy?" von Lubeck probed.

"I doubt it. He is a German officer and he believes in his country. He blames the Serbs for all this misery and he is determined to see Germany come out on top."

"Is that why you had an argument that was so terrible that it led to you taking your son and returning to Berlin?" the Oberst gently enquired. "Are you sure there is no other reason?"

"No," Rachel replied. "What other reason could there be?"

"Maybe your husband was not as loyal to you as you would have liked. Maybe he had a lady-friend," he suggested.

Rachel was shocked by the accusation. "Absolutely not! I know that he only had eyes for me, and I for him. Until we argued, he was the most loving and attentive husband any girl could dream of."

Behind that charming exterior the Oberst had a heart of pure steel. "The young lady; the daughter of the family Scholz, did he never show any interest in her. She is a very attractive young woman and we all know that boys will be boys!"

"Not my Adolphus," Rachel replied with a conviction in her voice that she did not recognise deep inside herself.

"Oh well," von Lubeck said, "let's leave that matter aside. You have another brother do you not?"

"I have two brothers. The older one Joe is a flyer in the Royal Flying Corp. He is missing after a flight over Belgium. Your people found his plane, so Adolphus tells me, but there was no sign of him or his Observer from the flight. As for my other brother I know that he will be obliged to join the British army next year when he is eighteen. God help him and God help us all."

"I am very interested in your brother Joe," the Oberst continued. "Do you have no idea where he is?"

"I don't, but you could not seriously expect me to tell you if I did, if I am to be honest." This was the old Rachel, the doughty fighter for women's rights in Manchester before the war.

"It would be difficult," the Oberst replied, "but surely now, your first loyalty is to your new country Germany, where you live and where your husband was commissioned as an army officer." The Oberst looked at her and continued, "I am now going to tell you something that I, an Oberst, could be in trouble for divulging to any civilian."

Rachel regarded him in amazement. "And what is that?"

"Where did we first meet?" von Lubeck demanded.

"On the train that was bombed. You were very kind to me on that occasion," Rachel replied, remembering with a watery smile.

"Ach so," the Oberst answered. "And who do you think was responsible for bombing that train, an act that could have killed you and your baby son? All our evidence points to a certain Flight Lieutenant Joseph Bergman of the RFC," he pronounced triumphantly.

This time Rachel was deeply shocked. She knew from Adolphus that Joe's plane had crashed and that both he and his Observer were probably still alive but in what condition, she did not dare to consider. Now this German officer was telling her that it was Joe who had bombed the train. Obviously he could not have had the slightest suspicion that she and baby Rudi were on board, but to her this was a cowardly act. At that stage in the war aerial bombardment was in its infancy. She could understand soldiers shooting at each other from the trenches; kill or be killed, but to destroy from the sky seemed incredibly wicked.

"I had no idea," Rachel replied.

"Do you have any idea where Joseph Bergman may be?" the Oberst asked.

"Absolutely not," Rachel replied. "He is still my brother and I hope and pray he is safe and well but if I saw him I would certainly wish to have a few words about the train bombing."

"Well my dear Frau Bergmann," the Oberst said, "I see no reason to detain you any longer."

"Can I now ask you one question," Rachel asked.

"And what is that dear lady?" von Lubeck replied.

"What has my husband done that he is in disgrace and confined to barracks?"

"All this may be nothing but he has behaved very strangely and we need to be sure that he is still loyal to his Imperial Majesty the Kaiser and his country, try not to worry."

The Oberst rose from his chair and escorted Rachel from his office.

She had entered the room with some disturbing information and all she had achieved was to add to it with more worrying intelligence.

Chapter Thirty-Eight

Southern Belgium 1915

Fellow Travellers

Joe made his way towards the open countryside outside Nieuwpoort. Twice he had been obliged to hide in doorways when two-man German patrols had sauntered down the streets he was trying to traverse. After a few hours he found himself quite near to the flooded area that divided southern Belgium from Northern France. If only he had a boat, he considered, he was sure he could navigate his way across. However, he knew that it was highly unlikely that there would be boats of any size moored on the edge of the flooded area, which was supposed to be a temporary feature to stop the Germans approaching the French coast. He decided that he must go east, but after just two days of trudging through fields and over rough paths he started to see large numbers of German soldiers, some in trucks and others marching. Joe watched their progress from a wooded area and felt some sympathy for these men, although the enemy, on their way to be slaughtered in the trenches. He had frequently seen the dreadful conditions in which all the armies toiled when he had flown his sorties as an RFC pilot over these self-same trenches. It was still summer and he dreaded to think what fate awaited all the combatants when the freezing rain arrived again, as in the previous winter.

His own predicament had begun to dawn on Joe. There was literally no way of by-passing the trenches and arriving in British or French controlled territory no matter how far he marched. If he tried to cross the lines, a German bullet would probably get him or a British or a French one, if he managed, by some miracle, to pass the German lines.

Adolphus had sent him off with a reasonable supply of food and drink but this was nearly exhausted. Fortunately there were lots of fruit trees to supplement his diet and he had been able to top up his water bottle from streams of pure water. However desperate Joe was to get back to Saint Omer, the prospect of doing so was growing dimmer and dimmer. He patted the two sets of identity papers in his inside trouser pocket. To access them he had to remove his trousers and he knew that the way he had sewn the pocket between his legs, at the de Vries farm before leaving, only a strip-search would discover them. If he was caught by the Germans he had decided to claim to be Private Gareth Jones, who had been killed by a stray Fokker bullet when this nightmare had first started. If the Germans were still looking for him after the train bombing, it would be far more likely that they would be searching for Lieutenant Joseph Bergman. This was especially so since his cover as a Belgian farm worker had been blown when he met up with Adolphus and the others.

If Adolphus helped me to escape, I am sure he will be in no hurry to identify me, but what of Smith and Bailey? Why would they protect me? Joe mused and decided he would be Private Gareth Jones from now on.

On the second night it started to rain and Joe took shelter in a deserted barn – or rather a barn that he assumed to be deserted. As an experienced dairy farmer, after the time he had spent chez de Vries, he could see no evidence of any living creatures, human or bovine and quickly settled down on a pile of dry hay. He awoke, after experiencing the quality of deep sleep that is usually only the province of the truly exhausted. He reached for his knapsack. He was certain he had placed it just to the left side of where he had lain but it was not there. He jumped up and discovered that all his belongings had gone. All he had was the shirt and trousers in which he had slept. Then he realised that he was barefoot. Wherever he was making for, he needed shoes to protect his feet. He looked around the barn and could see that someone else had been sleeping there. They must have arrived after he had succumbed to his desperate desire to rest his weary body and they had left at the crack of dawn. Joe began to look for some protection for his feet and eventually found some old rags in the far corner. He bound them round his ankles and then over his toes and heels and found he could walk like this, if not very quickly. In any case he now had no idea where he was making for. He found an apple tree and devoured three round rosy pieces of its fruit. With hunger and thirst temporarily assuaged he decided to set off and see what inspiration he might receive from the road signs. It was early afternoon when he heard footsteps, not marching footsteps as in German army footsteps, but he could definitely identify the sound of three or possibly four people coming in his direction. He crouched behind a hedge and watched as three men and a girl walked briskly by. They were speaking French which was of no significance as it was one of the two official languages of Belgium. Suddenly the one nearest to him stopped and said something to the other three. Then this man called, "Allo! We know you are there."

Joe of course stayed perfectly still and hoped against hope that the call had not been directed at him.

"Allo; we know you are there behind the hedge so you had better come out." This was said in French and then repeated in Flemish.

Joe stood up and made his way round to the path.

"Who are you and what are you doing hiding there?" the same man demanded in French.

Joe had learned French at school in Manchester and could converse fairly well in that language.

Joe had to give them some kind of answer. They were obviously French speakers and thus unlikely to have any sympathy with the Germans. "I am Private Gareth Jones of the British Army, Royal Flying Corp. My plane crashed further north and my pilot was killed," he explained.

One of the men flung his arms around Joe and kissed him on both cheeks. "So you are one of those brave British flyers who are helping to drive the Boche out of my country."

The other three, the two men and the girl were less demonstrative but shook his hand warmly.

The original man now started to introduce them all. "My name is Pierre Dubois and this young lady is Amelie Levi. We are both French nationals and our other two friends are..." Suddenly he stopped. "Sh! I can hear a motor vehicle coming. We must all hide."

Joe was both impressed and relieved to be with someone with such acute hearing; he had initially heard nothing and the Germans would have been upon him by the time he had realised.

Sure enough, from their vantage point behind the same hedge that had failed to conceal Joe, the five of them watched with open mouths as a brand new Mercedes 28/60 HP glided by, making short work of the bumpy road. Inside were three senior German officers and their driver, obviously on their way towards the front.

"Bloody Boche," the man called Pierre muttered. "If we had had more time and knew they were coming we could have relieved them of their lives and that beautiful piece of engineering."

Joe spoke up. "What are you doing here? All the main roads are crawling with Germans."

"That is precisely why we are here," the girl called Amelie explained. "We plant bombs along their routes and try to delay them from reaching the front."

"I did not introduce my other friends to you, when we were so rudely interrupted," Pierre remembered.

"Charles Guyon," said the taller man with a smile.

"Eduard Parmentier," said the fourth member of the group.

"Where are you based?" Joe enquired.

"We move around the area," Charles explained. "All of the people in this locality are very bitter about the way that Germany invaded the country and we have no shortage of help or hospitality. They have to be very careful though as the Boche regularly send out patrols to check all the farmhouses in the area. We tend to stay in the barns of our friends rather than risk them and ourselves by staying in their homes."

Joe nodded remembering the comfort he had enjoyed in the de Vries farmhouse. He realised that passing off one man as a farm worker was one thing, but to conceal four people was quite another.

"Now Gareth," Pierre said, "we are on our way to our base for the next couple of days. We need to know your story so will you come with us and you can tell us what happened to you. First however, I am sure you will understand that we need to see some identification."

"That goes two ways," Joe answered. "How do I know you are not working for the Germans?"

"Of course," Charles replied. "Come, let us start walking. The barn we are staying in is about three miles away."

On the way Joe became increasingly aware that Amelie, who had had much less to say than her three male companions, kept stealing little glances at him when she thought he was not looking. Eventually he fell into step with her.

"Where are you from?" he enquired.

"Oh," she replied, "My papers will tell you that I am a Belgium citizen; let's just leave it that, shall we? Where are you from?"

Joe was just about to say Manchester when he realised that Gareth Jones was of course from Wrexham in North Wales.

"Oh, so you're Welsh," Amelie commented.

Joe just nodded. This amazing young lady had the surname Levi and that was a Jewish name. However, he had decided to inherit the identity of the Welshman and he doubted that there were many Jews in Wrexham.

Joe nodded. "You kept looking at me. Did you think you knew me?" he enquired.

"Mais oui," she replied. "You strongly resemble someone I used to know but he was from Manchester. He was a liaison-officer between the British and French forces last year, at the very beginning of the war. Sadly, he was killed by the Boche while taking messages to our commander. He was a very brave man," she commented.

Joe felt a shiver run down his spine and then decided he was having ridiculous thoughts. *You really are going crazy*, he told himself. He decided to continue the conversation if only to satisfy himself that he was allowing his imagination to run away with him. "What was his name, your friend?"

"He was First Lieutenant Alfred Bergman," she replied quickly.

Joe felt dizzy and nearly fainted.

"Are you alright?" Amelie enquired. "Are you ill? You have gone absolutely white."

Joe knew that his beloved older brother had been killed. In Saint Omer the troops received frequent deliveries of mail and, soon after the event a letter had arrived from his parents, giving him the heart-breaking information.

"No," he replied, "I am fine. I think I must be exhausted. I have walked all the way from Nieuwpoort."

Amelie smiled, she had such a lovely smile. "So, what did you do before the war, Gareth," she enquired.

"I was a student," he explained. This at least was true. He hoped she would not ask him any more questions of this nature. After all, he was not Welsh, he had never been to Wales let alone Wrexham, spoke English as his first language where Gareth had been brought-up in a Welsh-speaking household. Furthermore, he was Jewish, whereas poor old Gareth had been what he described as 'Chapel.'

Fortunately Amelie knew even less than Joe about Wales and their conversation returned to the far more pressing matter of the war.

How weird it was, Joe pondered, that he should meet someone in a deserted part of rural Belgium who had known his brother. He longed to tell her but that would have made the entire group highly suspicious of why he had adopted the identity of Gareth Jones in the first place.

It was less than two hours of walking, from where Joe had encountered this group, when Pierre pointed and announced, "Do you see that barn? That is where we are going."

In the meantime the cloths that Joe had bound around his feet were in tatters and the skin below was red, raw and sore. Amelie had noticed his strange footwear or the lack of it, and once inside the barn she offered to examine the soles of his feet. Fortunately the skin had not yet broken but Joe was in no condition to undertake any more walking that day.

"Before I tell you my story," he suggested, "I need to see some identification from you."

They produced Belgian identity papers and said they had been officers in the Belgian army and Amelie a volunteer, to work with them on clandestine operations. They then explained that they were really French and if caught with that identity, they would automatically be shot as spies. However, they were in Belgium, and with Germany the occupying power, they might be taken prisoner but should avoid the firing squad.

Joe was entirely satisfied and went behind a sectioned-off part of the barn to remove his trousers and produce his identity or rather that of poor Gareth Jones. He also took the opportunity to bury his own papers in case he should be captured by the Germans,

They then sat in a circle as Joe related all that had happened to him since the plane had crashed. There were just two matters that he did not mention. One was the bombing of the train and the other was the burial of Gareth, which he told them was the burial of Joe.

Pierre and Charles then explained they were going over to the farmhouse to obtain supplies of food and replenish their stock of water.

"While we are there, Gareth," I will try and get you some footwear. "There is a farmer and three sons so I hope at least one of them has shoes or boots in your size."

Half an hour later, the two men returned. The three Frenchmen and their female compatriot enjoyed a substantial meal and so did Joe, once his poor feet had found adequate protection in a pair of sturdy boots that Charles had obtained for him.

This was a welcome respite for the five of them and they spent the evening chatting about the war and their experiences

Joe was fascinated by Amelie and it took great determination not to disclose his interest in the beautiful young woman. He wished with all his heart that he did not have to conceal his true identity.

They all settled down to sleep blissfully unaware of the events that would unfold the following day.

Chapter Thirty-Nine

Southern Belgium 1915

A Rude Awakening

Joe by now was quite accustomed to sleeping in the less than commodious barns that littered the Belgium countryside. The odour of previous animal occupants no longer troubled him and he curled up in the hay and was soon in a deep sleep. His three male companions had quickly followed suit and the delightful Amelie had retired at a decent distance where she could exercise just a modicum of feminine modesty behind a pile of hay.

Before drifting off Joe had allowed himself to speculate on why a middle-class Jewish young woman from Paris should be involved in such clandestine and dangerous activities. He also wondered whether there was, or had been at any time, a relationship with one of the three men who accompanied her. However, he re-assured himself that there was no evidence of this and they all seemed to consider her as 'one of the boys.'

He was awakened by a violent shaking and immediately tried to stand. It was still dark, probably about four o'clock in the morning and he quickly realised that someone was holding him down. In the dim light he was just able to discern that his three male friends also were being held down by shadowy figures.

"You may now stand but be aware that we have pistols pointing at you all so don't try to run or you will finish up dead, very dead," a voice announced in German.

There were at least twenty-five German soldiers in the barn including a Major. "People sleeping in barns are usually up to no good," he suggested. "You will now be searched by my men and I strongly advise you to co-operate."

Joe, of course, had no incriminating possessions with him as anything that could remotely be described as such had been stolen along with his clothing and shoes the previous night. As for the others, they lived permanently in fear of being discovered by the Germans and never took weapons or the explosives they used to undertake their attacks, with them into where they were staying. Such items were buried elsewhere in a location known only to Pierre and Charles.

It was then that Joe realised that the soldiers had not discovered Amelie sandwiched cosily between an outer wall and the haystack. They had quickly found the four sleeping men and a cursory search of the barn in the semi-darkness had satisfied them that they were the only occupants.

The Germans started to interrogate them and the three Frenchmen, knowing the game was up, told their inquisitors their names ranks and serial numbers in the Belgium army. They were, of course French not Belgians but their cover had been organised at the beginning of their mission. It was beyond most Germans to distinguish by accent the French from the Belgians and the subterfuge appeared to have worked. All Belgian soldiers had been imprisoned in Prisoner-of-War camps after the surrender the previous year. Many had then been released after interrogation, once the occupying power was satisfied that they would not give trouble.

As for Joe, he told them he was Gareth Jones and gave the interrogators his rank and serial number.

"If you are a British soldier why are you not in uniform?" the Feldwebel who interrogated him demanded. "If you are not in uniform then, as far as we are concerned you are a spy. Do you know what we do with spies?"

Joe nodded grimly. This was not a time to answer questions with the usual formula, name, rank and number. "I was in uniform up to last night," he lied, "but my uniform, shoes and all my possessions were stolen while I slept on my own in another barn; these kind Belgians took pity on me and borrowed a pair of boots for me from the farmer."

"If you are not a spy, how did you get here and what are you doing in Belgium?" the soldier demanded.

Joe would again have loved to resort to name, rank and serial number but the last thing he needed to do was to antagonise the German; that was if he was ever to see his parents and family again.

"I was an observer in a plane that crashed after being shot down by one of yours," he explained. "The pilot is dead and it is little short of a miracle that I survived."

The Feldwebel gave him a look that indicated that he did not believe a word of his story and went off to report to the Major. He, however, was delighted to have captured four enemy soldiers and told him that they were to be transported to a prisoner-of-war camp outside Roeselaar.

Joe and his new friends were then marched outside and for a minute Joe thought his time had come. However the four men were made to climb into the back of a truck, where they were outnumbered six to one by their captors and the rickety vehicle set off for their place of incarceration.

As they passed the farmhouse Joe spotted the Major standing with the farmer and handing to him a packet that he presumed to be money; the price for which his and his three friends freedom had been sold.

Well, my boy, Joe thought to himself, *you are still alive although a prisoner, but what will happen to Amelie if the greedy farmer finds her in his barn?*

So poor Joe, after so long avoiding capture, was now in German hands but at least they seemed to have accepted his assumed identity and would probably be happy to lock him up with all the others, as a soldier from the ranks. He was certain that if they had discovered his real identity, his treatment would be very different.

Chapter Forty

Antwerp 1915

Another Witness

The Oberst Otto von Lubeck was determined to come to a conclusion in the 'Bergmann' matter as he called it. Either the Hauptmann was innocent and should be returned to duty or he should be tried by a Militärgerichtsbarkeit (military court.) He began to go over the evidence before interviewing all the witnesses again and he read through his notes carefully. He then realised that there was one witness who had so far, not been interviewed. That was Gefreiter Hans Bach and he was sent for.

The Oberst decided to use the same form of questioning that he had employed with Leutnant Schmidt. As soon as the Gefreiter was seated opposite him, somewhat uncomfortable to be ordered to sit before such a senior officer, the Oberst began.

"So, Gefreiter Bach, tell me about the aborted trip to Saint Omer," the Oberst ordered.

"First, Sir, the British BE2b plane we were in, ran out of fuel."

"Yes, yes, I know that," the Oberst replied.

"It is normally a two-seater Sir, but this particular plane had been converted into a three-seater by our German engineers."

"Yes, yes, so then what happened?" the Oberst interrupted.

"Well Sir, Leutnant Schmidt was obliged to make a forced-landing."

"And what happened then?" the Oberst demanded.

"A man who looked like a Belgian farm worker approached us," Bach continued.

"And who was this man?" the Oberst demanded.

"Well Sir," the Gefreiter explained, "Hauptmann Bergmann knew the man."

"Don't you think that was rather surprising? You do not expect to bump into people you know in a field in southern Belgium do you? And who was that man?" the Oberst demanded.

"He was an English flyer really, a cousin of the Hauptmann, Sir, and he was on the run."

"So did you arrest him?"

"No Sir. The Hauptmann told him that we had defected to the British and were on our way to Saint Omer in our British uniforms."

"And did he believe you?" the Oberst queried.

"He seemed to," Bach confirmed.

"And then what happened?" the Oberst prompted.

"We set out together for Saint Omer in an abandoned Minerva Belgium Armoured Car. I got it going. I am a mechanic," Bach explained proudly. "After driving for a while we came to a flooded area. So then we marched to the outskirts of Nieuwpoort. The officers, the Hauptmann and the Leutnant, realised that because we were in British uniforms, our own German soldiers would think we were attacking them and open fire. So we got the British flyer dressed as a Belgian farm worker, to tell the Garrison commander in the town that we three really were German soldiers. That way we were able to stay at German HQ. And then we received orders to return here."

"So what happened then to the British flyer?" the Oberst demanded.

"Sir, he left on his own, in the middle of the night before we came back here."

"How did he manage that?" the Oberst asked feeling that he was at last arriving at the crunch question.

"I don't know," Bach answered feeling uncomfortable and aware that he was blushing.

"How many other people were sleeping in that room," the Oberst asked quietly.

"Just the Hauptmann, Leutnant Franz Schmidt and me," the Gefreiter stammered.

"I am afraid I don't understand how in a room containing just four people, one of them could get up, pack his belongings without disturbing the others, leave and just walk past the sentries." Then the Oberst decided to ask the most important question of all. "Did you not hear the British flyer get up and escape in the middle of the night?" he demanded, his icy-cold blue eyes staring hard into the soft brown ones of the Gefreiter.

"Well sir," Bach answered, "I did hear some movement but I thought it was probably just the Hauptmann coming back from relieving himself."

"How did you know it was the Hauptmann?" the Oberst queried.

"I opened my eyes and saw him getting back into bed," Hans explained trembling.

"And did neither the Leutnant nor the British flyer hear the noise?" von Lubeck asked.

"The British flyer was not in his bed then," the terrified Gefreiter explained.

"So, if you saw that an enemy officer had slipped away from your room why did you not alert others to find him?" the Oberst demanded angrily.

"The Hauptmann obviously knew he wasn't there so I assumed it was quite in order," Bach stuttered.

"Ach, so it looks as if the Hauptmann helped the British flyer, who was his cousin after all, to escape, does it not?" von Lubeck suggested gently.

The Gefreiter was beaten. He felt that he owed a favour to the British flyer. After all it was this man who had enabled them to safely enter Nieuwpoort. Hans Bach had been glad that Joseph had escaped but he knew that lying on such a matter to a senior officer would see him serving a long term in prison or even worse.

Hans Bach nodded sadly to the Oberst who told him that he may have to repeat this evidence in court. He was then dismissed and returned to his duties in the knowledge that he had probably caused serious trouble for the Hauptmann and possibly also for Leutnant Franz Schmidt.

Chapter Forty-One

Antwerp 1915

Militärgerichtsbarkeit (Military Court)

The Oberst was a man who had been blessed with the German characteristics of diligence and attention to detail and little by little the case against Adolphus was taking shape. The papers had now been passed to a Major who was to act as a prosecuting lawyer and another Major, a defence lawyer was appointed. His name was Ernst von Brandenburg and he was the scion of a distinguished Prussian family.

Adolphus was no longer confined to barracks. He was now incarcerated in an old Belgium army base used mainly by the German military as a prisoner-of-war camp. As an officer, remanded while awaiting trial, he was accorded certain privileges. His meals were served to him, and his room was of reasonable size and contained a comfortable bed. Sadly sleep was a commodity that was hard for him to locate. He spent all day brooding about his predicament and the process continued many hours into the night. He knew that if he was found guilty of the charge of Treason against the Emperor and people of the German Empire the only possible sentence would be death by a firing squad. Where had he gone wrong, he agonised? He loved Germany, it was his country and he had enjoyed the prosperity that had resulted from his father's success, as he grew to manhood in Berlin. He had joined the army reserve while still a sixteen-year old schoolboy and by the time his education was finished at twenty-two years old, he was already a reserve officer. His trip to England was solely to demonstrate his loyalty as there were those voices in Germany that still did not count German Jews as reliable and committed Germans. He would show them, and he volunteered to spy on the British military establishment in the north-west of England under the cloak of locating and visiting relatives in Manchester.

What he had not expected was to find a wife on the trip but he had fallen in love with his cousin Rachel the moment he had met her. After returning with him to Berlin after their wedding she had settled down well and produced young Rudi, who because of the war, he hardly knew. Now she was at an advanced stage in her second pregnancy as was evidenced conclusively by her substantial girth when visiting him in his prison.

Rachel had been relieved to know that now Adolphus had been charged she would be allowed to see him. However, the serious nature of the charge terrified her for her husband's sake, for her own sake and for that of her born and unborn offspring. She had dreaded what kind of condition she would find Adolphus to be in before the first visit. When she saw him, still in his uniform of a Hauptmann, she was almost relieved until she noticed the dark shadows under his eyes as a result of lack of sleep.

"Oh, Adolphus," she began. "What have you done that they should make all these terrible accusations against you?"

"My dear Rachel," he replied. "I wish I knew. I have worked tirelessly for my country and its Emperor and I still believe passionately in Germany. Indeed, didn't we argue about the war the last time we were together and that resulted in you returning to Berlin?"

Rachel nodded sadly. "Then what have you done my dear that made them treat you like a common criminal?"

Of course Adolphus knew exactly what he had done that caused the Oberst to suspect him of treason. He had deliberately allowed a man who should have been his prisoner to escape. That man was his brother-in-law and cousin and suspected of bombing a train and causing multiple deaths. Rachel must never know all this, so he was forced to make up a barely credible story about the failure of the Saint Omer mission which had hardly been his fault in the first place.

The day of the trial arrived. Adolphus had been interviewed on a number of occasions by his lawyer, Major Ernst von Brandenburg. The latter was confident that given Adolphus' military record and background, the evidence of Feldwebel Erich Braun, the first prosecution witness, about what he had overheard during the interrogation of RFC Lieutenant David Goldberg, could be easily disposed of. Adolphus had told him of the arrogance of the man and how quickly he could be provoked to launch into a diatribe about all his pet hates.

Erich Braun had been held in a far more uncomfortable military prison than Adolphus, until the trial. After that he was to be transferred to a fighting unit in the trenches. When called to give evidence he was seething with anger and made the most astonishing accusations about the court, the German army, the Jews and in fact just about everyone, as soon as he was cross examined by von Brandenburg. As a result, the presiding judge, General Ludwig von Nierstein, had Braun removed from the court and his evidence stricken from the record. That completely negated the evidence of Major Werner which was entirely based on a hearsay report given to him by the said Erich Braun.

However, the prosecution was still determined to call the Major.

After the first day's hearing the judge sat in his office reading through the evidence and depositions. He had been brought in from the Imperial Military Court in Berlin to try the case in Antwerp. He, of course, knew of the Bergmann family, mainly as a result of seeing their shoe shops on most major shopping streets in the larger cities and towns of Germany. However, he had never met Karl or his son the Hauptmann Adolphus, and he was determined to give the young officer a fair trial based on the evidence and not on who he was in the Berlin society hierarchy. This was important to him and he had been selected because he was neither a Jew nor an anti-Semite and he was a Judge known for his well-balanced verdicts.

The man Braun was a lunatic he had quickly decided and had the prosecution case rested on him alone the Judge-General would now on be his way back to Berlin with Adolphus returned to normal military duties. However, the Oberst von Lubeck was known to be a fine officer and would hardly have continued to investigate the Hauptmann without some justification.

As a good lawyer Judge von Nierstein quickly realised that Adolphus' most important misdemeanour appeared to be the incident in Nieuwpoort, when it looked as if the Hauptmann had engineered the escape of an English prisoner. That was undoubtedly a very serious matter and a crime against the Kaiser and his country. If proven, it was certainly treasonable, he decided.

The Judge had called for the military record of Adolphus and found his entire army career to be totally exemplary. Why would an officer of this calibre behave in this way, he conjectured. He sighed as he put away the papers until the following day and returned to his hotel room at the Kursaal Hotel. He hoped the case would not last too long as his daughter was marrying in Berlin in just two weeks time.

The next three days were taken up with hearing the evidence of prosecution witnesses including Major Becker and Major Werner. Adolphus' companions on the disastrous flight, Leutnant Franz Schmidt and Gefreiter Hans Bach gave their damning evidence. Major Bruno Feldheim and the hapless sentry, who had been severely reprimanded by Adolphus to facilitate the escape of Joe, were both brought from Nieuwpoort. Then it was time for Adolphus' commanding officer the Oberst Otto von Lubeck to appear. He had been responsible for requesting the army prosecution service to take the trial forward. He explained to the court under questioning, all the avenues of enquiry he had investigated. It was then Adolphus' lawyer's turn to cross examine von Lubeck. The Oberst described the Hauptmann as an exemplary officer and commented that it was hard to believe that a man like Adolphus could have displayed such disloyalty to his country, but the evidence could not be ignored.

Chapter Forty-Two

Antwerp & Saint Omer 1915

The Second Expedition

It was during the third day of the trial that Major Werner received confirmation that another British plane, a BE2c had been captured intact and it would now be possible to resurrect the Saint Omer mission. By now the British and French pilots were inflicting considerable damage on German troop movements with a new plane, the Sopwith 1½ Strutter. This was also being used with devastating effect on the German troops sitting in their trenches. The Saint Omer mission had originally been designated as a spying mission to gather intelligence; now it became a mission to infiltrate the air facilities at Saint Omer and to sabotage them in any way the members of the mission saw fit.

After giving his evidence against Adolphus, the Oberst Otto von Lubeck returned to his office and sent for Major Werner.

"I understand we have the ideal plane to resurrect the Saint Omer project," the Oberst said.

"Yes. That is so," Major Werner replied.

"I believe the court has finished with Leutnant Schmidt and Gefreiter Bach."

"Yes, Sir," the Major replied.

"Well, send them to see me at once," the Oberst instructed. "We have to curtail the activities of the British and French air services at all costs. The High Command tells me the situation is quite urgent."

The engineers in the hangar worked feverishly that afternoon to prepare the new plane for the flight. It was a two seater and von Lubeck had decided that for the type of sabotage they planned, two men would be sufficient. Schmidt was an experienced flyer and knew the old BE2b very well. This aircraft, the BE2c was an improvement on the previous model but still very similar. Major Werner gave them their orders. All German aircraft in the vicinity were told to look out for the British plane and allow it safe passage. The two men were once again in their RFC uniforms as they set out for the second time for their destination.

Just four hours later, after an uneventful flight they touched down in Saint Omer. They taxied over to the nearest hangar and told the mechanics who ran out to greet them that they had just flown over from England.

They then reported to the officer on duty. He was not surprised to find himself with two more airmen and another plane. RFC recruits were arriving daily from the UK and new aircraft were being turned out constantly and flown over to take their part in the war.

Lieutenant Frank Smith saluted smartly and introduced himself and Corporal Harold Bailey (Hans Bach.)

"When can we take a crack at the Hun?" he enquired enthusiastically in his thick Scottish accent.

"I understand your desire to get into the thick of it but first I need to see your ID cards."

These had been painstakingly forged by German artists and printers. They easily passed muster.

"Now Lieutenant," the officer began, "you will be housed in officers' quarters while your man here, Corporal Bailey, will be in the main barracks."

The officer was a Captain and Smith and Bailey both saluted him smartly and went off to find their accommodation.

Their arrival in their respective buildings caused no surprise. This was a daily occurrence and both men received a friendly welcome.

The following morning Smith was interviewed by a senior officer who seemed both surprised and disappointed to learn that they had only brought over a BE2c. "I thought those chaps in England knew how bloody useless these BE2s are. What we want are Sopwiths and lots of them. Anyway, if that is what they sent you with, you will have to fly it," he told Smith. "Later on we'll train you up on the Sopwith as well."

After lunch and a series of briefings, Smith met up with Bailey near one of the hangars.

"The first few days we need to keep a low profile," Smith said. "Just follow orders even if it means attacking our own German army. We cannot afford to raise suspicions."

Corporal Bailey nodded and grinned.

That night they were told to scramble and bomb German trenches not far to the east of where they were located.

Four planes set out that night, another BE2c and two Sopwiths. However, instead of finding an easy target in the German trenches they were met by six Fokkers. An aerial fight took place between the ten planes, which resulted in two Fokkers being shot down by the Sopwiths and two of the remaining Fokkers being chased off. Smith, or rather Schmidt, in the BE2c was almost relieved when he saw the two remaining Fokkers appear to turn tail. That was until he realised that they had doubled back and were now flying straight towards him with the rat-tat-tat of their machine guns clearly audible over the noise of the aircraft engines. He tried to drop altitude to shoot at the under-bellies of the planes that had suddenly ceased to be his compatriots and were now his enemy. He turned around to tell Bailey (Bach) to use his pistol and discovered that he was slumped in his compartment and almost certainly dead. Franz Schmidt felt sick as he took out his own pistol but as he raised his gun he was hit by a hail of bullets from the other Fokker. As the plane slowly plummeted towards the ground there was closure on the second unsuccessful German attempt to infiltrate and damage the allied air effort in Saint Omer. The destruction of the mission was down to Fokker aircraft who thought they had struck a blow against the British but had only struck a blow against their own German war effort.

Chapter Forty-Three

Southern Belgium 1915

Amelie's Flight

Amelie lay very still in her little nest wedged between a bale of hay and the rotting timber of the barn outer wall. Of course she was terrified but fear had in no way paralysed her thought processes. She listened carefully as her three male colleagues and the English flyer were first interrogated and then driven away to some prisoner-of-war camp. She knew exactly what had happened. She had told the three Frenchmen just before they encountered Gareth that she had a bad feeling about the farmer in their next port of call. They had met him the previous month, soon after a plane of the Service Aéronautique, the service arm of the French army had deposited them in northern Belgium, to make life more difficult for the Germans by interrupting the smooth flow of troops to their trenches. Their Belgian liaison had taken them to the farm and introduced them.

"I do not trust that man," Amelie told them after the initial meeting. "He has shifty eyes and did you notice his heavy gold watch and chain. Don't you think that is a strange possession for a working farmer to display, especially in wartime?"

Amelie was, of course, blessed with female intuition whereas her companions felt that if his barn had been recommended as a safe stop-over, he must be reliable. Now they were paying the price for their misplaced confidence.

She waited over an hour after she heard the German's trucks rattle and bump their way over the crude path leading out of the farm. Then she cautiously looked over the top of the bale of hay that had mercifully concealed her. All was quiet and she hastily gathered up her belongings. She was unarmed and had no idea where their guns and explosives had been hidden. She tiptoed to the barn entrance and looked out to right and left. Further up the path lay the farmhouse and behind were meadows where sheep and cattle were grazing. She knew there was another farm just three miles away where she was certain she would be safe. The farmer there was a Frenchman not a Belgian and she felt that was where she should go.

However, to journey in that direction she needed to pass the farmhouse of the man who she was now certain had betrayed them to the Germans. Fortunately the area between the house and the barn was wooded and she quickly made her way towards the building, keeping out of sight behind some of the large trees. However, she still needed to pass the kitchen door and the only alternative involved climbing over a fence into a meadow where she had already noticed a large black bull was standing. She crept through the yard adjoining the house keeping as near as possible to the walls of out-buildings from where she could hear the sounds of hens clucking away. She was level with the door when she heard the sound of the latch being lifted signalling that within a few seconds someone would be walking out into the yard. There was only one place to hide; in the hen-house. Once again she wedged herself into a small space. This was where the hen coops ended at the barn wall. She was grateful that she was slim, as none of her colleagues could have fitted into such a tiny area. Then she spotted the bucket containing hen-feed and realised that if anyone came into the barn to feed the clucking poultry, they would walk right up to where she was hiding to retrieve the container. Amelie reached out and dragged the bucket silently close to her so that it was no longer visible to anyone entering the barn. Then her worst fears were justified and the farmer entered the barn. He made his way towards her, whistling tunelessly and Amelie was sure that she would be discovered. Suddenly he stopped and turned back towards the door.

"Jacques," he bellowed, "where the devil have you left the hen-feed?"

Amelie could hear the muffled sound of an answer from outside the barn but not what was said. Then the farmer shouted again. "Well, it isn't there, you idiot. Where have you left it?"

Again there was a muffled reply and the farmer's response, "Come and find it for me then because I certainly can't see it."

Amelie realised that she was cornered and looked around for some implement she could use as a weapon. Then she saw what looked to her, like an extra large heavy metal soup ladle. This was on the ground near to where the bucket had lain and she silently leaned out of her hiding place to pick it up.

The farmer was still standing with his back towards her. Amelie was certain that if she did not seize the initiative she would finish up in the hands of the Germans at best, or even worse treatment from this man whom she remembered 'undressing her with his eyes', when they had originally met. Trembling with fear she crept down the passageway towards him. Fortunately the hens' clucking was increasing in volume as they complained vociferously about the delay in serving their breakfast. As a result she was able to get up to her target with the heavy implement raised above her head, and bring it down on him with strength that she did not know she possessed. Because of his height however, the blow had caught him on the back of the neck rather than the intended target of his head but he still fell to the ground writhing with pain. Then she saw that he had been clutching an open envelope that contained a thick wad of German Marks. She suspected that this was the 'blood-money' paid to him for betraying her friends and she pushed it quickly into her pocket.

Amelie knew she had not a minute to lose as the mysterious farm-worker Jacques, would inevitably be arriving, to locate the missing poultry feed. She dropped the metal scoop and ran as fast as she could out of the barn and towards the rear of the building intending to run across an open field behind the barn. Then she heard a woman's voice shouting, "Stop! You can't go in there. That field is newly planted."

Needless to say Amelie ignored the call but found that her progress was severely delayed by the soft earth in the rows of planted vegetables. Still, she ran on with her boots caked in a mixture of soil and manure. At least, she re-assured herself, the woman and Jacques would have enough to concentrate their minds on when they discovered the wounded farmer. What Amelie did not know however, was that she had severed the man's spine and he now lay dead among his chickens. She was now wanted for murder.

Chapter Forty-Four

Roeselaar & Antwerp 1915

A Change of Location

The four newly captured prisoners-of-war were taken to the camp outside nearby Roeselaar. There, they were interviewed by members of a German army interrogation unit. The three Frenchmen masquerading as Belgians came through their interviews with little difficulty. Their cover stories hung together fairly well and they were locked up with other defeated Belgium soldiers in barracks buildings which, if anything, were a considerable improvement, in creature comfort, on the series of barns which had been their recent domiciles.

Joe, aka Gareth, was initially questioned by a Feldwebel who carefully read the report prepared by his colleague when Joe was initially arrested in the barn.

"Ach, So," the new non-commissioned officer began, "What are you doing here in Belgium and where is your uniform?"

Joe patiently repeated the same responses. The Feldwebel nodded and returned Joe to his new accommodation. However, the following day he was sent for again and this time he was to face a Major; a man like Adolphus, skilled and trained in the techniques of interrogation.

"You may sit," the Major told him. "I am Major Horst Keller and I have a few questions for you Private Jones."

Joe nodded.

"What are you doing here in Belgium without uniform? We think you are a spy."

"My name is Private Gareth Jones, serial number 23778512," Joe replied.

"We know all that," the Major replied. "Please answer my question."

"The only information I am obliged to give you as a Prisoner-of-War is my name, rank and serial number. Shall I repeat them again," Joe answered.

"Well, I don't think you are Private Jones and we cannot accept the story about your uniform being stolen. Who in their right mind would steal a British uniform knowing the trouble they would get into, if caught with it?" the Major commented.

"You told the Feldwebel at the first interview that your plane had crashed and your pilot died in the crash. What was his name?" the Major demanded.

Joe had not been asked this question before. He thought quickly and answered, "Lieutenant Charles Hawkins. However, I should not have told you that. You are not supposed to question me on operational matters."

"Listen to me Private Jones," the German officer replied. "I don't think you realise how much trouble you are in. I do not think you are a Private and I do think you are a spy. I believe you claim to be Welsh. Please answer me this, 'Da iawn diolch (how are you today)?'"

"You should know that only a small number of Welsh people speak the language. In my family we speak English," Joe replied.

"Tell me another thing. Why don't you have a Welsh accent? You speak like an educated Englishman. If that is so why are you just a private, not an officer?" the Major demanded.

"Sir, I have to remind you again that I am only obliged to give you my name, rank and serial number," Joe answered.

"If this is going to be your attitude I am having you transferred to Antwerp where they have a unit to deal with people like you. They also have a very efficient firing squad there if you do not co-operate.," the Major threatened.

So once again Joe was on the move. He was sent handcuffed from Roeselaar to Antwerp on an empty troop train returning from delivering many more young Germans to the horrifying life or death of the trenches. He was accompanied by three military policemen who never left him alone until he was duly delivered safely into the charge of guards at the Antwerp prisoner-of-war camp. He was placed in the primitive conditions 'enjoyed' by other ranks prisoners, while officers received somewhat better treatment. If he was to continue with the subterfuge that he was Private Gareth Jones, this was the standard of accommodation he would have to accept. He could hardly have it both ways.

The morning after his arrival, he was escorted to a large makeshift shed where he was told to wait until his name was called. More and more of his fellow prisoners arrived as the clock ticked by the minutes, then the hours, until the whole morning had gone. Three German officers sat at a long table and spent no more than five minutes with each prisoner after his name was called. There were only five prisoners left when a trolley was pushed into the shed. This contained a large pot of some revolting looking stew and a jug of water. By now Joe was ravenous and wolfed down the food. He could not help thinking what his father would have thought of him eating non-Kosher food, but he had to remind himself constantly that he was now Welsh Chapel, not English Jewish and he had to survive somehow.

He had time to brood and think while waiting for his interview. He thought about his parents who would probably now think he was dead. He thought about his sister Rachel, married to a German. *I never trusted Adolphus,* he brooded, *but he did his best for me in Nieuwpoort so he cannot be all bad.* He also thought about the brave and beautiful young Frenchwoman he had met. He hoped and prayed that she was safe and he wondered what had persuaded her to become involved in this war.

It was mid afternoon when his name was called or rather the name Gareth Jones. He had to remind himself that they were calling him and he marched across the floor to the interview table where he saluted smartly and announced, "My name is Private Gareth Jones, serial number 23778512."

The officer sitting in the middle spoke first. "Jones, there seems to be some doubt about your identity according to the Major in Roeselaar. I need to see your papers."

Joe had expected this and had been asked to produce the identity documents on numerous occasions since his arrest in the barn.

The officer examined the papers carefully, showed them to his two colleagues and then handed them back to Joe.

"Those are in order but are you really Gareth Jones?"

Joe saluted again smartly and said, "Yes, Sir, Private Gareth Jones, serial number 23778512."

"I see you are in the RFC and your story is that your plane was shot down. I also understand that according to you, your pilot died. I now demand answers to two questions. Where is the plane? We have not found a British plane anywhere near Roeselaar and where did you bury your dead pilot?"

Joe had been dreading these questions and he had an answer ready.

"When the plane crashed I bumped my head and lay unconscious for many hours. When I eventually came round

I had no idea where I was or, for that matter, who I was and I wandered away from the plane leaving the body of my pilot still trapped inside. I think my idea was to get help but by the time I started to remember the crash, I was completely lost. I found my papers in my inside pocket and seeing my name Gareth Jones helped me to remember who I was."

"This is all very convenient, is it not?" the officer commented with heavy irony. "So do tell us how you came to lose your uniform; or don't you remember that?"

"Oh Yes," Joe replied. "I remember that exactly. I was exhausted from wandering around. I had no idea where I was and I was terrified of being picked up by one of your patrols. I found a barn and after checking it was empty I took off my uniform and boots and lay down to sleep. I must have slept about twelve hours and when I awoke all my belongings had been stolen except for the shirt and trousers I was sleeping in. It was extremely lucky that my papers were in my trousers pocket or I would also have lost those. I then found some old pieces of cloth which I bound around my feet. They are still very sore from walking without boots or shoes. Would you like to see them, sir?"

"Nein, Nein," the officer replied almost shuddering. "That will not be necessary. So then what happened?"

"Then I met three Belgians who kindly let me travel with them that day. They obtained boots for me from the farm where we were arrested the following morning."

"I have to say I do not believe a word of this whole story. You neither look like, nor talk like a Welshman. If anything you look to me like a Jew, an English Jew," the officer commented. "We do not accept your story and more investigations will be made. In the meantime you are our prisoner and will remain here. Do you understand?"

"Yes Sir," Joe replied and saluted.

So Joe remained a prisoner-of-war under the name of Private Gareth Jones. He was blissfully unaware that his old friend Lieutenant David Goldberg of the RFC and his cousin and brother-in-law Hauptmann Adolphus Bergmann were imprisoned just across the barracks square, but in somewhat more comfortable accommodation than he had to endure.

That was until he received some very worrying news from close-by.

Chapter Forty-Five

Antwerp 1915

A Verdict

The Oberst Otto von Lubeck was a troubled man. He had done his best to present his evidence to the court as sympathetically as possible. He was convinced that Adolphus was responsible for his cousin's escape from the German HQ in Nieuwpoort and that was a very serious offence for a German officer to commit. It really was inexcusable. However, he was also convinced that this would never have happened with any other prisoner. *When all was said and done, the man was also the Hauptmann's brother-in-law,* he told himself. *He is a damn good officer and is in every other respect a loyal subject of the Kaiser.* He was sitting in his office and, as he had done on previous occasions, he turned to stare at the portrait of his emperor, Kaiser Wilhelm the Second. Finally, he conjectured, *if we execute Adolphus I would hate to think of what kind of a noise his father would make. He has the ear of many people close to the Kaiser and that is how he became such a successful businessman.*

At the same time that von Lubeck was brooding about the 'Bergmann Affair' as the newspapers had started to call it, the presiding judge, General Ludwig von Nierstein was reading through all his notes. It annoyed him that a couple of the newspapers had hinted that because the Hauptmann was of Jewish origin he would not get a fair trial. This offended the Judge as he prided himself on making his decisions solely on the evidence. Not all German military judges were so fastidious which only served to make von Nierstein more determined to come to the right verdict. All the witnesses had now been called and he was due to hear the final pleas from the lawyer representing the Army and Adolphus' defence lawyer, von Brandenburg.

The Oberst von Lubeck came to decision. He would go and see the prosecuting lawyer, the man who he had originally called in, once his own investigation had run its course. "I don't think we should come down too heavily on Hauptmann Bergmann when you make your final plea," he said.

The man was surprised. He was only a Major but he was also a professional lawyer and he did not take kindly to being told how to conduct a prosecution by anyone, be they an Oberst or even a General. "Forgive me Herr Oberst, but it is my job to point out all the salient facts in this case to the Judge, and that is what I must do. The Judge General will then pronounce his final verdict after also listening to the defence lawyer." He saluted, clicked his heels and excused himself from the presence of the Oberst who, for once in his life felt embarrassed and belittled.

The day of the final hearing had arrived and Adolphus was escorted into court by his defending lawyer. The military court was held in closed session but such was the public interest in the case that crowds of German civilians and off-duty soldiers had gathered around the gates of the complex together with reporters from all the major German newspapers. They waited to hear the result of the trial and opinions among the crowd ranged from – *the Jew Officer is guilty and should get his just desserts* to, *he sounds like a fine officer. We need men like him to win this war.*

The verdict was announced. Hauptmann Bergmann was guilty but the Judge General had decided to postpone sentencing for a month while he considered every aspect of the case.

General von Nierstein also had personal reasons for delaying sentencing. He was due back in Berlin the following day for his daughter's wedding.

It was now winter and Adolphus had little to live for except the weekly visits of his wife Rachel, who had by now presented him with a baby daughter who they had decided to call Ruth. He knew that it was his own action in helping Joe to escape that had placed him in this position. However, no matter how many times he went over the events in Nieuwpoort, he could not believe that he would have acted any differently.

The Judge General had enjoyed the brief respite from the pressures of this trial and was now using the time before returning to Antwerp to read through the evidence once again and decide on an appropriate sentence. His new son-in-law, an army officer had just set-off for the front and his daughter was heart-broken to be parted from her new husband so quickly. She was tearfully expressing her grief to her father when he suddenly felt a violent pain in his chest and slumped forward on his chair. The daughter arose and quickly went over to him. "Papa," she screamed, "what is the matter?" but he could not hear her or any other sound. He had suffered a massive heart-attack and died almost instantly.

A new trial would have to be arranged and the whole 'Bergmann Affair' subjected to a further airing. However, it was not only the Judge General who had died, albeit from natural causes; two of the main witnesses Leutnant Schmidt and Gefreiter Bach had also departed this earth but in far more violent circumstances.

Chapter Forty-Six

Antwerp 1916

Face to Face

Adolphus had been dreading the final act of his trial when the sentence would be announced. He knew he was guilty of deliberately facilitating the release of a prisoner and he was terrified that, despite the special circumstances, the Judge General would be obliged to sentence him to death by firing squad. That was obviously the worst outcome but only a little better would be to be sentenced to a long period in a military prison. This would involve him being ignominiously stripped of his rank and reduced to the equivalent of a private soldier. He dreaded the disgrace this would be for his parents and even for his wife who, despite her natural sympathy for the British side in the current conflict, was very proud of his achievements in the army. He had long ago realised that the chances of walking away from all this with his character unblemished, were more than remote.

Then he heard that the Judge General von Nierstein had suddenly died and a new judge was to be appointed for a re-trial. Adolphus could not decide whether this was good or bad news. Nierstein had given the appearance of being scrupulously fair and he was deeply concerned to discover the name of the new judge. He agonised over what kind of treatment he might receive. In the end the army prosecutors' office appointed a Judge General Helmut Schwarz who was a protégé of the late von Nierstein.

General Schwarz asked for all the papers relating to the previous trial and studied them in great detail. He then had a private conversation with the Oberst von Lubeck when he asked him just one pertinent question. "Who was the officer responsible for the British flyer Joseph Bergman's arrest?"

The Oberst was shocked to be asked a question by the new judge that he could not answer. He had now been living with the 'Bergmann Affair' for the best part of six months and could not believe that anything as fundamental as the answer to the question he had just been asked could escape him.

"Sorry Sir," he began with a very unusual look of embarrassment on his normally stern face, "I don't know. In fact I do not know if the British Lieutenant was ever formally arrested."

"Well, I think you had better find out Herr Oberst, because the whole case against Hauptmann Bergmann hangs on this," the Judge General replied.

It, of course transpired that Major Bruno Feldheim in Nieuwpoort had never seen fit to arrest Joe and in fact he never knew until the original trial that he was not a Belgium national. In addition, neither Adolphus nor Leutnant Schmidt nor Gefreiter Bach had any intention of arresting Joe. They were only grateful that he had managed to manoeuvre them all into the safety of the German HQ in Nieuwpoort. To then arrest Joe as an enemy officer just did not occur to them.

A date was set for a new trial but one which the judge suspected would be over very quickly unless some evidence of another misdemeanour was discovered against Hauptmann Bergmann. Having read his army service records he certainly did not anticipate that would be the case.

It was just two days before the trial when Adolphus came face-to-face with his recent past in the shape of his cousin and brother-in-law RFC Lieutenant Joseph Bergman.

Joe had been ordered to cross the square to the officers' quarters with a message for the Feldwebel in charge of stores there. Under his assumed name of Private Gareth Jones he had proven to be an ideal prisoner and was entrusted with many errands on behalf of his jailers.

He had just left the stores adjoining the main officers' accommodation block and he glanced through the window just to see for himself how higher rank prisoners were housed. And there was Adolphus sitting on a chair reading. For some reason Adolphus looked up at that moment and glanced towards the window and then he saw that face, the face of Joseph Bergman of Manchester staring at him. For Joe the question was why would Adolphus be sitting in quarters allocated to allied officer prisoners-of-war? And for Adolphus the question was how did Joe get here and where and when had he been caught? Both men were deeply shocked.

Joe quickly recovered his equilibrium and continued across the square to the 'other ranks' barracks. His mind, however, was in turmoil. Would Adolphus identify him as Joe Bergmann rather than Gareth Jones? It was late afternoon and most senior German officers would have left the camp for their billets in homes in Antwerp. Why, oh why was Adolphus sitting there, looking very much at home in prison?

Adolphus' mind was also in turmoil? Apart from the obvious questions about how and where he had been captured, had Joe been brought there to give evidence at Adolphus' trial?

Neither of the cousins had any answers or knew how to obtain answers to the questions that were tormenting them.

Joe was due to be interrogated again the following day and the interviewing officer was following up on a hunch. It was now nearly a year since the train bombing. That had been carried out by a 'rogue' RFC BE2b pilot who had abandoned the plane when it ran out of fuel not many miles from its final act. They had no way of proving that Private Gareth Jones was in fact Lieutenant Joseph Bergman. However, the man Jones had admitted to being an observer in a similar plane. Maybe he had been the observer in the plane that had bombed the train and would then know all about the fate of Bergman, if he was not that man himself. And if he would admit to this they would at last have one scalp from the train bombing.

Predictably Gareth Jones had been entirely uncooperative when these allegations were put to him but the interviewing officer told him he would be placed in solitary confinement until he told them the truth. He would also be placed on a diet of bread and water.

After numerous interrogations his tormentors had been obliged to accept that Gareth Jones was Gareth Jones and he was released from solitary, but he was always under special surveillance for any evidence that would confirm his true identity.

Chapter Forty-Seven

Southern Belgium 1916

A Temporary Haven

Farming had always been a hard way to make a living, Raoul brooded, and in wartime under the heel of the Boche it was even harder. It had been a cruel winter with the ground frozen solid for months on end. Now it was all changing to mud but at least he had been able to make a start on planting his crops in the soft soil.

He was constantly reminded of the greatest worry in his life; his son Albert. He was fighting with the French in the trenches, just seventy or so miles to the south of the farm. God help him and God help them all, he thought, imagining the conditions.

He had just entered the farmhouse, to have a good wash before his wife called him for dinner, when there was a gentle knock on the door. He opened the door to find a young woman, covered in mud and shivering from the cold, or so he assumed.

"My name is Amelie Levi and my friends and I were due to stay in the shelter of your barn tomorrow night," she explained.

"You had better come in," Raoul said quietly. "Where are the others?"

She entered, and looked down at the spotless tiles on the hallway floor.

"Shall I remove my boots?" she enquired timidly.

Raoul smiled although anticipating that the news the young woman brought would be far from good. "Yes please," he nodded, "and maybe you should take off that muddy coat as well or Monique will be horrified."

He ushered her into the living room. "Please sit down," he said, "Maybe you would like a cup of coffee?"

Amelie nodded gratefully and Raoul left the room for a moment, returning to tell her that his wife Monique would bring her coffee and some food.

"Where are the others?" he repeated.

"The Germans have them," she told him in flat voice, seemingly devoid of emotion.

"How come?" Raoul asked. "Were you caught while carrying out an operation against them?"

"No," she answered. "The farmer over there," and she pointed in the direction from which she had just arrived, "He called them. It was only good luck that they did not catch me as well. I am sure the Boche paid him well for his treachery," she commented bitterly.

"That bastard Jan de Smet," Raoul replied. "I have never liked him. Even as a farmer he is a crook. People say he waters down his milk and sells horsemeat as mutton."

"Not anymore," Amelie replied in the same flat voice. "I hit him over the back of his neck and I think he is quite badly injured," she explained.

At that point Monique opened the door and entered with a tray containing a cup of steaming hot coffee and a plate of delicious looking cakes and biscuits.

Amelie was still feeling somewhat sick as a result of her recent experiences and she sipped the coffee slowly and carefully. The more she imbibed the better she felt and after a few minutes she felt strong enough to try a biscuit. The fare was all delicious and she sat back managing a little smile at her audience of Raoul and Monique, who silently and with satisfaction watched the girl recover from her ordeal.

Then came a loud knock on the farmhouse door; Monique rose and peeped through the window. "It is the police," she said. "Quickly, take Amelie upstairs and hide her in the attic loft."

As soon as Raoul and Amelie had climbed the stairs Monique opened the door.

"Good day," she began. "What can I do for you today?"

"We are looking for a young woman," the police sergeant explained. "She is probably in her mid to late twenties and dressed in trousers like a man. She is probably covered in mud as she was seen running in this direction over the newly ploughed and muddy fields."

Then Monique glanced to her left and realised that Amelie's filthy boots and coat were just behind the front door.

"There has been no one of that description here and if she turns up later we could let you know," she enquired pleasantly. "Can I ask what you want to see her about?"

"Murder," the policeman replied. "She was seen running away from the scene after your neighbour Jan de Smet was killed."

"Oh, that is terrible", Monique replied, thinking, *good riddance to a nasty dishonest traitor.* "You can be sure I will contact you if she comes here but I would doubt it. If she has killed de Smet she will surely want to get as far away as possible from his farm don't you think?" She smiled sweetly at the policeman who nodded in agreement.

As soon as she was sure that the Sergeant had gone she quietly called up to her husband and to Amelie that they could now come back downstairs.

"Well you killed him," she told Amelie grimly. "Now what are we to do with you?"

Amelie looked at her nervously as if she thought she might be about to hand her over to the authorities.

"Don't worry my girl," Monique reassured her. "We knew he was working with the Boche. Who told you it was safe to stay there?"

"I don't know," Amelie replied. "One of my friends, Pierre, was told by a Belgian called Thomas that de Smet's barn would be safe."

"Would that be Thomas Maartens?" Raoul enquired.

"Yes, that's the man, Thomas Maartens. I never met him myself but Pierre was told that he was reliable," Amelie explained.

"Reliable! We now know he is working for the Boche. I need to make sure that Paris knows that he is a traitor to Belgium just like his late unlamented friend de Smet," Raoul said angrily. "Anyway, what are we going to do with you?"

Before Amelie could reply Monique spoke up. "Firstly I am going to show you to our bathroom. You can have a good wash and clean yourself up. I am going to give you some clean dry clothes, and then we will all sit down and decide where you can go from here."

Chapter Forty-Eight

Antwerp 1916

The Second Trial

Judge General Helmut Schwarz wanted the Bergmann Affair to be dealt with expeditiously. Until 1912 he had been a civilian judge and had then applied for an appointment with the military. He saw this as a significant advancement of his career.

Schwarz discussed the case with senior military figures who agreed with him, that they needed promising young officers like Hauptmann Bergmann to ensure ultimate victory in the war. Of course Adolphus had made a terrible error of judgement in facilitating the escape of his wife's brother. They were however, convinced by everything about the Hauptmann's career that he was, and would remain dedicated and loyal to the Kaiser and the German Empire.

The war between the Central Powers and the Allies was not working out as General Count Schlieffen, who had been Chief of the Imperial German General Staff, had originally planned. Schlieffen's successor, Helmuth von Moltke the Younger, was a realist and had already given up any ideas Schlieffen had had of invading Holland. He wanted a neutral Netherlands to ensure German accessibility to the North Sea ports. He was also well aware of the fast developing importance of aerial warfare. The Germans needed bi-lingual intelligence officers to seek out the latest developments in this field by the allies. Men like Adolphus were not easy to find.

Judge Schwarz told senior officers that the British flyer Joseph Bergman had never been arrested and therefore Adolphus could not be accused of allowing a prisoner-of-war to escape. This was a technicality but one that should enable the Hauptmann to quickly resume his important work.

The date of the new trial was set for May 3rd 1916 and the witnesses were again examined in court. There were now far fewer witnesses available as Leutnant Schmidt and Gefreiter Bach had died, shot down by their own German comrades while on the second espionage and sabotage mission to Saint Omer. As for Feldwebel Erich Braun, if he was still alive, he would be somewhere in the trenches and certainly not available as a witness. So the witnesses were the Oberst Otto von Lubeck and the two Majors, Werner and Becker. The judge also insisted on the Major and sentry from Nieuwpoort being brought to Antwerp. The sentry was a prosecution witness as he still smarted from the dressing-down he had received that night from Adolphus. The Major, however, aware of the fact that as the senior officer in Nieuwpoort, he should have taken far more interest in the identity of the 'Belgian' and arrested him as a British spy, was on the defensive for himself and also for Adolphus.

As for the Oberst Otto von Lubeck, it would be a profound relief to have this entire matter disposed of in the manner suggested by the new judge. He was delighted when Judge General Helmut Schwarz told the court that he was stopping the trial, as there could be no case to answer when there had never been a prisoner-of-war to escape. He ordered the immediate release of Adolphus having told him that his conduct, if somewhat unwise, was hardly treasonable.

Adolphus resumed his interrogation of allied officers and once again took up residence at the Scholz home where he was delighted to be re-united with his wife Rachel and their two young children.

There was, however, one matter still causing Adolphus sleepless nights and it was a subject he could not discuss with his wife. He had seen Joe Bergman in the prisoner-of-war camp and he wondered why he had not been called as a witness. He decided that the authorities in the camp did not know Joe's real identity and the fact that he was not imprisoned in officers' quarters confirmed this. One thing was certain, the Hauptmann was not again about to risk his career and maybe his life for the sake of his cousin and brother-in-law. Joe would just have to remain in the 'other ranks' billets. At least he was safe there, Adolphus decided, and he did deserve punishment for bombing the train, he convinced himself.

Chapter Forty-Nine

Southern Belgium 1917

Amelie's Story

Amelie was really happy to be a guest of Raoul and Monique. They had persuaded her to stay with them for at least a few months after the terrible and terrifying experience that had resulted in her, Amelie, a middle-class Jewish girl from Paris, being sought as a murderess. Each night in the comfort of her bed she re-lived the experience and then, in the knowledge that she was now safe, managed to drift off to sleep. However, she needed to return to France somehow and to obtain new instructions as to how she could once again play her part in defeating the Boche. She wondered constantly what had become of her three companions. Would the Germans accept them as Belgians or discover that they were really French saboteurs? And then there was the Englishman on the run who had joined their party for just one fateful day. She was sure he was Jewish although he had told her he was Welsh.

Early in 1917 after numerous discussions with her hosts a plan was agreed to enable Amelie to return to France. Monique had tried to persuade her to stay with them for the duration of the war but the Frenchwoman was utterly determined that she must leave and once again take her part in striking blows against the Boche.

Amelie had long dark hair and Monique suggested that, as part of her disguise, at least until she was well away from the area where she was still wanted as a murderer, her hair should be cut short and bleached blonde. It was fortunate that the two women were of a similar height and figure and Monique insisted on providing Amelie with some of her own clothing. This included a hooded cape, a popular fashion item at that time and one which would help to keep her from being recognised by the police whose description of her would now bear little resemblance to her new image.

"Now, we come to the most important question of how you are to leave Belgium," Raoul considered. "I have been giving the matter a lot of thought. I have also been talking to one or two trustworthy people. This is what I now suggest..."

With the route mapped out in great detail Raoul came to his final question. "You will need some money. You may be on this journey for two or three weeks. Fortunately we can help..."

"That is not necessary," Amelie replied with a sad, gentle little smile. "Jan de Smet dropped the money that the Germans had just paid him as a reward for reporting my friends and me to them, when he fell. It is blood-money and I will use it for my journey. I only wish there was a way to use it to get the others out of the prisoner-of-war camp; that would have been even better."

"Amelie," Raoul continued. "Can I ask you why you feel so strongly about the Germans? We French and the Belgians obviously hate the way they attacked us, occupied Belgium and much of northern France and most of us detest them for this. I know you are from Paris and I can understand that you are like everyone else in wanting our countries to be free, but it is unusual for a young lady of your background to put her own life in danger as you do."

Amelie nodded and tearfully explained. "I was married just over two years ago to a wonderful young man, also from Paris. We had been childhood sweethearts and were wonderfully happy. Then the war started and my husband Gerard immediately volunteered. He had a university education and had started a career as an Avocat (lawyer.) He was granted a commission in the army as a Capitaine and posted to the front with his men. Coming out of the trenches to drive back the Boche, many of his men were killed and he himself received terrible injuries which resulted in him losing both legs. The army brought him home. I was pregnant with our first child and when I saw the condition of my poor Gerard, I collapsed. The result of all this was I lost my unborn baby. Gerard would never have been able to make me pregnant again as a result of his injuries. However, he died after just two months at home and I vowed that after all that, I would offer my services to France as an Espion (spy.) So now you know why I must continue my work in ridding France and Belgium of these evil Germans."

Both Raoul and Monique reached for handkerchiefs and wiped away unbidden tears. "Please, my dear girl," Monique said, "I am sorry you were asked that question but we are truly honoured that we have been able to be of a little assistance to you."

"Tomorrow you will start your journey and tonight, at dinner, we will open a bottle of 1935 Burgundy I have been keeping in the cellar. It was to toast 'peace,' if and when it arrives, but instead we will toast you, a remarkable and brave daughter of France," Raoul promised.

Chapter Fifty

Antwerp 1917

An Escape Plan

Joe Bergman spent his twenty-second birthday in prison. After all his experiences on the run and after his capture, he was not in a great place to celebrate. He lay in bed early that morning taking stock of his situation. He could not use his real name and had by now become quite used to his assumed identity of Gareth Jones. His thoughts wandered to the lonely unmarked grave under rocks, by a river bank, where the real Gareth Jones lay. If ever this war ended and he had the opportunity to take the poor dead observer's family to find the remains, would he be able to locate them? Having been a Lieutenant in his former life, his new identity had resulted in demotion to the rank of Private. This meant that he was among 'other ranks' prisoners most of whom were good fellows but lacking the interests and education he had achieved before volunteering. He also had to keep his Jewish religion to himself as Gareth Jones was known to be 'Chapel.' At least their Sunday services were fairly simple, not the heavily symbolic and ornate services of the Catholic prisoners. However, he would have given anything to attend a Jewish service along with a few of the prisoners who were his real co-religionists. He gave them a wide berth as he was terrified of being recognised as a Jew. He even tried to cultivate a sing-song Welsh accent to confirm his claimed origins.

Joe had lots of time on his hands to worry and wonder about the fate of his parents. He was sure that they had long since given him up for dead. Even his sister Rachel, married to cousin Adolphus probably assumed he had been killed. He knew his brother-in-law had seen him through the window that day, some months ago and wondered if he had reported this to Rachel or if he had his own reasons for not doing so. It was quite obvious that the Hauptmann would not wish to have any contact with him as that would incriminate him, himself, in facilitating Joe's escape from Nieuwpoort. *If Adolphus has any sense*, he decided, *he will give me a wide berth.* In any case, what on earth had the Hauptmann done that justified him being held with enemy officers? He hoped this had nothing to do with him. A few months had now elapsed since that one sighting, and on his occasional visits to that side of the camp, he had never seen Adolphus again.

Then his mind wandered to the young French woman he had met months ago on the day before he had been captured. There was something very special and very sad about her and also great charm. He could never forget her name, Amelie, although they had only been in each other's company for a few precious hours.

Joe would never forget his birthday that year. True it was his twenty-second but it was also the day he was approached by two other prisoners who wanted his opinion about a plan to escape.

Jimmy Jackson was twenty-five years old and had volunteered to 'fight the Hun' as soon as war was declared. He was one of the many loyal and patriotic young men from his Lancashire town and they were all given the title of 'Accrington Pals.' From the age of fifteen he had been a mill worker and had recently been promoted to the role of 'Tackler' where he could make good use of his ability as a mechanic. He had an unblemished employment record and his wife and family were all very proud of him.

Tom Hudson was a very different personality. He had never held down a job for more than two or three months in his twenty-seven years and had been out of work when the call to arms came. He came from Ancoats, an inner city area of Manchester known more for its hard drinkers than its hard workers.

It was Jimmy who had initiated the conversation. "Tom and I want to 'ave a chat with thee," he said. "We can see thou art someone with some brains and we want to ask thee what tha thinks about an idea we 'ave to get out of this bloody place. Will tha meet us behind number three barracks an hour before lights-out tonight?"

Joe desperately wanted to escape but was terrified of doing anything that brought him to his captors' attention and could possibly provoke them into more questions about his identity. Naturally he agreed, intrigued to discover what the two young men had in mind.

Tom began the conversation. "I 'ate these German bastards," he began. "If I can't get away from 'ere soon I am going to swing for one of them guards."

Joe nodded sympathetically although he had never experienced any trouble himself from the men who ran the camp. Most of them were disciplined German soldiers, tough but not unreasonable.

Tom continued, "Shall I tell 'im or will you?" he enquired of Jimmy.

"All reet," Jimmy answered, "I'll tell 'im what we 'ave in mind. Listen Gareth," he continued. "Does tha know that a horse lorry comes every Thursday to take away the laundry?"

Joe nodded again.

"Does tha also know that Tom and me works in't warehouse where all the laundry is packed and sorted?"

This time Joe shook his head. So far he had not needed to utter one word in exchange for the information he was being given.

Tom now took over the narrative which was something of a relief to Joe who found Jimmy's broad Lancashire accent hard to follow. *This Tom looks like a bit of a scoundrel but at least he speaks with a Manchester accent and I am used to that,* he decided.

"The laundry is packed in huge 'man-size' bundles," Tom explained, grinning. "Do yer get it, 'Man-size' bundles," he emphasised. "There are at least thirty bundles sent out to the laundry each week and I reckon we could be in three of them ourselves. The guards are so used to seeing the horse-lorry coming and going that they hardly even notice it, let alone check it."

"Well, that seems like a plan," Joe replied trying to put on his best Welsh accent. "But what do you want me for? You two already work in there."

"We don't need you to get out of the place but once we leave we have no bloody idea how to get out of this bloody country," Tom explained.

Jim took over. "We noticed that tha seemed different to most of the other lads in here, more educated, like! We thought tha would know how to get to 'Olland where there is no war and we could get a boat back to Blighty."

"What you are proposing is very dangerous and we could all finish up in front of a firing squad. Let me think about it anyway," Joe replied.

Tom looked angry. "We thought you'd jump at the idea. If you tell anyone about this, I'll kill you myself. Do you understand?"

"I have no intention of telling anyone," Joe replied, "and if you ever threaten me again I will not answer for the consequences. Do you understand? I never asked you to tell me your half-baked plan in the first place."

"Eh, come on Lad," Jim turned to Tom, "there's no need for that kind of talk. It was thee that suggested bringing in Gareth in't first place. He is reet to want to think it over. Just behave!"

Tom obviously had a short fuse but one that burned out quite quickly. "Sorry Gareth," he said, holding out his hand. "It's this bloody place getting on top of me. Are we friends?"

Joe nodded. "This is a lot to take in. I will be in touch with you again in the next few days."

Joe started to give serious consideration to the plan. *It all sound so simple*, he decided. *Too simple! But then the best plans usually are simple. If we were to make good our escape as the boys suggest, how could we get back to England?* Everyone knew that the Germans had decided not to invade Holland. It had no common border with France. Belgium was different; it had a long border with France and that country was the ultimate target. The French government had sided with the cursed Serbs and that was enough to earn the wrath of the Kaiser.

Joe knew that Antwerp was not far from the Dutch border. They would need to be disguised as Belgians but if any of them were challenged he did not have a single word of Flemish and he could not imagine that working men like Tom and Jim would ever have learned that language. Joe spoke French but with a strong English accent and the minute he started to converse, they would be discovered. Then he had an idea. What if they were disguised as orthodox East European Jews? He had a friend in

Manchester who had emigrated from Antwerp and he had told him all about the community there and the beautiful Eisenfeld Synagogue. It had only been built in 1907 and, until the war, had been catering for a growing population. If he decided to join Jim and Tom in their escape bid, they would need to go straight there, once they had slipped out of the bundles of laundry. What they needed was a map of Antwerp but how to get his hands on such an item when locked up in a prisoner-of-war camp was a real problem. Not surprisingly this was a seriously restricted item and anyone found in possession of such a map would be in deep trouble.

Joe asked Tom and Jim to meet him behind the hut again that evening and he told them he had a plan and would give them details once they were on the outside. However, he also told them that his plan would only work if he had a map of Antwerp.

"How, the bloody hell, do you think we could get hold of one of them?" Tom demanded.

"I really don't know," Joe replied. "But I do know that I will not leave without one. It is vital that we know where we are going if we are to have any chance of getting out of the town without being arrested."

In the end it was impossible to obtain a map but another solution was found in the name of one, Artur van Hoeven, a Belgian prisoner who spoke good English and had been a resident of Antwerp for almost four years before the war.

Artur loved to speak English and spent more time with the British prisoners than the French or, come to that, his own fellow-countrymen. He had chatted to Joe on a number of occasions, but Joe had tried to avoid him when he discovered he had visited North Wales many times before the war. He was terrified that this intelligent young Belgian would soon discover that he was not really Gareth Jones from Wrexham.

Joe told Jim and Tom to look out for Artur and tell him they needed to know the way to Oostenstraat. This was where the new Eisenfeld Synagogue was located, but Joe simply told his two comrades that this was the address of someone reliable who could help them. However, before seeking out Artur, the boys were to find out the address of the laundry. Joe only hoped the two places would be in the same direction.

"Well that's one thing that's easy," Jim explained. "All the bundles have labels on them so all we need to do is to read it off."

Tom nodded his head but looked a little uncomfortable.

"What's problem Tom lad?" Jim enquired.

It was the first time that Joe had seen Tom look really embarrassed. He turned to Jim and replied, "You'll 'ave to read it, I'm not much of a scholar."

They found Artur the following day at mealtime and asked for a chat.

"There is something we want to ask you, Artur," Tom explained. "This is just between us and I 'ope you won't rat on us to the bloody guards."

"Of course not," Artur replied. "I am a prisoner too and I certainly won't do anything to help the Germans who have stolen my country."

He was naturally intrigued by Tom's question. "Do you know de Boeystraat, (where the laundry was located) and Oostenstraat here in Antwerp? Which one is nearest to here?"

Artur replied, "From here, you pass Oostenstraat on the way to de Boeystraat, and neither of them are more than a few minutes from here. But why do want to know?"

"Oh, we just heard some of your Belgian mates talking and wondered," Tom replied quickly.

Artur grinned and said with a conspiratorial wink, "I think you have a plan to get out of this place but don't worry I am not telling. However," he continued, "if you do know how to escape, you really need a good guide to show you how to leave Antwerp and I could be your man."

The two English prisoners looked at each other and went off to report back to Joe.

"This feller Artur told us that the two places are very near each other and we pass your street on the way to the laundry. However, he guessed why we wanted to know and asked if he could come with us," Tom explained.

"Did you tell him we had an escape plan and what it was?" Joe gasped.

"We're not that daft," Jim answered, "but he seems a clever lad and he knew straight away why we were asking."

"He told us that having him with us would be very useful as he knows his way around and speaks the language," Tom added.

Joe thought for a moment. "I think we should all go away and think this through properly. Then if we still want to go ahead, I think I should have a chat with friend Artur."

It was three weeks later when the usual weekly laundry lorry, hauled by a huge shire horse, made its way through the gates of the prisoner-of-war camp and onto the streets of Antwerp. Buried among the other huge bags of laundry were an extra four bags, which as soon as the lorry was out of sight of the prison camp developed a life of their own.

The occupants slid out of the covers and re-buried themselves among the other large bags awaiting the lorry's arrival on Oostenstraat.

Chapter Fifty-One

Antwerp 1917

Four Men in a Cab

For Adolphus and Rachel the last year had been one of healing. The time they were apart was becoming a bad memory. The Hauptmann was still stationed in Antwerp and they were domiciled as a family unit in the home of Herr Scholz and his good lady. He no longer had to avoid the daughter of the house, Romilda, who had moved in with the Oberst von Lubeck when his wife, wearying of his dalliances, had returned to her parents' home. Romilda's father, always impressed by rank was secretly honoured that a man of such importance should have taken up with his daughter. His wife, however, with a strong Lutheran streak of morality, was embarrassed and ashamed and felt that Romilda appeared to be little better than a prostitute.

From time to time Adolphus' thoughts turned to Joe Bergman and he puzzled over why he had not been called as a witness in the Hauptmann's second trial. He was absolutely certain that it was Joe who he had seen peering through the window of the allied officer's barracks. It looked as if the German authorities were not aware of Joe's identity, which was confirmed by the fact that he was not imprisoned with other allied officers and must be with 'other ranks.' *Anyway*, Adolphus brooded, *the least said about Joe and the effect he had on my life for a while, the better.*

His children were a delight to him and although committed to a very heavy schedule with more and more allied officers to interrogate, he was able, now and again, to accompany Rachel and the little ones to synagogue on a

Saturday. He would attend in full uniform and was assured of a warm welcome from the Rabbi and other congregants. He was by far and away the most senior Jewish officer ever to visit and the members felt honoured by his presence.

Then he had the strangest of experiences. Adolphus had left his gloves in the cloakroom and decided to pick them up on his way home the following Tuesday evening. As he arrived he noticed a group of four East European orthodox Jews just leaving the premises. There had been an influx into Belgium and Germany of Jews from Poland and Russia, fleeing persecution under the Czar. This had started some thirty years previously and it was not an uncommon sight to see them, noticeable in their black garb, on the streets of Antwerp. Germany was, of course, at war with Russia now and this had stopped the flow but those who had arrived before 1914 were delighted to support Germany after the pogroms they had experienced in countries under the harsh rule of the Czar.

The four men were just getting into a cab when the second one spoke and in excellent Flemish asked to be taken to the Railway station. The last one to climb in glanced round to take a lingering look at the newly built synagogue. He had a short beard and wore a wide brimmed hat but there was no mistaking that handsome young face, it was Joe. Adolphus was deeply shocked and his first reaction was to step out in front of the cab and stop him leaving. However, there were four of them and if it came to a fight on the quiet street he was sure the Belgium cab driver would also support them. So, he stood there and watched the cab chug away. When he recovered from the shock he was horrified. Was this Nieuwpoort all over again? *What have I done? Am I going to be tried again, and this time found guilty of aiding and abetting four prisoners to escape?* Then he realised that this was nonsense. No one, including Joe, had seen him standing there and in no way had he helped the escapees. All he had to do was to keep quiet.

And then he thought about Rachel. She worried constantly about Joe and did not know if he was alive or dead. Adolphus hated having secrets from his wife but this was the one big one that he dare not confide to Rachel. *One day*, he hoped, *the truth would come out.*

Chapter Fifty-Two

Northern Belgium and Southern Holland 1917

A Circuitous Route

The plan had worked like a charm. The four men had easily slid off the back of the horse-lorry as it made its slow unfaltering progress past the Synagogue. Fortunately this was an era of bearded and/or moustachioed men and to let their facial hair grow a little longer did not provoke any comment from their jailers in the prisoner-of-war camp. It was summer anyway and until they arrived at the Synagogue their only clothing was shirts, trousers and, of course boots. They were not at all sure what kind of reception they would have there. Many Belgian Jews had some sympathy for the Germans if only because they were the enemy of their greatest enemy, the Czar. However, the more established Jewish families considered themselves as Belgians and deeply resented the way that the Kaiser's army had marched in and taken over their country. The Synagogue secretary was from an old Belgian Jewish family and when he received a visit from Artur, who of course, was not Jewish but a Belgian nevertheless and Joe, a British Jew, he was delighted to help. The Synagogue had a collection of old black coats and hats from before the war. These were to provide for new, poverty-stricken arrivals from the East and had now lain un-wanted in a store cupboard behind the Synagogue office for the last three years. Once Joe and Artur were sure that they had a sympathetic friend there, they called for Tom and Jim to come in through the rear door.

Jacob Kaplan, the secretary, also insisted on providing the four men with a good meal before they left and while they were eating, he walked round to the cab office nearby to organise their transport to the railway station.

"Have you any money?" he enquired on his return.

The four men looked at each other and shook their heads in embarrassment. They had intended to walk all the way to the Dutch border or jump freight trains – a dangerous undertaking even in peace time.

"Just a minute," Jacob said and left the office. He returned a few minutes later with sufficient cash to pay for the train tickets and a little left over for food.

"I am sorry that is as much as I can put my hands on at the moment," he explained.

The two non-Jewish British soldiers were astonished and Jim from Accrington had never met a Jew before. "I thought Jews were supposed to be tight," he said. "Bloody hell, I don't think we would find many Christians as generous as yon man."

"How can we ever re-pay you for your kindness?" Joe said.

"You just get yourselves to safety and that will be sufficient repayment," Jacob answered.

And so the journey to freedom commenced with four unlikely fellow-travellers making their way to the main railway station in an Antwerp swarming with German soldiers.

At the ticket office Artur left his three companions standing as inconspicuously as possible, near a wall. A continuous stream of German soldiers passed by; most of them looked about sixteen years old, Joe decided. Obviously with the huge losses both sides were sustaining in the conflict, the Germans were recruiting even younger men than hitherto as 'cannon-fodder.' None of these terrified youngsters even glanced in the direction of the three 'Jews' standing back by the brick wall of the station.

After ten minutes Artur returned with the tickets. Despite the strain they were all under, he was laughing as he explained that the man in the ticket cubicle had complimented him on his Flemish. "He thinks I am a foreign Jew. Little does he realise I am as much a Belgian as he is. I hope that is a good sign that our disguises are working."

Although Antwerp was far nearer to the Dutch border, the route Joe had agreed with Artur was to firstly take a train to Bruges. He was certain that the border just a few miles north of Antwerp would be heavily guarded and Joe was sure that their absence from the prisoner-of-war camp would have now been noticed. There would be military police looking for them and the first place they would look would be the Dutch border.

The journey to Bruges was uneventful. Most of the passengers were French speaking Belgians and they seemed to be wary of engaging the four 'Jews' in conversation. That certainly suited Joe and his comrades. There were very few Germans on the train and all the troops they had seen at the station were being sent south to the trenches (and almost certain death.) As a result the trip was uneventful and the four waited at Bruges station for the next train. This was to take them to Sluis, a somewhat unusual destination for four East European Jews but they had a cover story ready, should they be questioned. How well that would have worked was debatable. It was early summer and the story Joe had come up with was that a famous Rabbi from Amsterdam always took his holidays in Breskens, just across the border and they were to meet with him to discuss matters relating to the Belgian community while under German occupation.

In Sluis they persuaded, (or rather Artur persuaded) a man who rented a horse and trap to take them across the fields, thus avoiding the official crossing which would be manned by German and Belgian border police. Artur's method of persuasion was, of course monetary and that disposed of almost all the funds so generously given to them by Jacob Kaplan in Antwerp. However, they were free at last. All they had to do was to make their way along the coast to Handelhaven and somehow persuade a kindly Dutch fisherman to take them back to dear old England.

The four men looked for overnight accommodation and found a primitive rooming-house in Handelhaven. The man on the desk was most unfriendly and Joe wondered if he was a German spy. However, his collarless shirt, unbuttoned waistcoat and unshaven appearance made Joe think that if he was a spy he would hardly be likely to persuade anyone to relinquish military secrets to him.

"How many rooms?" he demanded without removing the soggy cigarette from his mouth.

Money was now very tight and after glancing at the ancient tariff of room charges on the wall behind the desk, Artur said, "Just one room with four beds."

This seemed to be a not unusual request and the man grunted, shuffled over to the keys hanging alongside some grubby shelves and said, "Here you are. Number four. There are four beds in it already. That'll be twenty guilders."

The room was just as awful as they had all suspected and even Tom, who had probably visited establishments like this before, remarked on just how bad the room was.

Anyway, it was still better than being in a German prisoner-of-war camp. At least they were free.

It was then that Joe decided to check out the bathing facilities, such as they were and left the others to find the bathroom. Then it happened! He came face-to-face, in the dark dismal corridor outside the men's room, with the girl who had been the secret subject of so many dreams during the long days and nights in the camp.

Joe could not believe his eyes and neither could the young lady who had provoked such a surprise. "Amelie," he gasped. "It is Amelie isn't it?" Her long black flowing hair was gone; it was bleached blonde, but there was no doubting her identity. That beautiful oval shaped face, those dark eyes and that olive coloured skin could only be Amelie.

"Gareth?" she said with her eyes wider than ever in wonder. "What?... How?... what are you doing here?"

"My friends and I are on our way back to England. Come; let me introduce you to them."

He knocked on the door of the bedroom they were sharing and called, "Are you decent as I have a lady with me." He assumed they would probably think it was a woman who worked in the hotel; maybe a chamber-maid.

The reply came back, "Come in!" and in they went.

The three men simultaneously jumped to their feet.

"This is Amelie," Joe explained. "We met in the south of Belgium last year when she was doing her bit for her country, France. Unfortunately her three comrades were caught by the Germans together with me and that is how I finished up in the prisoner-of-war camp."

Tom and Jim both seemed to be overawed to be in the presence of such a beautiful lady. Joe was sure they weren't normally tongue-tied with pretty girls but there was something very regal about Amelie.

Artur greeted her in French and Joe then introduced her to the two other Englishmen.

Amelie glanced around the room with its peeling wallpaper and threadbare carpet and then noticed with a shock the East European Jewish clothing lying on a chair.

"What on earth are those?" She enquired, pointing to the big hats and black coats.

"We travelled here wearing them," Joe explained. "And nobody bothered us."

Joe then turned to his three travelling companions and said, "I would like to spend a little time with Amelie, over a cup of coffee, catching up on what has happened to us since last year. I am sure you will find a way of passing the evening and I will be back by eleven."

The three men nodded and grinned and Joe was sure that Tom was thinking that Joe was after more than coffee and a chat. He was the first to reply."Sure, Gareth, you go off and enjoy yourself. If we can scrape together a little change I think we will check out the pubs and bars round here."

Joe left the seedy hotel with Amelie who looked totally out of place in such an establishment, but neither of them cared. They had found each other again.

Chapter Fifty-Three

Antwerp & St Quentin 1917

An old Friend?

When Adolphus arrived at the base the following morning the whole place was in turmoil. "What on earth is going on?" he asked the Feldwebel who was his assistant.

"Three British prisoners and a Belgian were missing at roll-call last night," the man explained.

Adolphus feigned shock and horror and said, "How could this have happened?"

"Nobody has any idea, Sir," the Feldwebel told him. "They have just disappeared. Apparently all the perimeter fences are secure and at the moment the military police have not been able to discover how they could have escaped."

"Are they officers or enlisted men," Adolphus enquired.

"All four of them are what we call 'other ranks,'" the man informed the Hauptmann.

"Who is in charge of the investigation?" Adolphus demanded.

"I don't know, Sir, but the Oberst von Lubeck has called a meeting of the security committee."

"Right, Herr Feldwebel. Well we'd better get on with our work. I believe you have two new British flyers for me to interview," Adolphus replied briskly. "Please let me have their files and by the way, when the Oberst has finished with them, I would like to see the files for the three British prisoners who have disappeared."

"What about the Belgian, Sir?" the Feldwebel enquired.

"No, just the British ones, Feldwebel, do you understand?"

Adolphus was intrigued. Joe had obviously been living under his nose for the best part of a year and he was curious to try and discover which of the three escapees had been Joe Bergman masquerading as a private soldier.

The Oberst kept the files for four days during which time the camp was literally turned upside down but their captors still did not have a clue how the four men escaped. Other prisoners from their barracks were questioned extensively, some gently and some being threatened with torture, but all to no avail.

On the fifth morning Adolphus' assistant turned up with the files. "Major Becker says you can only have them for this morning and then the Oberst wants them back again," he informed the Hauptmann.

Adolphus started to read through the details on file for Tom and quickly realised that he was hardly the type of man whose identity Joe could assume. He had been captured between the lines lying among dead comrades and in a drunken stupor. It was a miracle that he had not been buried with the rest. It was only a sudden movement that alerted the Germans, clearing the newly captured area that the man was alive.

Next Adolphus started to read about Jim. He was a good soldier and had fought bravely but had been captured when his trench was overwhelmed by a German force out to take the territory. Somehow this did not seem like Joe the flyer and the Hauptmann opened the third file. This was of a Welshman called Gareth Jones and he had been picked up in southern Belgium. He was described as an observer which meant a flyer and there it was. Obviously, without a shadow of a doubt, Gareth Jones was really Lieutenant Joseph Bergman.

Adolphus snapped closed the folder. He was determined to keep this piece of knowledge to himself. Joe had escaped anyway and Adolphus hoped and prayed he would avoid re-capture and travel as far away as possible from the Hauptmann. He had caused him enough trouble already.

It was now April 1917. Their enemy in the East, Russia was in total disarray. The Tsar, Nicholas the second, had abdicated the previous month and the new government was already putting out feelers that it wished to sue for peace with Germany and the other central powers. Then the news was received in Berlin that the United States of America was entering the war on the side of Great Britain and her allies. Just two weeks later Adolphus received notice that his whole unit was to be transferred to army headquarters just north of St Quentin in German-occupied northern France. This town, an ancient and thriving community had been virtually destroyed in the continuous trench fighting in the vicinity during the battles of the Somme. Large numbers of allied officers had been captured and the interrogation unit was to interview them.

The Hauptmann was obliged to bid a sad farewell to his wife Rachel and two children who were then to return to his parent's home in Berlin. As for Adolphus he was billeted in officers' quarters in a modest chateau in the area. Even this beautiful example of traditional French architecture had suffered in the fighting and only one wing of the building was habitable.

The first morning at breakfast he sat with brother officers at a long table and, as was customary, they were to be served by 'other ranks' soldiers, many of whom had been transferred from the front-line after injury. He was just enjoying his coffee before leaving for the interrogation centre when he glanced up at the man who was pouring the black liquid. They recognised each other instantly and neither could say it was a pleasure. Serving his coffee was none other than Erich Braun, the man who was largely responsible for his year of agony and anguish in Antwerp.

Braun had been stripped of his rank of Feldwebel and as instructed by the Oberst Otto von Lubeck he had been sent as a private soldier to fight in the battles of the Somme. Secretly, he was still determined to make it to the British lines and re-claim his British nationality having, at that time, developed a hatred of Germany and everything German – especially German Jews. His opportunity came when his unit was ordered to come out of the trenches and attack the British troops in their trenches. Hand to hand fighting occurred and he tried to tell various British soldiers that he was British, from Bradford and would fight alongside them. This was, not surprisingly, ignored in the heat of battle, and the Germans drove their opponents back to other trenches further to the south. Erich was then discovered lying injured with a bayonet wound to his side that luckily for him had missed vital organs. He was admitted to a field hospital where he found a Gefreiter by the name of Adolf Hitler in the next bed. Erich was spellbound by this rough Austrian with his never ending flow of invective against the allies and Erich's other pet hate, the Jews. They were kindred spirits and although only together for three weeks, Erich became, once more a loyal German.

His 'bravery' in the face of the enemy was observed by a number of his comrades who thought he was shouting curses at the British, not trying to change sides and he was decorated with the Iron Cross second class, the same award that his new hero Adolf Hitler had received two years earlier.

The Hauptmann was determined to ignore Braun's presence and continued with his breakfast without another glance. Braun however, as the embittered and prejudiced man he was, now blamed Adolphus for everything that had happened to him since he left Antwerp. He was obsessed with the idea of getting even with the Jewish Hauptmann either by plotting his downfall or somehow arranging Adolphus' death or serious injury. Before, his hatred had been personal but now, after the time spent with the other Adolphus, known as Adolf, he considered himself to be on a crusade against German Jews generally and Adolphus Bergmann in particular.

Chapter Fifty-Four

Handelhaven 1917

Getting to Know You

Joe and Amelie eventually found a cafe that looked reasonably respectable and clean and they ordered two coffees. Amelie explained to Joe how she had become involved in helping the French cause as a saboteur. She bravely told him the story she had recounted to Monique and Raoul of how the war had robbed her of her husband and unborn child and then she asked him for his story.

But before he had a chance to respond, she told him smiling, "I cannot believe you are Welsh. I visited the country with my parents when I was fifteen and the people neither looked like you nor sounded like you. The place was beautiful and the local population seemed to like us all the more when we told them we were French. They were lovely and friendly but quite different to this Gareth Jones who you claim to be."

"I can now tell you the truth and you are going to find it quite amazing," Joe replied sadly. "My real name is Second-Lieutenant Joseph Bergman of the RFC. I come from Manchester," and here his eyes brimmed over with tears, "and yes, Alfred Bergman was my brother."

Amelie looked at him in shock and she too hastily dabbed her eyes. "I knew it," she said. "Didn't I tell you, you reminded me of him?"

They both sipped their coffee in silence trying to come to terms with the incredible coincidence and Amelie's loss of a friend and Joe's of a dear brother.

Eventually Joe spoke again. "Firstly everyone calls me Joe and I would be very happy if you would do so. Secondly, I think I must tell you how I came to be wandering about and hiding behind hedges in the south of Belgium when we first met."

He then proceeded to tell her about his plane crashing, the death and burial of the real Gareth Jones, his meeting with his German officer cousin and how he had spent over a year languishing in a German prisoner-of-war camp outside Antwerp.

They decided between them that it was nothing short of miraculous that they had both escaped to Holland at the same time and to the same place.

"My father is very religious," Joe told her. "He would say it was the hand of God that brought us together and I must say that if I saw him now, I would agree with him one hundred per cent."

Amelie nodded and simply said, "And so would I."

Towards the end of the evening Joe admitted, "I want you to know that ever since I met you, I have not been able to get you out of my mind. I would like to think that we could be very close friends."

Amelie leaned across the table and gave Joe a gentle little kiss on the cheek which was received with the broadest of smiles.

They walked back to the hotel hand in hand knowing that tomorrow they must start the difficult task of finding a ship prepared to ferry them all over to England and safety.

Breakfast in the Badhotel in Handelhaven was not an entirely exciting culinary experience. Tom and Jim were both convinced that the Badhotel was called by that name because that was exactly what it was – 'bad.' However,

Artur and Joe insisted on explaining that 'Bad' meant 'bath or pool.' Jim felt that even so, 'bad' described it, as it was so seedy and run-down. Tom, however, had other ideas and suggested that hotels of this kind probably let out their rooms by the hour and many naughty and 'bad' activities almost certainly took place there. When the four men were joined for breakfast by Amelie, other residents started to arrive and judging by the fact that many of them seemed to be sailors accompanied by women of a certain profession, it looked as if Tom was right.

The men knew that finding a ship to cross the channel would rely more on the sympathy and dedication of the captain and crew than any monetary award they could offer. Their money had all but run out and Joe explained this to Amelie.

"You do not have to worry about that," she told him in a whisper. "I have more than enough money. I told you that I took the money the cursed Boche had given the evil farmer for betraying us."

"We cannot take that," Joe replied. "You will need it yourself to get back to France."

However, Joe knew he would probably be forced to accept her help and it did, of course, also benefit Amelie in ensuring her safe passage to England. If she did have to pay for their passage it would mean that she would have four strong men to escort her and ensure her safety.

There was a chill wind blowing in off the sea as the five potential passengers walked along the shore after breakfast. They quickly arrived at a rickety old jetty and on both sides a few even more rickety-looking fishing boats were moored. They decided that they must leave no stone unturned and two of them had small crews busily preparing to go out to sea that night.

Joe did not much like the look of the first man they approached. However, the question was asked by Artur in his Belgian Flemish.

The man looked them all up and down and his inspection lingered far beyond decency on the shapely figure of Amelie. "Nee!" he replied in Dutch and then continued with a leer, "Dat hangt er van af..." (That depends) staring lasciviously at Amelie.

Artur turned to them and said,"Come on! I wouldn't feel safe with this fellow myself and certainly not with the lady."

The next boat captain just said, "Nee," in a gruff voice and returned to mending his nets.

There was no crew visible on the other boats and they returned disappointed to the hotel. Another man was now at the reception desk and he appeared to be pleasant and sympathetic. In fact they all wondered why a good-looking, well-dressed young man like him should be doing such a menial job in such a run-down establishment. Joe suspected that he might be the Manager or owner but even that seemed a step down for a man of his apparent calibre. They asked him for five coffees and sat down in the now deserted breakfast room to consider their next move.

Holland was, of course neutral during the war and this had been of considerable benefit to the Germans who had made great use of the Dutch ports for the import of vital supplies. However from 1916 onwards the British Royal Navy had started to blockade all Dutch ports. Like all neutral countries in wartime it was a hotbed of spies from all countries involved in the conflict.

The man from the reception returned a few minutes later with five steaming mugs of coffee. Much to their surprise he pulled up a chair alongside their table and sat down.

"Where are you from?" he enquired pleasantly in Dutch.

"We are a mixed group," Artur replied. "I am the only one who speaks Dutch. Do you speak English; then we can all understand."

The man answered in accentless English. "Who is actually British here?"

Joe replied, pointing to Tom and Jim, "we three are and may we know who you are?"

"My name is Clive Sanderson and I am originally from Cheltenham. Now who are you and what are you doing here? This is a dangerous place, especially for a lady."

"I am afraid I must ask you the same question. What are you doing here?" Joe replied.

"Look," Clive replied. "I am going to show you my identification and then you must show me yours. I do not know what you are doing here but even in peacetime this is not exactly Brighton or the south of France."

Clive reached into his pocket and produced an official looking British government card. Joe read it carefully and handed it back. "I am Second Lieutenant Joseph Bergman of the RFC and I was stationed in Saint Quentin France before crashing my plane and being captured in Belgium."

Joe then asked the other men to identify themselves with their names, ranks and serial numbers.

He then turned to Amelie who told Clive she was a French national and gave no other details.

Clive seemed to be satisfied. "Now why are you here?"

"That is easy," Joe replied. "We want to find a boat to take us back to England."

"Well Joe," Clive replied, "I am afraid that is not easy. We are blockading all Dutch ports to stop vital supplies getting through to the Germans and that means the only ships allowed in are British or allied ones. In addition the Germans are still trying to use their submarines to attack our ships but now they are rarely successful. Friendly foreign ships know how dangerous these waters can become and mainly keep well away from the Channel and the North Sea. However, I will see what I can do to help but it may take a little time."

"Thank you Clive," Joe replied. "We are all desperate to get home and in my case I do not know if my family think I am alive or dead."

So it looked as if the five escapees from German occupied Belgium would be in for a long wait and the Badhotel no longer looked so 'bad' now that they knew they had a friend who apparently worked there. However, after a few days marooned in Handelhaven time was really dragging, at least for three of the party. For Joe and Amelie, on their voyage of exploration of each other, the passage of time was rather less torturous.

Chapter Fifty-Five

St Quentin 1917

Planted Evidence

Adolphus was deeply shocked to find Erich Braun now acting as a steward in the officers' quarters at St Quentin. He knew the man had a personal vendetta against him and that there were enough like-minded men in the 'other ranks' barracks to encourage him. By 'like-minded' he meant anti-Semitic and there had always been an undercurrent of prejudice in the German nation but in good times this tended to become dormant. However, there were more than enough sensible men among the middle and upper echelons of German society, men like the Oberst Otto von Lubeck, to keep these hot-heads in check. They loved their fatherland and anyone, from whatever origin who displayed the same loyalty, was one of them, a good German. Adolphus was sure that in his present subservient role, Braun would cause no trouble. How wrong he was.

A number of men in St Quentin had become 'infected' with Adolf Hitler's ideas on the inferiority of certain races and the superiority of those who claimed to be part of the larger German nation. One of those was a man called Heinrich Muller, a Bavarian gardener before the war. He was somewhat over-fond of 'good Bavarian beer' and as a result of a drunken outburst in the garden of Rabbi and Frau Wertheimer, he had been dismissed. That was enough to strengthen his already intense hatred and resentment of the 'Jewish race.'

Muller had met both Hitler and Braun in hospital and he was delighted to find himself working with Erich Braun when they were discharged.

It was the evening of the day when Braun had come face to face with Adolphus.

"What on earth is wrong with you, Erich?" Muller had demanded. "Judging by the expression on your face, you look as if all the worries of the world are on your shoulders."

"The Jew-bastard Hauptmann Bergmann who got me sent to the front is here now. I had to serve his breakfast this morning and just the sight of him sitting there really pissed me off," Erich explained. "If I had had poison, I would have put it in his coffee."

"Well," Heinrich replied. "If you want to really get the Jew, we must be cleverer than that. If you poisoned him they would soon find out that you knew him before and you would be in front of a firing squad in double-quick time."

"So what do you suggest?" Braun enquired.

"Let me give it some thought and I will get back to you," Muller replied.

Muller was not the greatest 'brain' in the German army but a few days later he had come up with a simple plan.

"You were born in England weren't you?" Muller asked.

"Ja!" Braun confirmed.

"So you speak good English and could write a letter in English that would look like a genuine English letter," Muller suggested.

"It would be a genuine English letter if I wrote it," Braun replied a little irritated by the comment. It must be remembered that Erich Braun was not famous for his patience.

"You told me that the Jew Hauptmann had been in trouble in Antwerp, something to do with a British cousin."

"Ja! That is correct," Braun confirmed and immediately went into one of his rants about the Jews having foreign connections. "You can't trust these people. They are everywhere and only work for the good of their own race. Everyone else can go to hell..."

"Ja! Ja! I know all that just as well as you do," Muller cut him short. "Do you want to know my plan or are you more interested in making speeches?"

"Sorry!" Braun replied. "So what is this plan of yours?"

"You write a letter in English making out it is to the Hauptmann from the English cousin. Do you know this cousin's name?" Muller enquired.

"Oh, Ja! It was Joseph Bergman but the Jew called him Joe," Braun quickly replied. He remembered almost every word of the interview he had heard when Adolphus interrogated the British flyer David Goldberg.

"Gut! So this is what you do. You write a letter something like this." And Muller dictated in German a fairly short letter that Braun then translated into English.

Dear Adolphus,

Thank you for the information about troop movements. I have passed this on to the British and Americans and the air-forces will be able to make very good use of it.

I am glad you have realised that we Jews should support the Allies not the Germans.

Your cousin,

Joe

"So," Braun enquired when the letter was done. "How do we get this letter to the Hauptmann?"

"We don't," Muller replied a little surprised that his much better educated friend should be so slow on the uptake.

"So what is the point?" Braun demanded.

"You make the letter look as if it has been well read by folding it as if it has come from an envelope," Muller explained patiently. Braun was always quick to anger but Mueller was patience personified except when he had been drinking and then he was capable of flying into violent rages.

"Ach so!" Braun replied. "And then we plant it where other officers will see it, right?"

So the plan was put into implementation and the following morning at breakfast Braun 'accidently' dropped the letter on the ground near to where the Hauptmann had been sitting. He then ostentatiously retrieved it as soon as Adolphus had left the room. This was just when the officer in command of the base General Horst von Kulm was passing.

Satisfied that the General had seen him bend down to pick up the letter, Braun said, "Excuse me Herr General. I think the Hauptmann Bergmann has dropped this piece of paper. Can I be excused to go and find him?"

"Nein," the General replied. "Give it to me and I will pass it on to him."

Exactly as planned, the General glanced down at the letter and remarked to himself, but out loud, "That is strange, the letter is written in English."

He then stood still as he carefully and slowly read the contents. As he digested the words his face turned a puce colour and Braun was sure he was about to have a heart-attack.

Suddenly the General straightened up and marched out of the room summoning one of the military policemen standing at the entrance to follow him.

Adolphus had just called for the first of the allied prisoners he was interviewing that day to be brought to his office when General Horst von Kulm burst in with a military policeman.

"Seize that man," he bellowed, pointing at Adolphus.

The Hauptmann was deeply shocked and stuttered, "Is something wrong Sir?"

"Is something wrong?" the General shouted. "Jawohl! Something is definitely wrong. This is wrong," he exclaimed as he banged the letter on the desk.

"What is this?" Adolphus replied, totally mystified.

"You know exactly what this is," the General answered. "Why not read it out for me. I speak English."

Adolphus picked up the letter and as he read it he went pale. At the end he felt sick.

"Take him to the lock-up," the General ordered. "You will be tried by a Court-Marshall tomorrow morning and with this evidence you might as well start saying your prayers now."

The news quickly circulated around the old chateau that had become German military headquarters. The trial was over in less than two hours. Adolphus protestations of innocence were hardly credible against the damning evidence that Erich Braun and his accomplice had so easily manufactured.

The following morning at dawn, with no hope of a reprieve, Adolphus Bergmann, a loyal officer of the Imperial German Army was to face a firing squad.

Chapter Fifty-Six

Handelhaven 1917

HMS Erebus

They had now been stuck in Handelhaven for ten long days. Even Joe and Amelie longed to be able to leave the little coastal town and they, at least had used the opportunity to get to know each other. For the others there was just boredom.

They were all certain that Clive was a British agent stationed there for a very specific purpose but he refused to discuss this possibility. All he would say was, "Wait and see and please be patient," when quizzed as he frequently was, especially by Tom and Jim.

On the eleventh morning Joe rose early and opened the curtains in the room he shared with the other three men. The window was stained with years of salt-laden rain and looked as if had never been cleaned since the building was originally constructed, probably in the mid nineteenth century.

Joe peered out to look at the small harbour and jetty and noted that the same fishing boats were still moored there as they had been on the day they all arrived. Then he saw movement on the horizon. Until then, all he had viewed from the window was a vista of grey, choppy sea. He knew there were ships out there, large ships, destroyers and he had also heard about the German submarines that stealthily glided under water towards unsuspecting British vessels. However, as he watched, the movement on the horizon grew larger until he could identify it as a ship. With his training as an RFC pilot he recognised the craft as a Royal

Navy ship usually described as a Monitor. Satisfied that the approaching visitor was friendly he called his three room-mates to the window to watch as the ship moored alongside the jetty. Then they saw the gang-plank placed against the jetty and three naval officers disembark. At that moment Joe saw a figure sprinting along the jetty and realised that it was Clive, their host. He saluted and greeted the naval officers and then all four men went aboard again.

"Come on lads," Joe said. "Get dressed and we can go and see what is happening. Maybe, just maybe, we could catch a lift back to dear old Blighty on the ship."

A few minutes later the four men were walking briskly along the jetty to inspect the new arrival. The Monitor was called HMS Erebus and as they approached two armed sailors came down the gang-plank. "That's near enough," one of the sailors called. "Who are you and what do you want?"

Joe saluted and his three companions followed suit. "I am Second-Lieutenant Joseph Bergman of the Royal Flying Corp." Tom and Jim gave their identification and regiments.

Artur then saluted a second time and introduced himself as a member of the defeated Belgium Armed Forces.

The sailor who had spoken told them to wait where they were and he went back on board. He returned just minutes later with Clive who told them to return to the hotel and await further orders.

In the meantime Amelie had awoken and dressed and knocked on the men's room door to ask if they were ready for breakfast. When there was no reply she had opened the door and was somewhat surprised to find that none of the four men were still there. For a second the thought entered her head that they had gone back to England without her and then she realised that all their possessions were still in the room. She was also sure that Joe would never do that to her. At that moment she heard voices and realised that they were returning.

As soon as Joe came into sight she asked him where they had been. He told her about the newly-arrived ship and explained that Clive had instructed them to return and await orders.

"I do think you might have told me where you were going," she remonstrated gently. "I really thought you had gone off without me."

"Sorry," Joe said. "You are right. Of course we should have told you about the ship. Am I forgiven?"

"Of course," she smiled. "Do you think they will take us all back to England?"

"We are all hoping so but Clive is on board and obviously he is something to do with them being here," Joe commented.

After half-an-hour they decided to go back downstairs for breakfast and await Clive's return. They were served by the man they had seen the first night and it seemed unlikely that he had washed or shaved in the interim. However, they were hungry and thirsty and cared little who served them.

The four men and Amelie sat around the table all morning discussing the likelihood of being rescued from boredom. Joe pointed out to them that this was a ship that would be heavily involved in operations against the Germans in Belgium. It was probably only because Handelhaven was literally a backwater that the ship had docked there. In truth its presence was compromising Dutch neutrality.

Lunchtime arrived and still they were sitting there. Once again they were served by the same scruffy man and they all enjoyed the light meal, despite his appearance.

Then at 2pm Clive returned. He came marching into the dining-room and said, "I thought I would find you all here. The Captain of the Erebus is Gordon Crawford and he would like to meet you. Please therefore follow me back to the ship."

As the senior officer, Joe fell into step with Clive as they made their noisy way along the rotting timbers of the jetty.

"Is she sailing back to England now?" he enquired quietly so that the others would not hear.

"I think so but you had better ask him all those questions yourself," Clive replied in a voice just above a whisper.

Two different armed sailors were now stationed on either side of the gang-plank and when they saw Clive they swiftly stood to attention and saluted.

"We are all on our way to have a meeting with Captain Crawford," he announced.

They stood aside as the entire party climbed up to the deck.

There was scarcely room for the party of five, plus Clive, the Captain and another naval officer, but somehow they squashed around the table and waited for Captain Crawford to speak.

He was Scottish, as his name indicated and he spoke with what Joe recognised as an Edinburgh accent.

"May I firstly welcome you aboard HMS Erebus," he began. "I am sorry we are a relatively small ship with limited facilities. Our main job is to fight the Germans and we have just returned from action just along the coast in northern Belgium."

They all smiled and nodded.

"I understand from our friend Clive that you are all desperate to get back to Blighty so that you can have another crack at the Hun," he continued.

Once again they all smiled and nodded.

"I also understand that the senior officer here is Second-Lieutenant Joseph Bergman of the RFC. I assume that is you," he continued.

"Yes Sir," Joe replied.

"Well the short answer to your main question of whether we can ferry you back to England is YES. I have received a signal from the Admiralty giving me permission to take you across to Harwich. We need to pick up supplies anyway so this trip will not affect our schedule," he announced to the smiling group. "However, Petty-Officer Thomas and I need to interview you all separately before we leave. The Admiralty insist on this. So, I suggest we start at once as we must put to sea tonight."

Chapter Fifty-Seven

St Quentin 1917

Firing Squad

Adolphus lay in his cell contemplating how suddenly his life had changed. In fact the following morning, it would no longer be a life – just another death in this horrible war that was claiming the lives of so many young men from across Europe.

He had been a good son, if an only one and hoped that he had made his parents proud; so proud that they would be unable to believe that he had suddenly become a traitor to his country. He hoped he had also been a good and loving husband and here too he had been loyal despite temptation (except for the night with Romilda when he seriously suspected that all he had done was to sleep away his drunken stupor.) He had also tried to be a good father and if young Rudi would be able to remember him, it would be fondly. Sadly little Ruth had no chance of remembering him at all. She was still far too young. He wiped away a tear and wondered where he had gone wrong.

The fact that he had been set up was obvious. The incriminating letter was a forgery. He had tried to tell the court that Joseph Bergman, his British cousin was either dead or a prisoner but they never believed him. The comment in the letter about the Jews supporting the Allies rather than the Central powers did not help but then, even without this, his fate was sealed. He knew who had hated him so much that they would have planted the letter. It could only have been that cursed madman Erich Braun. But he had won and Adolphus had lost; so much for justice, both German justice and divine justice!

He would die blindfolded and tied up in front of a wall early in the morning. He had witnessed a couple of such executions himself and it had sickened him. The way the body suddenly lurched forward when the bullets hit, was terrifying and he just hoped that the first shot would extinguish his short life. Then he remembered that, with the second execution, the man was not dead after the volley of bullets. An officer had finished off the poor devil with a pistol shot to the brain.

He had just decided to pray when the cell door was unbolted and a military policeman entered with one of the Jewish Chaplains to the German armed forces.

Adolphus looked up to see a young Rabbi standing there and surveying him sadly.

"I am Rabbi Blumberg and I can't tell you how broken-hearted I am to find you in this situation," he began.

Adolphus nodded. "I had just decided that I must say some prayers and you arrive. I wish it was an omen that I am to be reprieved but I hardly think that will happen."

"Would you like to tell me what happened," the Rabbi said.

Adolphus was glad to talk and told him how the letter had been discovered and how it was so damning that his trial was over in very short time. "I know who must have done this to me," he explained and told the Rabbi about Erich Braun.

"I don't think that if the court did not believe you that they will listen to me," Rabbi Blumberg commented. "If I thought there was anything I could do, I am sure you know I would try. You must know, however, that once a verdict is decided by a military court, the sentence is immediate. All we can do is to pray to God and would you like me to do that with you now?"

Adolphus nodded and the Rabbi pronounced with him the age-old prayers usually reserved for those about to depart from this world from natural causes.

"Would you like me to accompany you out of here?" the Rabbi asked.

"Yes please," Adolphus replied feeling sick but trying to appear brave. "Please can you contact my wife and parents and tell them the full story of what happened. I am not a traitor. I love my country and have worked hard for our Kaiser and the German Empire."

The Rabbi nodded and they waited for dawn to come reciting Psalms together.

At precisely six o'clock the door of the cell was unlocked and four military policemen entered. They told him, as if he did not know, that he was to be escorted to a place of execution by a firing squad and with Adolphus, accompanied by Rabbi Blumberg, the six men marched out to the drill yard where the sentence of the court was to be carried out.

Adolphus was instructed to stand against a wall pock-marked by bullet holes from previous executions and facing a detachment of soldiers armed with rifles. His hands were tied behind his back. He was offered a blindfold which he gladly accepted and the Rabbi blessed him and then withdrew to let him meet his maker.

The sergeant in charge of the execution detail then instructed them to raise their rifles and prepare to fire...

Chapter Fifty-Eight

HMS Erebus 1917

An Eventful Voyage in More Ways than One

The four fugitives from the Antwerp prisoner-of-war camp were once again accommodated in one room but in even less comfort than in the Badhotel. If their facilities were less than ideal, poor Amelie had to make do with what was virtually a cupboard; it was just long enough to hold a narrow bed. However, if the five passengers on HMS Erebus were really on their way to England, any discomfort was a tiny price to pay for their freedom.

In comparison with many of the Destroyer ships in the Royal Navy, the HMS Erebus was not a small ship. She carried a crew of approximately two hundred and twenty men. It was quite surprising therefore, if not bordering on the miraculous, that it was only an hour after they had put to sea that Joe came face-to-face with a certain Petty Officer. The man was drilling a number of obviously newly-recruited seamen. Joe was on his way to see the captain and he glanced at the group of men on deck. The Petty Officer glanced at Joe, and Joe at him and they both realised simultaneously that they were both looking at their one surviving brother. Ike Bergman was still in his nineteenth year but had volunteered to be in the Royal Navy a year earlier. He had impressed his officers and had been quickly promoted to the rank of Petty Officer.

"Stand easy," he called to his men. His face was as white as a sheet, almost as if he had just seen a ghost. Indeed, having presumed for all this time that Joe was dead, it was like seeing a ghost. "My God," he spluttered. "Joe, it is you, isn't it?"

Joe surveyed his younger brother smartly attired in his Royal Navy uniform and with tears in his eyes he demanded, "Ike, I really can't believe it. When are you off-duty? We have so much to tell each other, but one thing I must know now, how are Mum and Dad?"

Ike nodded and said, "Well, but sad. We lost poor Alfred in 1914 and they had long since decided that you too were dead. I can't wait to tell them that you are here, alive and well. I am off duty at four o'clock, so why not meet me outside the non-commissioned officers' mess then?"

Joe could not believe his good fortune and went to tell Amelie his news. He knocked on the door of her tiny room and she appeared, looking remarkably fresh and lovely.

"I would ask you in but there is hardly enough space for one in here, let alone two," she explained as she stepped out of the 'cupboard.' "Is everything alright?"

"I have some amazing news for you," Joe replied, smiling broadly.

"The fact that we are on the way to England on a British ship is more than enough amazing news for me," she answered.

"But I have some even more amazing news," Joe protested. "My younger brother Ike is a Petty Officer on this ship. I have just spoken to him and I am meeting him this afternoon."

"That is wonderful," Amelie said and gave his hand a little squeeze.

It was then that the siren started to whoop and howl.

"What on earth is that?" Amelie said with a terrified look on her face.

"We must be under attack. Go back in your room and I will try to find out what is happening," Joe instructed.

Amelie nodded and re-entered her tiny domain.

Joe started to make his way on to the deck and then had to hastily stand aside as large numbers of seamen were dashing up the steps to take up battle stations.

Once all was quiet below deck, Joe tried again to ascend to see what was transpiring. However, as he emerged into the fresh salty air of the Channel he encountered the Ensign that he had seen with the Captain the previous day. "You had better return to your quarters Sir," the officer said. "Our sonar has picked up an approaching U9 submarine. Please tell your comrades to stay below until we have dealt with the little blighter."

The Erebus carried four depth-charges. These were explosive devices dropped over the edge of surface ships and timed to explode when an attacking submarine was estimated to be near. Sadly, because of the weight of these devices even a fairly large ship like the Erebus had to make do with four. On this occasion three of them had been activated without success. The last one was launched when the sonar indicated the submarine was dangerously near the Erebus and in a position to fire a torpedo at the British ship. This last depth-charge achieved its mission and the German U9 was destroyed. It sank to the bottom of the sea where a sandy grave awaited its crew. However, the explosion had seriously damaged the hull of the Erebus which, as a consequence, had lost much of its manoeuvrability.

Once the initial emergency had passed the Captain sent for Joe. He explained that they were now an easy target for any other submarines in the vicinity and all he could do was to limp slowly towards Harwich, so near yet so far away, and hope for the best.

Under cover of darkness the Erebus finally arrived in Harwich.

Because of the emergency Joe had missed his meeting with Ike and as they disembarked on to British soil he looked out for his brother.

They were met by representatives of the Royal Flying Corp (for Joe), the army for Tom and Jim and a messenger from the Free Belgium Government in exile awaited Artur.

Joe, Tom and Jim were granted a full week's leave before re-joining their units. The three British soldiers were supplied with a little cash and train tickets to their home towns. Artur made his adieus and hoped they would meet again when Belgium was again free from the yoke of the German invader.

The French authorities were not, at that stage, aware that Amelie had arrived in England and as her work had been entirely clandestine it would be up to her to make her way home. Firstly, however, she was invited and immediately agreed to accompany Joe to Manchester to be introduced to his parents. They, at that stage were still unaware that not only was he alive and well, but that he had found the lady who he hoped would agree to become his wife.

By now it was three o'clock in the morning and the three British soldiers and Amelie decided to make their way to the Railway station to catch the first train home.

Joe was still sad that having found his brother Ike he had been unable to see him again. However, as they walked away from the damaged ship Joe heard the sound of running footsteps and a young Petty Officer ran towards him shouting, "Joe. I am here, Joe!"

The brothers embraced and Joe introduced Ike to Amelie and also to Tom and Jim.

"Are you on leave now?" Joe enquired.

Ike shook his head sadly. "No, I have to stay on board until the ship is repaired and ready to set sail again. Please give my love to Mum and Dad. Please God the next time we meet, the world will be at peace."

Chapter Fifty-Nine

St Quentin 1917

Attack!

Adolphus had never been raised with much religion but his time with his wife Rachel had given him a love for the faith of his ancestors. As the firing squad raised their guns he recited out loud, "Shema Yisrael, Hashem Elokaynu Hashem Echad." (Hear Oh Israel, The Lord is our God and the Lord in One) Then he flinched as the order to fire was given and was astounded by the sound of a huge explosion. He had never anticipated that guns could be quite so noisy. Then he realised he was still alive and unhurt and now there was the sound of shooting but it was all missing him. He tried to release the cord that bound his wrists so that he could remove his blindfold but that proved impossible. As he struggled unsuccessfully to free himself, the noise of more explosions, of shouting and shooting continued until finally he freed his wrists and tore away the blindfold.

A pitched battle was in progress and he recognised the khaki uniform of literally hundreds of British soldiers fighting with fixed bayonets and overcoming the much smaller number of German soldiers. The ground was littered with the field-grey clad bodies of the dead, the dying and the wounded. He was the one who was supposed to die that day and he was alive, uninjured and almost inconspicuous in the melee. He thanked God for his deliverance and then began to wonder what his fate would be at the hands of his enemy, the British.

His feet were still tied and he made no effort to release them. He just stood there against the wall, half spellbound and half revolted as he watched the carnage of the battle for St Quentin unfolding. Adolphus was an officer in the army of his Royal Highness the Kaiser but he had never seen fighting before. Of course he had been combat-trained but his entire military career had been spent in military intelligence. His battlefield had been his office where he interrogated captured allied officers. Suddenly he realised that if the British were winning the battle he was watching, he would probably be their prisoner and subjected to the same interrogation methods that he had employed on them. At least he hoped that would be what would happen. He knew the British were just as fond of the firing squad as the Germans and he had heard numerous tales of them shooting their own men when they were too shell-shocked to continue fighting; were they blood-thirsty barbarians, or would they treat him with humanity?

The Hauptmann kept his hands behind his back to give the impression that they were still secured by a cord. His feet were still bound and he hoped the British would not see him as a threat or his death sentence would have just been postponed, not cancelled. Eventually he saw two British officers approaching him.

He heard one say to the other, "Look at this poor bugger. Looks like one of their own officers and the bastards were about to shoot him."

Adolphus recognised one officer was a Major and the other a First-Lieutenant. "Do you speak English?" the Major asked.

The Hauptmann nodded.

"You are now a prisoner-of-war. We need your name rank and serial number," the Major demanded.

Now where had I heard that before? Adolphus thought wryly. "My name is Adolphus Bergmann and I am a

Hauptmann in the army of His Majesty, the Kaiser of the German Empire. My serial number is 70896357."

By now the battle was over. Most of the Germans had been killed or wounded but there were a number of casualties among the British forces. A small group of German prisoners sat disconsolate on the dusty ground. They were shackled to each other with metal chains and handcuffed.

"As a Hauptmann," the Major told Adolphus, pointing towards the chateau, "if I have your word that you will not try to run, the Lieutenant here will release you and you can take your place over there with the other two surviving officers."

"You have my word as a German officer," Adolphus replied in a low voice.

"Herr Hauptmann," the Major continued. "We know you were about to face a firing squad and you have had a very lucky escape. I hope you realise that you now owe your life to the army of his Majesty King George the fifth of Great Britain."

Adolphus nodded uncertainly. In truth, the events of the last few hours had taken their toll and he was in a state of shock.

The British Lieutenant untied Adolphus' ankles and after stretching his legs gently he found he could once again walk. The officer escorted him over to where the two German officers were standing. He recognised them both from the officer's mess but had only been on nodding terms with them. One was a Major and the other a Hauptmann like him. When they saw him approaching, they both turned their backs on him. Obviously, as far as they were concerned he was a traitor to his Kaiser and country.

Adolphus had nothing else to do but watch as the British soldiers and medical orderlies buried the dead and tried to help the injured.

Then a British army truck rattled its way into the courtyard and the 'other ranks' German prisoners were told to climb aboard. There had been many German casualties that day but somehow Erich Braun had survived and was being hurried onto the truck to be driven away to a prisoner-of-war camp.

I hope I never set eyes on that evil little man again, Adolphus prayed. *He nearly destroyed me but God was on my side.*

The three German officers were then marched into the Chateau, now being used as a base for the British army. They were told to sit outside an office which Adolphus recognised as the one that had been occupied only yesterday by General Horst von Kulm. They were there to await interrogation. During all this time his two fellow German officers completely ignored his presence which suited him. He needed peace and quiet to restore his equilibrium.

Well, Adolphus, he said to himself, *where do I go from here?*

Chapter Sixty

Manchester 1917

A Brief Homecoming

It was two o'clock in the afternoon when the train ferrying Joe and Amelie, together with Tom and Jim, pulled into London Road Station in Manchester. Tom went off to catch a tram to his home just a mile away and Jim had to walk across the city to Victoria to pick up another train for the final leg of his journey to Accrington. They had said their goodbyes and they all wondered if they would ever meet again.

The station was heaving with service personnel and the main concourse resembled a veritable sea of khaki uniforms. There was a long queue for taxis and it was half an hour before they could continue onwards to the Bergman home in Broadoak Street.

As soon as the cab pulled up outside number twenty-seven Joe jumped out, left Amelie to disembark in a more dignified way and bounded up the steps. The taxi driver carried their bags and deposited them on the top step. In the meantime Joe was knocking and ringing the door-bell for all he was worth but to no avail. Not surprisingly, there was no one in. Both Jacob and Leah were at work. Fortunately the weather was warm and dry and, accepting that there was no way he could gain entry, they both sat down on the top step to wait. It was to be a long wait, but having completely missed a night's sleep, they both nodded off in the warm sunshine.

It was a quarter past six when Joe felt himself being shaken and awoke.

"What are you doing on my step?" a male voice demanded in anger.

"Dad, it's me, Joe," he answered.

"Joe! Oh my God!" Jacob replied. "How long have you been sitting here? Why didn't you send me a telegram to say you were safe and coming home? Who is this lady?" All the questions just tumbled out of Jacob's mouth, almost without him taking a breath.

The two men embraced and Joe told his father that this was a very dear friend, Amelie Levi from Paris. Amelie shook hands formally and then pulled the surprised Jacob towards her and kissed him on both cheeks.

"Where is Mum?" Joe enquired.

"Oh, she won't be back from work for another hour," his father explained and pulling his keys from his pocket, he opened the front door and ushered them in.

Suddenly Jacob burst into tears. "We thought you were dead," he explained. "The man came from your unit and told us about your plane crashing and we feared the worst."

"Thank God, I was ok," Joe told him. "My poor Observer, a Welsh boy did not fare so well. He bought a bullet from a German plane and I had to bury him. However, I was a prisoner-of war in Belgium for over a year but enough about me. How have you both been?"

"Better for seeing you," Jacob replied. "I do not know why we are standing in the hall. Come into the front room and I will make you both a hot drink. Is tea alright?"

Amelie and Joe both said in unison, "Yes, please," and Amelie then added, "Without milk for me please."

They enjoyed their drinks in silence with Jacob just staring at them with his face bathed in a permanent smile.

"Now, I will show you to your rooms and you can freshen up. Mum will be home soon and then we can really start to catch up with all that has happened to you," Jacob suggested.

"Dad," Joe said, "There is one important piece of good news I must share with you right now. Yesterday, on the ship that brought us back to England we met Ike, and Dad, he is fine. He sends his love to you both."

Once again Jacob dabbed his eyes and showed them upstairs. Joe was back in his old room and Amelie was in the spare room; the same spare room that Adolphus had lived in, but she knew nothing of Joe's cousin the Hauptmann in the German army at that time. That was soon to be rectified.

Feeling much better for a wash and change, the pair descended and called to Jacob that they would wait in the front room for Leah to return.

Jacob, quite understandably would not leave them on their own for a minute and the three waited the final half hour for Leah to come back from her work.

At last they heard the front door open and close and a pleasant female voice call out, "Jacob, where are you?"

"In the front room my dear," he answered. As the door opened she was saying, "What are you doing in there?" And then she saw Joe. "Joe?" she enquired, peering at him. "Joe, is it really you?" Then she ran across the room and flung her arms around him, sobbing. "Joe, Oy, Joe! My boy; you have come home, and who is this young lady?"

Joe introduced Amelie who once again in French style kissed Joe's mother on both cheeks.

Jacob then spoke up. "Leah, Joe saw Ike yesterday and he is fine, so that is two worries we can forget for now. I will help you to prepare some supper. These two young people must be starving."

Leah turned to Joe smiling. "You should come home more often; your father is not always so keen to help in the kitchen."

That evening, was the happiest that Jacob and Leah had spent for many a long year! They could never forget Alfred, their first-born, but having Joe and his charming French lady-friend home and knowing Ike was fit and well, gave them some confidence that they would still have a family when the awful war ended. There was one other person constantly in their thoughts, their daughter Rachel. She was on the wrong side of the European divide in the enemy capital, Berlin. It was some time before she was even mentioned as neither Jacob nor Leah would have believed that Joe had seen Adolphus, her husband.

Joe decided to tell his parents of his experiences in reverse chronological order. This was mainly to explain how Amelie came into his life. Eventually he returned to the way that he had met Adolphus in a field in Southern Belgium and how Adolphus had more than proved his loyalty to the family by facilitating Joe's escape from the German Headquarters building in Nieuwpoort.

"So, what did he tell you about Rachel?" Leah interrupted.

This was at the time when Adolphus and his wife were estranged and Joe saw no reason to mention that. He did know, however, that all was well, at least at that time, with the German Bergmanns. He also mentioned catching a glimpse of Adolphus outside the Synagogue in Antwerp when he was escaping from Belgium.

"Adolphus going to Shul on a weekday," Jacob commented with satisfaction. "It sounds as if he is becoming more religious under Rachel's influence."

The news that Joe had to tell could hardly have been better. There was only one piece of bad news that he had saved until the end of his story, namely that they were only in Manchester for a precious few days. Then Amelie must get back to France and Joe to an RFC base.

The following morning Joe left Amelie at home and reported as instructed to an RFC office to obtain his new orders. These turned out to be better than he could have ever wished. He was to report to Blandford Forum in Southern England not to Saint Omer as he had expected.

"You will receive your full orders in Blandford, Lieutenant Bergman. Here is your travel warrant and you must report there next Monday at 0800 hours."

Chapter Sixty-One

North-West France 1917

The Interrogator is Interrogated

There probably never was a prisoner-of-war as happy to be captured as Adolphus. He was taken with a number of other German officers to a British base near Saint Omer in Northern France; this was the area that had already figured so much in his military career, but which he had never actually visited as a German soldier.

The other two officers who were captured during the British raid on Saint Quentin were, happily for Adolphus, sent elsewhere. There were three other officers with him now and they chatted with him in a friendly manner being entirely unaware that he was to have been shot as a traitor.

Eventually the truck carrying the four officers, and a detachment of British troops to guard them, arrived at their destination and Adolphus was relieved to see that the Allies were treating captured enemy officers similarly to the way the Germans had. They were, of course locked up but in an old French army billet with accommodation, if not luxurious, at least tolerably comfortable.

Adolphus was grateful to be issued with basic requirements such as soap and toothpaste, shirts and trousers. He would not have been allowed to use his own belongings anyway, but he had lost everything in Saint Quentin.

There were just fourteen German officers and two Austrians in the billet and the prisoners already there, welcomed them. It transpired that apart from one Hauptmann they were all Leutnants of different grades so

Adolphus immediately became one of the two senior officers.

At the crack of dawn they were instructed to join 'other ranks' British prisoners for drilling. Then, as Adolphus expected, he was interrogated.

The interviewing officer was of the same rank as Adolphus. He was a Captain Algernon Denton-Carruthers. *And I thought German names were long,* Adolphus mused.

"Good morning Hauptmann," Denton-Carruthers began, pleasantly enough. "I trust you are comfortable in your accommodation. I know you were captured in a French chateau and I am afraid we cannot equal that. Now may I firstly have your name, rank and serial number?"

Adolphus was fascinated. He had been doing the same job as Denton-Carruthers for the last three years and the Captain appeared to be starting the interrogation in exactly the same way as Adolphus always had, in other words, pleasantly.

"My name is Adolphus Bergmann and I am a Hauptmann in the army of His Majesty the Kaiser of the German Empire. My serial number is 70896357." Adolphus told him.

Denton-Carruthers looked down at his notes. "Yes, that is all correct and there is nothing unusual there. However, the other information I have about you is far from usual. I understand that if our troops would have attacked just thirty seconds later you would have been executed by a firing squad. So you owe your life to the British army, wouldn't you agree, Hauptmann?"

"My name is Adolphus Bergmann and I am a Hauptmann in the army of His Majesty the Kaiser of the German Empire. My serial number is 70896357." Adolphus replied.

"Herr Hauptmann, I repeat and I expect you to at least agree that you owe your life to the British army," the Captain demanded.

"My name is Adolphus Bergmann and I am a Hauptmann in the army of His Majesty the Kaiser of the German Empire. My serial number is 70896357." Adolphus once again replied.

"Herr Hauptmann," the Captain said. "This really will not do. I understand that we saved your life, and you refuse to co-operate. This is all rather disappointing. Are you prepared to confirm this information and tell me why your own army was about to have you killed?"

"Captain Denton-Carruthers," Adolphus replied. "You know just as well as I do that my only obligation is to supply you with my name, rank and serial number."

"Very well but I think you are going to be here for a long time and I advise you to show me a little more co-operation. You can go back to your billet now but, I warn you, I want an explanation and I will have an explanation."

As the Hauptmann walked briskly back towards his barracks he passed a party of 'other ranks' German soldiers who were being drilled by one of their own Feldwebels under the supervision of a French officer. There was something familiar about the man in the last row. As he strode passed he had a better view of the face and realised with a shock that it was none other than Erich Braun. The same Erich Braun who had managed to torment his life for two years and had been within a hair's breadth of bringing about Adolphus' death just one day earlier. He rarely wished anyone dead but he had been convinced that Braun must have been a fatal casualty at Saint Quentin and that prospect hardly caused him any regret. Now he was here and although they were both prisoners, Adolphus was convinced that Braun would be looking for a way of targeting him, once again.

He wondered if Braun had seen him and he decided that if he had not seen him then, it was only a matter of time before they came face-to-face. He made a quick decision and returned to the office of Captain Denton-Carruthers. However, the British officer was now engaged in another interrogation and Adolphus explained to the sergeant who ran the Captain's interviews that he wanted to see him again as he had more information to supply. The sergeant was somewhat surprised but allowed Adolphus to wait outside the office of the Captain until he had finished interrogating the German officer.

"Captain Denton-Carruthers," Adolphus began when eventually, he was in front of the officer's desk again. "I would like to be transferred to another camp."

"Hauptmann Bergmann," the Captain replied. "You know that is out of the question. May I remind you that you are our prisoner and it is up to us to decide where you are to be held."

"Sir," Adolphus tried again. "I think my life will be in danger if I remain here."

"Really Bergmann, don't you think you are being rather over-dramatic and quite frankly I consider your request to be an impertinence? If that is all you have to tell me you are dismissed."

"Sir," Adolphus tried again. "You asked me at our earlier interview to explain why I was before a firing-squad when your troops attacked. I am now prepared to tell you."

The British Captain sat back in his chair stroking his moustache and peering into Adolphus' eyes. After an eternity, or so it seemed, he said to the Hauptmann, "Very well; talk!"

"How long have you got?" Adolphus asked.

"How long do you need?" the Captain replied. "Just give me the outline."

So Adolphus told the British Captain about the most recent events, those that had just occurred at Saint Quentin.

"But why did this man hate you so much, if I am to believe this tale. Did he know you from before Saint Quentin?"

"That is why I asked you how much time you had. This story really started in 1915 in Antwerp," Adolphus told him.

"Look I will have to see you again late this afternoon," the Captain eventually said. "Just tell me one thing before you go, what is the name of this man?"

"Erich Braun and he was born and brought-up in Bradford, England," Adolphus replied.

"Come back here to the interrogation centre at 17.00 hours and you can tell me the rest. In the meantime I will make some enquiries about this Erich Braun," the Captain said.

Chapter Sixty-Two

Blandford Forum 1917-1918

Promotion

The following Monday after their all-too-short leave, Joe and Amelie bade farewell to Jacob and Leah and to Manchester. They took a tram to Central Station and then caught a train to St. Pancras Station in London. Amelie had been in touch by telephone with the French Embassy in London and had been told to report there for further orders. Technically she was still a civilian but she was happy to consider herself to be under military discipline.

Joe was to walk to nearby Paddington station to catch another train that would take him to the RFC base at Blandford Forum.

The couple bade each other a tearful goodbye and promised to write whenever possible and to meet up again after the war.

The Royal Flying Corp base at Blandford Forum was used for training pilots to fly the new war-planes, now being manufactured by the British at an unprecedented rate. When the war had started both the French and the Germans had vastly superior aircraft, but the British learned quickly and by the time Joe arrived in Blandford they had aircraft that were able to inflict severe damage on their enemies.

Joe was to be trained to fly the Sopwith Camel, a single seat biplane which could achieve concentrated fire from twin synchronised machine guns.

It was a fighter and Joe could not resist the temptation of mentally comparing it with the BE2b which had crashed into trees in Belgium in what now seemed like a lifetime ago. If only he had had the Camel then he would have made short work of the Fokkers and his life over the following three years would have been so different. But then, he mused, I would not have met Amelie and I am sure she will be a very important part of my life in the future.

After a month's training he was considered competent, indeed more than competent, so it came as something of a surprise to be ordered to report to the RFC commanding officer in charge of the Blandford Forum base.

"Well, Lieutenant Bergman, you are certainly a fast learner. You seem to have mastered the intricacies of the Camel with consummate ease. We are also aware of the fact that you escaped from a German Prisoner-of-War camp and amazingly found your way back to England. Having now had the opportunity to study your record I am recommending you to be promoted to Captain."

Joe saluted and said, "Thank you very much Sir. I hope I can fully justify your confidence in me."

"I have not finished yet. We need bright young officers to train men to fly the Sopwith Camel and I feel you can contribute more to the war effort by remaining here and ensuring we have a steady flow of well-trained new pilots. How do you feel about that?"

Joe was disappointed. He had spent so much of the war as a prisoner or on the run that he had been longing, with the new plane, to have 'a real crack at the Germans.' He told his commanding officer this but he would hear none of it.

"I understand how you feel but you can do far more good here; so that is settled."

So Captain Bergman became an important member of the team who were training new pilots.

It did not take long before it dawned on him that that he now had the same rank as his cousin Hauptmann Bergmann, but in a very different army.

Captain Bergman sent many young men to France and other theatres of war during the course of the following year and was present at Blandford Forum when, on the first of April 1918 the Royal Flying Corp and the Royal Naval Air Service ceased to exist and were amalgamated into the Royal Air Force.

Jacob and Leah were delighted to hear Joe's news. At least one member of their family appeared to be out of danger. He spent most leaves with them in Manchester but he constantly thought of and worried about a certain French young lady called Amelie. He hoped and prayed that she would survive the war and then they could find each other again.

Chapter Sixty-Three

Outside Saint Omer 1917-1918

Braun's True Colours

When Captain Denton-Carruthers saw Adolphus again he was prepared to thank the Hauptmann for the information previously supplied. "You have been very frank and I know from the way you speak that you still consider yourself a loyal member of the German army. I am however, very grateful to you for telling me the story of Erich Braun."

Adolphus nodded. "Why does that concern you so much?"

"The man is a dangerous lunatic and if not for you telling me about him, he would now be working with the British army," the Captain explained. "He was interviewed by Lieutenant Johnson and he told him some cock and bull story that he had been working for the British government as a spy throughout the war. I have to say that the Lieutenant found him very convincing and he is, of course, a British subject. So, early this morning I interviewed him and also found his story quite credible. However, armed with the information you had given me, all I had to do was to mention that you were a prisoner here and he started to rant and rave about you being a traitor to Germany. Why he would think that would worry me, I cannot think. And I must tell you he is virulently anti-Semitic and started cursing the Jews both in Germany and Bradford."

"So what are you doing with him now?" Adolphus asked.

"Well at the end of the day he is a British subject and he saw fit to join the German army to fight against his own people. I would call that treachery, wouldn't you? You are a born German and I expect you to be loyal to your country. Braun is a real traitor and he has been placed in solitary confinement pending a trial."

"I can tell you," Carruthers continued, "that if we were in battlefield conditions here, he would have been summarily executed as soon as his treachery was known. Many British soldiers have been shot for far less."

Adolphus was obviously very relieved to hear that Braun was out of circulation and for the next few months, well into 1918 his main worry was trying to find a way to contact his wife and children in Berlin. He wrote to them frequently not knowing if any of the letters would get through and eventually a reply arrived from Rachel, through the good offices of the Red Cross, telling him that all was well. She obviously had no idea that he had been sentenced to death by a firing squad and only rescued as a result of the British attack on Saint Quentin. That was one piece of information he never mentioned in his letters.

He formed a friendship of a kind, bearing in mind the Captor/Captive relationship, with Captain Denton-Carruthers. He quickly discovered that Adolphus had no military secrets to impart, having spent much of his army career questioning British officers just as the British Captain was now doing with German prisoners.

Life, however, was tedious for Adolphus. He had always been a man of action and now the days dragged by with painful slowness. He drilled and he ate and he slept. He read whatever he could find to read and he enjoyed the occasional chats with his jailer Captain Denton-Carruthers. He worried about his family, his parents and he often wondered if his English cousin Joe had managed to get back to England.

In March 1918 he learned from recently captured German prisoners that Russia was out of the war having signed a peace treaty with the Central Powers. He still hoped his country could prevail despite the fact that the United States of America was siding and fighting with his enemy.

In July and early August the flow of German prisoners-of-war increased. They explained to Adolphus that their attack on allied positions along the Marne had been a disaster. The French forces had counter-attacked with several hundred tanks and inflicted severe casualties.

There were now so many German prisoners to contend with that Adolphus' occasional chats with Captain Denton-Carruthers became a thing of the past. From the German side the news was of one disaster after another culminating in the British officer in charge of the hugely extended camp calling the prisoners to an open air assembly. Here he told them on November the ninth 1918 that their Kaiser, Willem the second, had abdicated and fled Germany.

Two days later, on November the eleventh (the eleventh hour of the eleventh day of the eleventh month) Germany signed the armistice at Compiegne in France.

It came as a profound shock, just a few days later when the German 'other ranks' prisoners were told that they could not return home yet as they were required by the French government to assist in the re-building of areas of France ravished by war. Many of the officers were treated in like manner but Adolphus, no doubt through the friendship of Captain Denton-Carruthers, was told to take his kit and make his way home. The Captain supplied him with a series of travel-warrants but such was the chaotic state of the rail system in northern France and Belgium that the journey was far from easy. On the way, through a France and Belgium devastated by the war, he came across large numbers of British and French troops travelling in the opposite direction. He was still in uniform but all evidence of rank had been removed. He was just another defeated German soldier; no longer the Hauptmann, just plain Adolphus Bergmann.

Chapter Sixty-Four

Brussels 1918

Franks takes a Long view

In Brussels he found the Jewish community and asked for their help. He was dirty, dusty and his field-grey uniform had turned an altogether darker shade of grey. He was questioned by the Synagogue secretary who asked him what he had been doing during the war. Once again the interrogator was being interrogated but this time by a civilian. At first the man was more than a little suspicious. How did he know that he was really a Jew? However, thanks to Rachel taking him to Synagogue both in Berlin and Antwerp he was easily able to convince the secretary that he was genuine.

"So, you want to get back to your family in Berlin," the man eventually conceded.

Adolphus nodded. "My wife and parents will wonder what has become of me. Do you have the telephone installed here?" he enquired.

The man shook his head. "We are only a poor congregation and we cannot afford such luxuries. However, I will take you to the post office and from there you can send a telegram."

The secretary, who told Adolphus that his name was Lucien Cohen, then explained that the only other help he could offer was to show Adolphus the way to the railway station.

Adolphus shook his head. "I have no money for a ticket. A British officer gave me some travel-warrants but these have been used up on the roundabout route I had to use to get here."

Cohen looked at him in shock and pity. Everything about the conversation and deportment of Adolphus said 'wealth and privilege' except, of course for his tattered uniform and current plight.

"I think I may know someone who could help," Cohen replied. "Come with me. We will go and see M Georges Franks. If you were British or French I know he would help you but a German; I don't know how he will react. He was a very wealthy man before the war but the occupation of Belgium by you Germans resulted in him losing large amounts of money."

Franks lived in a large villa, a good half hour from the centre of Brussels and welcomed Cohen warmly.

"Ah, my dear Lucien, this is indeed a surprise. And who is this young man?" he enquired taking in the filthy German uniform.

"This is Adolphus Bergmann from Berlin. He has been a prisoner of the British for over a year and now that the fighting is over he wants to return home," Cohen explained.

"And what has that to do with me?" Franks demanded. "He may be a Jew but he is also a German and you know how my businesses suffered during their occupation."

Then Franks turned towards Adolphus having studiously ignored him during the earlier conversation with Cohen. "Bon Jour, M Bergmann," he said in a voice dipped in icicles. "And what were you doing during the war?"

"I was in charge of the interrogation of allied officers in Antwerp," Adolphus explained nervously.

"Look, M Cohen obviously brought you here to see if I could help you get back home to Berlin. Why should I? I have lost three quarters of my assets during your occupation and if this war had gone on any longer I would have been totally ruined. And if I did help you get back home what would you do? Plan how to attack Belgium and France again with your army friends?"

Adolphus was not used to pleading for financial help. He was too proud to talk about his time as a prisoner-of-war and all the other events that had marked his life over the last four years. "I want to go back into the shoe business with my father," was all he said.

"Shoe business?" Franks replied thoughtfully. "Are you connected to the Bergmann who had all those shops and factories?"

Adolphus nodded. "Ja. That is my father Kurt Bergmann."

"Alors, you are Kurt's son. In 1911 before all the madness of the war took over, we were in negotiation to open shoe shops in Belgium for him," Franks explained, suddenly softening his attitude.

Once again Adolphus nodded.

"So how is Kurt?" Franks enquired.

"I have no idea but I hope he and my mother and my wife and children in Berlin are all well. They will be worried about what has become of me," Adolphus replied.

Franks turned to Cohen. "You can leave young M Bergmann here with me. I will see that he gets home safely. Thank you for bringing him to me." He then turned to Adolphus smiling. "You know I have the telephone installed here in the house. Let us try to get the operator to connect you with your family in Berlin; while we wait, how about a cup of coffee and something to eat?"

Adolphus thanked M Cohen for bringing him to Georges Franks and followed his host into an office where the call was placed with an operator who would call back as soon as she had a connection.

Adolphus sat in the comfort of Franks' office sipping his coffee and thinking how important it was to know the right people. He was astonished by the transformation of M Franks from an aggressive unfriendly man to a beaming convivial host, just because he knew his father years earlier. And then he realised that what had really happened was that Franks had smelt a whiff of a business deal to be resumed after being interrupted by war, all those years ago.

Two hours later, the telephone rang in the hallway of Bergmann house in Berlin. Rachel was just preparing the two children for a walk to a nearby park. It was more normal for the housekeeper to answer the new gadget and then announce the name of the caller to the intended recipient. However, it was Rachel who by taking the call received one of the most wonderful surprises of her life.

"Hello," she said after carefully unhooking the earpiece from where it hung. "This is the Bergmann residence."

And then she heard that voice, the voice of her husband Adolphus. "Adolphus is it really you?"

"Ja. It is really me, my darling. How are you and how are the children?"

"Oh, Adolphus," Rachel replied. "I can't believe I am actually speaking to you. Are you coming home?"

"Ja, ja, my darling I am coming home. Is everyone well?"

Then Rachel heard another male voice; a voice with a strong French accent which said, "Madame Bergmann. My name is Georges Franks. I am an old friend of your father-in-law. I will personally organise the return of your husband to you and your family within the next twenty-four hours."

Early the following evening Adolphus arrived back at the family home in Berlin to a hero's welcome and to resume a life so rudely interrupted by a war that he had embraced so enthusiastically, when it first started. He was one of the lucky ones. Millions of other young men, British and French, German and Austrian, Russian and Belgian and a multitude of other nationalities never came home at all.

Chapter Sixty-Five

London & Manchester 1919

Unexpected Visitors

The queue started somewhere in the dark interior of the building and snaked its way out of the main doors, onto the street and around the block. Most major embassies in London were besieged at that time by people desperate for their many services but the French embassy claimed the longest queue, day after day.

Joseph Bergman, now a civilian, had tried five times to get into the building, let alone to see someone who could help him with his enquiries. It was now June 1919 and Joe had decided that the only way to gain an interview was to take up a position by the Embassy's huge oak double doors, the night before. He had being staying with an old RFC/RAF friend, Hugh Bertram, and he begged from him the loan of a deck-chair. So, complete with sandwiches and a flask of coffee he took up his position.

It was now over a year since he had bade farewell to Amelie and since that time he had not heard a word from her. Joe had expected that once the war ended she would quickly be in touch but month followed month without news or contact. He hoped that, as an undercover agent for the French government, they would at least be able to confirm if she was alive.

At last morning arrived and the doors opened. Joe dashed over to the enquiry desk to state his business. He was told to go to the second floor and wait outside an office labelled 'Missing Persons.' Half an hour later he was in front of a rather sour-faced middle-aged French woman to explain his errand.

When Joe told her the purpose of his visit she opened a drawer and produced a form which she started to complete.

"Name?"

"Who me, or the missing person?" Joe enquired.

This produced a withering look from the woman. "You, of course; if we have information we need to know where to send it."

Joe then supplied his name and address in Manchester.

"Now, who is it that is missing?" she demanded.

Joe gave her the name Amelie Levi and could not help but notice the sniff of disdain when the Jewish surname was supplied.

"And why should the French government know where she is?" she enquired.

Joe proceeded to tell her that Amelie was an under-cover agent and how and where he had met her. During the whole of this story the woman uttered not a word and when he had finished she wrote just a few words onto the sheet.

"Merci Monsieur," she again sniffed. "If we have any news we will be in touch but there has been a war on for four years and many people have disappeared so don't hold out too many hopes for this Amelie Levi." Again the name 'Levi' provoked another sniff.

Joe left the Embassy feeling angry and disappointed. *Was this how the French government cared about people who had been prepared to risk their lives for the country?*

He was sad. He had fallen in love with Amelie and he knew she cared deeply for him. What could have become of her? He agonised.

The following day, after discussing the situation with his friend Hugh, he decided to return to Manchester.

There was one other matter weighing heavily on his conscience. His Observer, Gareth Jones was still buried in an unmarked grave by a river bank in Belgium and Joe needed to contact his parents in Wrexham. The old RFC records had now been taken over by the newly formed RAF and Joe, as an ex-officer applied for details about the Jones family. Contacting them proved to be well nigh impossible as they had moved home without leaving a forwarding address and to find a specific Jones in Wales was like looking for a needle in a haystack. In the end he resolved to visit Belgium himself the following year, find the grave and have him receive re-burial in one of the vast Army burial sites now being established.

Firstly, however, in September, he was to resume his studies at university and he must try, as best he could, to see a future in which Amelie would not feature.

Joe tried to be positive. Apart from his studies there was the impending visit, in August from Berlin, of Adolphus, with his wife, Joe's sister Rachel and his nephew and baby niece. His brother Ike had decided to remain in the navy and had signed on for five years with an appropriate promotion. He had managed to arrange a leave to coincide with the visit of the Berlin family. Joe was also happy to see how his parents had started to blossom again. The sadness of the loss of Alfred would never leave them but they squeezed every ounce of pleasure out of the remaining members of their family including poor Alfred's wife and children who were frequent visitors to the Bergman house.

It was just two weeks after Joe had returned from London when there was a ring on the doorbell.

A young telegraph-boy stood on the step. "Telegram for Mr Joseph Bergman," he said.

"That's me," Joe replied and signed a receipt for the small envelope. *This is it*, he decided. *They have found Amelie.*

He anxiously tore open the envelope and read...

```
Magda   and   your   young   son   Joseph   junior
arrive  in  Manchester  on  12th  August  -  stop  -
you  can  meet  her  at  exchange  station  -  stop
-  the  11am  train  from  Hull  -  stop  -  regards
Kurt de Vries
```

Joe stood dumbfounded staring at the telegram and reading it over and over again. Of course, Kurt knew his name and location. He would have been easy to trace. Joe had often thought about Kurt and Magda and wondered what had happened to the baby she was carrying, his baby. How was he to tell his parents? Somehow he had to break the news that he had a baby son before Magda arrived. That was unless he could keep them away from the family.

Jacob came into the hall and glanced at Joe staring at the telegram. "Good news about Amelie?" he enquired.

"N...no," Joe answered. "It is just from an old friend I knew during the war."

"Is it bad news?" Jacob asked, studying the pale and worried appearance of his son's face.

"N...no," Joe repeated. "Everything is fine." But his expression and lack of conversation said something else.

Joe started to rehearse how he would tell Jacob and Leah. Would he tell them together or separately? If the latter, who would he tell first? Eventually he decided that he would have to face telling them both at the same time.

"I am sure that something is worrying Joe," Leah said to Jacob. "I know the lack of news about Amelie is gnawing away at him all the time, but the last few days he has been so pre-occupied. I am sure there is something else."

Jacob nodded and agreed. "I think we should have a word with him. I wonder if it has anything to do with the telegram that came the other day."

Jacob had now returned to his jewellery business and usually only came home after nine pm, tired and constantly distressed to see the poverty of the people in the towns he visited. However, those of his old customers who had survived the war, and were back in work were delighted to see him and he was constantly refusing the cups of tea they offered in welcoming him back into their lives as an old friend.

That Thursday night Jacob was even later than usual and missed the evening service at the synagogue. It was ten o'clock and before joining Leah and Joe for supper he had said his prayers alone in the front room of the house. Finally at half past ten the three of them sat down to eat. Joe had decided this was the night he must break the news as it was only ten days before Magda and the little boy arrived. Jacob and Leah had also decided that they must try to discover the reason for the sudden mood change of their son.

Leah opened the conversation by staring deep into her son's eyes and with a look of serious concern on her own countenance. "Joe," she began. "We don't like secrets and something is wrong. I know you are constantly worried about Amelie but there is something else troubling you these last few days."

"We are your parents," Jacob took over the conversation. "We love you and we can share whatever problem you have. Just tell us."

Joe nodded with a look of misapprehension on his face.

"You are not going to like this. You remember I told you that I spent some months living on a farm in Belgium while I was on the run from the Germans. The farmer's name was Kurt de Vries and he had a daughter called Magda."

Leah and Jacob nodded in unison. The mention of a daughter was already signalling problems ahead of what Joe would say next.

Joe decided there was no easy way of saying this so he just blurted it out. "Well, I got her pregnant and then I left to try to get back to England."

Neither of his parents could disguise the shock of the announcement.

"I suppose she was a good-looking young woman," Jacob said quietly but feeling anything but quiet inside. "It is not impossible to understand how such a thing could happen. Have you seen the baby?"

Joe shook his head. "No. I left well before he was due to arrive. I could not take a farmer's life for another minute. Her father was using me virtually as slave labour."

"How then do you know it's a boy?" Leah questioned.

"This is how," Joe replied and produced the telegram from his inside pocket.

It was one thing to be told of their son's 'wild oats' while on the run from the Germans and quite another to see the result in print before their eyes, in their own home.

Jacob looked grave. "I never thought that with your upbringing as a Frum (observant) Jew you would produce a non-Jewish grandson for us. I spend most of my business life with non-Jews and I have many close friends among my customers. However, their ways are their ways and our ways are ours. I need to give this some thought. Let's try and eat the supper your mother has cooked for us and we can talk again tomorrow."

Chapter Sixty-Six

Manchester August 1919

Family Reunions

<u>Tuesday August 12th</u>
Joe had purchased a platform ticket and was pacing up and down, awaiting the arrival of the Hull train. After much discussion his parents had decided that it was only right and proper to allow the girl; the mother of their son's child, together with the baby boy himself, to stay in their home.

Joe had made his feelings very clear to Jacob and Leah. He would never consider marrying the girl. Apart from the fact that it would have meant marrying out of the faith, he did not really like her. He also deeply resented the way that her father had plotted with her to keep him on the farm as an unpaid labourer. *I certainly never seduced her,* he reminded himself. *If anything, she seduced me.* However, the son was certainly his and for that reason and that reason alone, Jacob and Leah were prepared to entertain Magda.

The train was ten minutes late when the huge steam engine rolled noisily into the station. Hull – Manchester was a popular route and hundreds of people started to disembark. Joe peered carefully at all the young women with small children as they went by. He had left Magda a plump young farm girl, always with an apron over her unfashionable dresses; her hair loose and perpetually greasy as if it never saw a comb. It was nearly four years since he had last seen her and he expected a change. But he was totally unprepared for the fashionably dressed young woman who approached him. She was accompanied not only by a handsome four year old boy but also by a man.

"Joe," she said, peering closely at him. "You haven't changed." She then proffered her hand for a formal handshake. Considering how intimate they had been on the farm, Joe found this both reassuring and puzzling.

"Ah," Joe replied. "It is Magda, isn't it? You have changed beyond all recognition."

She smiled and said to the little boy, "Joseph, this is your Father."

The little boy looked up and said in excellent English, "Pleased to meet you Sir."

Then Magda spoke again. "This is my husband Jan van Guilder."

The man then smiled and also shook hands formally with the somewhat bewildered Joe. "Pleased to meet you Sir," he exclaimed.

Then the man spoke again. "We are staying at the Exchange Hotel just five minutes from here. I have business in Manchester and we will be here for at least a week. I hope you will join us for a cup of coffee."

"Yes. Thank you," the still shocked Joe replied.

A few minutes later they were sitting in the lounge of the Exchange Hotel sipping piping hot coffee and exchanging news.

"What do you do for a living," Joe quizzed Jan.

"I am in the diamond business in Amsterdam," he explained.

"Oh, that's interesting. My father is also in the jewellery trade."

Eventually Joe said, "I really must be going now. My parents are expecting you all for dinner tonight. It may be a little late for young Joseph, but I hope that will not deter you from bringing him along."

The dinner was a huge success on a number of levels. Joe was delighted that Magda had married and married well by the look of it. He felt as if a huge weight had been lifted from his shoulders. Young Joseph was hardly the wild young toddler that Joe had expected, more used to cows and sheep than city people. He was brought up in the atmosphere of Amsterdam and Jan was obviously a good disciplinarian.

Magda explained that she had always told young Joseph that his father was English and called Joseph, just like him. Jan was happy to accept this as he loved Magda and his little stepson.

Joe's parents were also delighted, Jacob particularly so when he retired into the front-room after dinner for a very promising business discussion with Jan.

Magda told Joe that she felt the right place for young Joseph was with his mother but she would like to ensure that he was able to spend at least a few days with his father each year. Joe accepted this suggestion with alacrity.

Jacob and Leah told Magda and Jan that their daughter Rachel from Berlin, with her husband Adolphus, were visiting in three days time and she would love for them to all get together over dinner the following Sunday night.

Friday August 15th
Once again Joe had purchased a platform ticket and was pacing up and down, awaiting the arrival of the Hull train. This time it arrived punctually and once more Joe stood scrutinising the people as they made their way along the long platform. Then he saw them. Adolphus was as well-dressed as ever, but now had the appearance of a prosperous German businessman rather than the young dandy of 1912. Rachel, Joe's dear sister who he had not seen

for over five years was elegantly dressed and although no longer the young blushing bride who had left Manchester in 1912, she looked well and happy and as beautiful as ever.

They were accompanied by Rudi, now five years old and Ruth, a pretty little three year old.

Rachel saw Joe first and ran over to where he was standing dragging the children with her in her excitement.

"Joe, oh Joe," she said. "How wonderful it is to see you again after all these years. You look well."

"So do you," Joe replied grinning from ear to ear. "And these are my little niece and big nephew. How do you do, children?"

Rachel had been teaching them English since they were old enough to speak and as a result they were both bi-lingual. However, the expression 'how do you do,' was a little difficult for Rudi to understand.

"How do I do what?" he enquired with a puzzled expression. Rachel quickly explained and Adolphus arrived with a porter to carry their luggage. Joe could see that they did not travel light.

"Hello Joe," Adolphus said smiling. "We meet again in rather better circumstances than last time."

Rachel looked from her husband to her brother and back again and could make no sense out of the comment. *Surely,* she thought, *the last time they met was at our wedding.*

However, the joy of their reunion again, as a family, made her put the comment to the back of her mind.

Joe had hired a taxi and within twenty minutes they were back at the house in Broadoak Street. As soon as the cab pulled up outside the family home, Leah and Jacob rushed down the steps and pulled open the cab door. They all embraced and Rudi and Ruth were introduced to their English grandparents for the first time.

All Jacob could think about was taking young Rudi to Synagogue on Shabbat morning and introducing him to his friends and their grandchildren. Both grandparents were determined that the children would enjoy a visit they would always remember.

A trip to Belle Vue, then the largest amusement park in England, was scheduled for the Sunday morning and Jacob and Leah let it be known that this was a grandparents' treat; no parents allowed.

During dinner that night Joe explained about the other visitors who were joining them on the Sunday night.

Adolphus found the fact that Joe had been in hiding on a Belgian farm and produced a son there, quite amusing.

"So, my dear fellow," he commented, laughing, "we Germans did you a favour. We left you to have some fun there for quite a while."

"It was far from fun," Joe replied gently. "However, I do now have a charming little boy to introduce to my German nephew and niece when they come for dinner."

After dinner Joe took Adolphus aside. "I cannot thank you enough for what you did in Nieuwpoort. You probably saved my life. I hope there were no serious ramifications as a result."

"Not at all, my dear man," Adolphus lied. "However, I had to survive some pretty difficult questions from Rachel when she overheard what I said to you at the station today. You see I had never told her about our meeting in southern Belgium. I can tell you she was far from happy that I had kept from her the fact that you were safe and well." He paused. "You know I also saw you in Antwerp in the prisoner-of-war camp," Adolphus commented.

"Yes," Joe whispered, "but why were you also locked up there?"

"Oh, that's a long story and one I wish to forget," Adolphus replied quickly. "But what you don't know is that I saw you again outside a Synagogue there, after you escaped."

At that moment Jacob came over to the two men. "Will you stop whispering like a couple of old ladies and re-join the rest of us."

Adolphus and Joe both grinned and nodded and returned to the dining table.

Chapter Sixty-Seven

Manchester Sunday August 17th 1919

The Family Party

Sunday August 17th 1919

This was becoming a habit, Joe mused. *I wonder if they give you a reduced price if you buy your platform tickets by the dozen.* Here he was yet again, pacing up and down, awaiting the arrival of the Hull train. However, this time he was there to meet his young brother Ike and as far as he knew he was coming alone.

Joe was looking for a Royal Navy Petty Officer but suddenly standing before him was the youngest Lieutenant Commander in the British navy.

"Hello Joe," the naval officer said. Joe did not know whether to salute him, kiss him or shake his hand and decided on the last option.

"Ike, my dear chap, how are you?" Joe asked.

"Absolutely fine," Ike replied. "Now the war is over I am really enjoying the navy."

"Well they obviously like you," his brother replied. "I did hear you had been promoted but, my little brother a Lieutenant Commander, that is really impressive."

Ike just had time to quickly catch up with his parent's news when the Berlin Bergmanns arrived for the dinner party. They still had no idea of the existence of young Joseph and the van Guilder family and as the latter arrived hot on the heels of the German branch of the family, they had to be introduced without an explanation.

Finally Anne, the widow of Alfred, arrived with her young sons, Arnold and Malcolm. Again she was introduced to the van Guilder family without explanation and she was very curious to know why they were there at this Bergman re-union party.

The table was set for fourteen people and Jacob asked them to take their places. He then suggested that as not everyone there knew the van Guilders and why they were included, that Joe should introduce them. Adolphus and Rachel, Anne and Ike had no idea that they had a Belgian nephew and in the circumstances they all took the amazing news very well.

Leah had spent the whole day preparing the food and was more than grateful for the assistance given to her by her daughter Rachel.

Towards the end of the four course meal, Jacob stood up and started to make a speech of welcome. He reminded them that the official end of the war had occurred on June the twenty-eighth, just six weeks earlier with the Treaty of Versailles. However, when he tried to mention his first son, Alfred, he broke down in tears and both Leah and Rachel had to comfort him.

Eventually he resumed his speech and said, "I think the ancient blessing, Shehechiyanu, that we Jews reserve for special occasions really summarises everything I have said; *Blessed art thou oh Lord, King of the Universe, Who has preserved us, sustained us and brought to this day.*"

It was now half past ten and well past the children's bedtime. Jacob finished his speech by saying that he prayed that the terrible war they had all just endured would be *'the war to end all wars,'* as the politicians had promised. "Let us hope that we may all live out our lives in a world at peace, and that includes all our little children."

Jacob had just sat down to applause when there was a ring on the front door bell.

"Who can that be at this time of night?" Jacob said.

"I will go and find out," Joe answered. It had better be important or I will give them a piece of my mind."

Then they all heard Joe's voice once again, as he opened the door and shouted out in excitement, "I don't believe it; is it really you? Come in, Come in!"